BREAKS

Corpus Christi Mysteries, Book 2

By Alice Marks

"Good Breaks, Bad Breaks and Spring Break"

a suspense novel

DEDICATION

This book is dedicated to my former home of Port Aransas, Texas, which was decimated by Hurricane Harvey. A favorite destination for Spring Breakers and one of the settings for this novel, be assured the island community will be even better than before as it rises from the horrifying rubble left by Harvey.

ACKNOWLEDGEMENTS

It is readers of <u>Missing</u> who are responsible for this book as they asked for a sequel. Thanks to them and all of my readers for your support.

With all my heart, I thank my editor, David Marks. Additional deep gratitude goes to my sponsor, Pamalee Ford.

Deserving thanks are my Beta-readers, Pamalee Ford and Devorah Fox. Others whose critiques I appreciated are Judy Budreau and Megan Finlayson.

Lake Superior Writers, the Ink Slinger Writers Group, Alesha Escobar, Devorah Fox and the Zenith Bookstore are constant sources of inspiration. My husband and my family, close and extended, are my magnificent support system.

And, last but not least, a praise goes to Erika M Szabo and Golden Box Books, publisher supreme.

PRAISES OF BOOK 1, MISSING

"One day Dr. Rhonda L. Collins walked away from her job at the Cielo Vista Clinic in Corpus Christi, Texas. Well, someone walked away. In "Missing," author Alice Marks has created an intriguing "who done it," and a disturbing "who's who." Page by page, the reader is drawn into the gripping maze of lies and deceptions until the revealing and surprising end." ~Michael Stephen Daigle, author of the Frank Nagler mystery series.

"Missing" is an intriguing, suspense-filled novel. Alice Marks is an excellent storyteller who keeps the reader on the edge of their seat. She guides the reader through the search for a beautiful, popular physician by a "rookie" policewoman who is assigned to the missing person case. Many other well-developed characters are intertwined as the plot develops. The author's clever approach to developing a credible story of multiple personality is critical to the success of this novel. The twists and turns in this novel maintain the reader's interest and keep them guessing the outcome until the very end. I truly enjoyed reading "Missing" and look forward to the sequel and other writings by this author." ~Ann Redding Justus, Reviewer

"Finished reading a book by Duluth author, "Missing" by Alice Marks. I loved it! Great mystery, well-written, engaging plot, colorful characters." It's available at Zenith Carol Halenbach Hall, Staff, Zenith Bookstore, Duluth

"Rhonda attracts attention. She's charming, compassionate, a beloved doctor and a best friend. Or so everyone thinks. How could she fool so many and seemingly get away with it? Her schemes along with her dreams take us

along on a page turning adventure." ~ Pamalee Ford, Writer, Integrated Mental Health Consultant

"What happened to Rhonda? What's Sandra running from, and will she overcome the obstacles to making her escape? What secret is Dr. Linda's husband hiding? Even more interesting to me was the fate of Maria Gonzales. Would the young officer, pressed into service on a case that looks like a career-killer, solve the mystery and gain the respect of her partner, a veteran detective? I had great fun following the story's interwoven threads all the way to the end. A huge fan of Alice Marks's shorter works, I was delighted to have an entire novel of hers to read, and hope that there will be others." ~ Devorah Fox, Author of BeWilliam Fantasy series, Detour, first in Big Rig Series, The Zen Detective and numerous short mysteries and fantasies.

INTRODUCTION

It is almost November. Just two months ago I, author of <u>MISSING</u> met my heroine, Sandra Lewis. I went along as the unseen narrator while this determined young woman experienced a variety of misadventures on-the-run from Texas. Most believed this woman really was Dr. Rhonda Collins, the notorious "Missing Doctor", who left the Cielo Vista family clinic in Corpus Christi on her lunch hour and never returned. This woman whom I first met at the shabby Liberty Motel called herself the sister of the Missing Doctor and for good reason. I learned that Dr. Collins had designated Sandra Lewis as the sole beneficiary of her estate. A rookie detective, Maria Gonzalez, from the new South Corpus Christi Police Headquarters, attained rock star status when she proved that Sandra Lewis and Dr. Rhonda Collins actually were the same person. Clever! Rhonda could "die" and still retain all her assets, plus she had reason to make others believe she had died to avoid a likely prison sentence. Fleeing Corpus Christi, Sandra, among other adventures, bought a stolen car, battled a hurricane, tossed out evidence that a volunteer highway clean-up crew found, was detained at the San Antonio as a suspected terrorist and finally reached a safe haven in Chicago. She didn't know charges against her had been dropped because the owner of the Cielo Vista Clinic, wanting to avoid bad publicity, refused to press charges.

The last time I saw Sandra she was on a bus heading from Chicago to her home state of Arkansas, and who was on that same bus? Sandra's half-sister, the real Rhonda Collins who looked remarkably like Sandra before she cut and dyed her hair. Sandra used the name of Rhonda Collins, a real person who had no idea that for eight years Sandra had borrowed her name. This name-change is confusing. Dr. Rhonda Collins who was Sandra is now Sandra again, but there is a real person named Rhonda Collins sitting beside her on the bus.

Throughout Part One of this novel I kept track of both women and another look-alike sister, Rainey, in the small town of Harmon, Arkansas. Except for a having their own missing woman, life in the little Arkansas town proved pretty mundane. While I watched the newly arrived sisters stir up things in Harmon, I also trained an eye on Brian Cavendish, who finds himself in big trouble, and Maria Gonzalez, who tries to convince her partner Stan that they needed to revisit the Missing Doctor case in order to nail the one who provided her false credentials.

But, I'm getting ahead of myself. We need to step back and hop on the Byways bus to experience the reunion between two sisters, Sandra Lewis, formerly known as Dr. Rhonda Collins, and the real Rhonda Collins.

PART ONE

Chapter One

Reunion

Rhonda Collins recognized her half-sister, Sandra Lewis, even with the different hair color and style. The minute Sandra boarded the Byways Bus. Rhonda called out to her, "Sandra!" When Sandra turned towards her sister, Rhonda eagerly added, "What a coincidence! Are you headed home, too?"

Rhonda, the real Rhonda Collins, whose name Sandra Lewis secretly had appropriated for eight years, couldn't contain her excitement about this chance meeting. All eyes on the bus focused upon the attractive blonde woman who looked like she had fleas by the way she jumped up and down in her seat, waving her arms.

Sandra Lewis's first inclination was to tell the woman hailing her, as coldly as possible, that she was mistaken. When Sandra owned a beauty salon in Tulsa eight years earlier, Rhonda, her older half-sister, had found Sandra through Facebook. They hadn't seen each other since Rhonda was six and Sandra was four. Sandra couldn't forget how her long-lost sister took advantage of her kindness when she showed up in Tulsa with her hand out. Sandra had hoped she'd never see Rhonda again after she moved to Texas. *Why now,* she thought, *when I want to put my past behind me?*

A small sigh escaped Sandra's lips. Remembering a pledge of honesty, she'd made to herself, she smiled broadly as the passengers waited to see what would happen next. Her half-sister stood and indicated Sandra should sit in the window seat. Rhonda resumed sitting in the aisle seat and gave Sandra the expected hug as both wondered how this would turn out.

Sandra answered her half-sister's question. "Yes. I'm going home. I'm determined to find my, I mean, our mother and our . . ." She paused, totally unsure of this reunion with Rhonda, but continued, "Now we've found each other again, we'll be able to see Mama together, and I'll be able to introduce you to the little sisters, Rainey and Midge."

"Oooh, I'd love that," Rhonda squealed, "but I'm going home to see my daddy first." Quickly changing the subject, she inquired where Sandra had been since they last saw each other. Sandra explained that she had worked at a medical clinic in Corpus Christi for eight years, the absolute truth. *Someday I will tell her the whole story when I'm certain she will understand and forgive me for using her name. But not now.*

"What about you? What have you been doing, Rhonda?"

"When was the last time we saw each other?"

"Ten, eleven years ago. I still had my hair salon then."

"That's right. You did my hair like you always did, but it turned out to be the last time. I went back to California, and when I came back the shop had a 'For Sale' sign." Rhonda's voice filled with resentment. "I asked around, but no one could tell me exactly where you'd gone. Then someone said she thought you mentioned wanting to go to Texas."

Lost in thoughts of how her half-sister had taken advantage of her in Oklahoma, Sandra didn't answer. Rhonda, not one for pauses in conversations, had another question. "Did you like it where you were?

Taking a deep breath, Sandra had a faraway look in her eyes. "I loved Corpus Christi. Wonderful weather, the beautiful bay with shrimpers bringing in their catch of huge shrimp, best I've ever eaten. I adored the Hispanic culture, their colorful traditions, and incredible Tex-Mex food. I've never been happier."

"Wow! I'd love to see that place. What did you say you did there?"

Sandra had the same wistful look in her eyes." I had a job I did well, a lovely townhouse, a great car, a dog, friends; I even went to church and loved the people there. But, you still haven't answered my question. What did you do for ten years?"

"Nothing significant." Then grinning, "I sure didn't get religion or hold a satisfying job!"

Sandra couldn't help giving her sister a disparaging look. "Surely you did something during the last ten years."

Both sisters were developing cricks in their necks from facing each other. In unison they turned to look forward. Sandra noticed it had begun to rain, as Rhonda answered her sister's question.

"Back and forth between California and Oklahoma, with a few stops in Missouri. Tried to reunite with my second husband, he seemed to have matured but turned out to be the same loser he always was. I almost married another guy but if the third time wasn't the charm, I didn't think the fourth would be either. I guess I wasn't meant for marriage."

"I could say that, too,"

"Didn't you meet any guys in Corpus Christi?"

"Sure. I fell in love with a handsome Latino and I would have married him in a minute, but he already was taken." (Sandra refrained from adding, *His wife was the best friend I've ever had.*) She said instead, "I did have an incredible girlfriend. We went on trips together, even Mexico, and had such good times together." Tears welled in Sandra's eyes. *I betrayed her in the worst possible way. I was unbelievably cruel to one who meant everything to me.*

"You must miss her."

"I do, but we had a misunderstanding." (*That's an understatement for having an affair with her husband)* and I'll never see her again. She included me in all their family activities. Sandra's voice cracked. With guilt, she continued, "She and her husband had three wonderful boys."

Rhonda yawned, always more interested in her questions than the answers of others. "We have a long way to go. I think I'll take a nap." She reached for a pillow she'd been leaning on and put it behind her head. As she settled down to sleep, she thought her sister seemed a little secretive; but she had her own secret, a big one, about their mama.

Chapter Two

Dueling Detectives

"What's on your mind, Gonzalez?" Detective Stan Belkin asked his partner.

Maria looked startled to see her partner standing over her cubicle. She spun around in her chair. "Actually, I was thinking about our first case together."

"The one that got away," Stan laughed. "What's there to think about? You figured out why the famed Missing Doctor took off, and the clinic refused to press charges. Case closed."

"I know there's more. Where is she now? Putting other patients in jeopardy with her false credentials? And who created those documents for her?"

The two detectives, the veteran and the rookie, had started out with a volatile relationship but had gained definite respect for each other as they solved their first cases together. A trace of the old irritability erupted when Stan answered, "Drop it, Maria. We still need to finish the summaries on the last case."

The case to which he referred had been related to the first. Maria had found the connection between a teen that almost lost his life to illegal drugs and his sale of a car to the Missing Doctor to obtain drug money. The high school student, now clean, helped them finger the small-time dealer who brought drugs from Mexico and targeted kids in Corpus Christi high schools. His arrest had little impact on South Texas' drug problem, but for the moment there was one less dealer on the streets.

"I know we have the report to finish and one of us will have to testify at the trial, which was necessary because we used entrapment to arrest the dealer but," she said through gritted teeth, "that doesn't mean we can't discuss a couple things related to the Missing Doctor."

"You're not thinking of asking to have the case re-opened, are you? You know that's not happening." Belkin was getting steamed.

"Why not?" Maria's dark eyes flashed anger and frustration with the man she grudgingly had come to admire. Her voice became shrill. "There still are unanswered questions."

"There are unanswered questions to every case!" Belkin also raised his voice.

"Keep it down, you two!" came from a desk cop, who hadn't heard an exchange like that between the two detectives for some time.

Chagrined, Maria asked as calmly as she could, "Couldn't we just discuss my need for more closure with the case?"

"Sure. It's almost lunchtime. Let's discuss it over Whataburgers."

"No, I want to discuss it now." Maria could be a pain when she wanted her way.

Belkin pulled up a chair. "Make it fast."

"We need to find her to make it possible for justice to be served. We need to find out where she obtained false documents and arrest that person."

"I concede that your concerns are legit, but is it worth the time to try to find her when she'd probably plead insanity? As for the documents, there's a huge underground…"

Maria interrupted. "I want to talk personally to her friends in Chicago."

"Do you have reason to think they're criminals who provided the documents?"

"No, I've checked out both. No priors. She's a housewife; he works for an international banking company. He and Sandra Lewis had the same address in Tulsa before he moved to Chicago. I'm guessing they might have been more than friends.

Stan Belkin, master of sarcasm, said, "Obviously you're already working on the closed case. Count me out. I'm going to lunch."

* * *

14

As Stan wolfed down two Whataburgers with a shake and large fries, he wondered just what his partner had up her sleeve. She was the most stubborn woman he had ever met and that included Diana, his current, independent wife, who lived in Houston most of the time because she played with the symphony.

Maria had questions about The Missing Doctor case; he had some about this current case. The kid Maria knew identified the drug dealer, but he felt certain there was another man involved. He had no proof, but he thought the man they'd arrested wouldn't have had the amount of capital needed to set up the operation. He would have needed someone to back him, maybe accompany him to Mexico to get the drugs. This guy didn't seem smart enough to get past the border guards and their drug-sniffing dogs. Even though the dealer had insisted it was a one-man operation, Stan doubted it.

Every case has unanswered questions, just as he had cautioned Maria. The Missing Doctor case was over and this one was also. To wipe out all the drug dealers getting rich by spreading their poison would be akin to vanquishing the independent corps of people providing false documents for a price. The occupation of the latter probably wasn't responsible for any deaths of their customers even though those opposing the Missing Doctor feared that she could have harmed her patients with her impersonation of a doctor. *Maybe Maria is right. The bogus doctor could be using her false credentials in another state putting more patients at risk. When we finish this case it might be a good idea to continue to track down Dr. Rhonda. She could still be in Texas or in any other state. Or Mexico.*

Stan deliberated about having another burger, but his wife had been nagging him about his high cholesterol. Reluctantly he resisted another juicy, flavorful Texas icon. Considered so delectable, more than one Huntsville prisoner on death row had requested a couple for a last meal before the Lege eliminated that courtesy.

15

Chapter Three

Introspection

With her chatty sister asleep, Sandra had time to reflect. Having Rhonda by her side made it easier to resume her old identity, the identity it was necessary to claim now that she had given up her name and position as a doctor under shadowed circumstance.

She closed her eyes to reminisce. *Who am I? Just a few months ago I was Dr. Rhonda Lewis, an award-winning physician at the Cielo Vista Family Clinic run by Dr. Ronyl Brooks in Corpus Christi. How happy I was working there but leaving was the only thing I could do. Now I am back to being Sandra Lewis, formerly of Modell and Tulsa, Oklahoma. I spent most of my teen years in Modell with Lurene, the woman who took me in when I ran away from home. I changed my name to Sandra when I took off from Arkansas.*

Sandra flexed her long legs, trying to find a more comfortable sitting position. *I met Brain Cavendish when he happened to stop in Modell. It was love at first sight for me, still a teenager.*

A tear dripped down her cheek. Cancer killed Lurene and I moved in with Brian. I helped him with his on-line occupation of making false credentials for people who requested them. Sandra looked out the window at the changing colors of the trees; at the time helping people change their lives seemed just as natural, not dreadful or illegal. *With Brian's skills in documentation, I became a third-grade teacher and then a hair stylist and wound up with my own successful salon. When I grew bored with that, I became a doctor and moved to Texas.*

Now I am on my way to my hometown, where I was born thirty plus years ago. My parents Roy Lee and Martha Mae Jackson named me Ronnie Lee. Their first child, as it seemed then, is seated next to me. She also is returning home. Our mother named her Sue-Ella, but she said she changed this to

Rhonda, to honor me with a grown-up version of Ronnie. Now she's Rhonda, and I'm back to being Sandra.

Looking out the window, Sandra continued to think. *I borrowed my sister's name when Brian refused to give me documentation I needed to be a physician. I tricked him by saying my sister wanted the same thing and would he do it for her? He agreed to do it for a stranger and I appropriated my sister's name and credentials.*

Dark clouds bullied away the sun that had been streaming through the bus windows. As passengers muttered about the weather and turned on their reading lights, Sandra glanced again at her sleeping sister. *Until she found me* in Tulsa, *we hadn't seen each other since she was six and I was four, back when she was Sue-Ella and I was Ronnie Lee.*

Sandra's earliest memory had to do with her big sister pulling little Ronnie Lee in a small green wagon. They lived in a pretty frame house in a rural Arkansas town called Harmon in the northern part of the state, where sometimes it snowed enough to cover the ground. Sandra almost laughed out loud as she recalled vividly Daddy showing his girls how to make skimpy snow angels in the thinnest layer of snow.

She had strong memories like this of growing up in a happy home until alcoholism infested and destroyed the family like weevils infest and decimate a solid oak. She didn't understand why Daddy started drinking so much. He had a good job at the mill, but the company fired him. Mama insisted it wasn't his fault, but they had to move from their home into a trailer house across town. Ronnie and Sue-Ella couldn't understand why Mama cried about moving there because they were excited that the trailer park had a big playground.

Shortly after they moved there, the cute little blonde sisters played at the playground in the trailer park. They saw a strange car pulled up beside their new home and an angry looking man got out. Weaving in and out between neighbors' small yards, the little girls ran the short distance to tell Mama, but she already had opened the door and stood talking to the man.

"Mae, this is too much. I'm not having my daughter grow up trailer trash with a thief for a father. She's going home to Gurney with me."

Without any argument or comment at all, Mama called to Sue-Ella and said, "Honey Bun, this is your real daddy Big Jake; you're going to live with him."

"No!" Sue-Ella wailed and kicked at the man who picked her up and whispered kindnesses into her ear as he rushed her to his car. Little Ronnie Lee cried for weeks because she missed her sister, her playmate. One day Mama told her that in a few weeks she would be a big sister, and she had been so overjoyed about having a new baby to help care for that she gradually forgot about her big sister.

It wasn't until Rhonda found her in Tulsa twelve years earlier that Sandra learned the whole story about their relationship. Two men were in love with their Mama, who often said she couldn't help being too darned beautiful and charming. She decided on Roy, the man who would become father of her four daughters. He really wasn't the father of the first, Sue-Ella, but he forgave Mama for her not telling him and the real father, Big Jake, right away. Roy Lee Jackson loved baby Sue-Ella like his own.

Now Sandra studied her sleeping sister. They looked amazingly alike. Rhonda was an inch or so shorter and her features were more rounded than Sandra's; she also had a tiny mole by her left ear. Both were slender, had green eyes and naturally blonde hair. Rhonda wore hers long. Admiring her sister's hair, Sandra, with the short brown dyed hair, made the decision to let hers grow out to its former length and shade. The sisters dressed well though Sandra's outfit was of a classic line while it looked as if Rhonda shopped in the junior section in an attempt to look younger and flashier.

I wonder how my little sisters look now they're grown. Rainey favored Mama like Rhonda and me. The baby, Midge, looked like Daddy with his dark hair, short stature and sturdy body.

The bus stopped for gas and new passengers. The driver said there would be time for everyone to stretch their legs or buy a snack. Sandra felt hungry and wakened her sister who protested she wanted to keep sleeping. Sandra squeezed past her and went into the convenience store that reminded her of being on the run from Corpus Christi. The tantalizing aroma of burritos tempted her as it had then, but she resisted and bought an egg salad sandwich and two energy bars, one for her sister. As she left the store, new passengers mounted the stairs of the bus. One man in a business suit glanced at her with a look of recognition. Sandra's heart careened to the pavement. *Is he an undercover police officer or journalist from Corpus Christi? Will I ever feel safe? Will I ever quit feeling guilty for doing what I've done?*

Chapter Four

Memories

Rhonda scarcely moved when Sandra crawled over her again. Sandra studied her half-sister. She looked sweet as she napped, like a child, like the child Sandra always had dreamed of having. With a disgusted look, Sandra acknowledged that based on her sister's visits to Tulsa, sweet was the last thing she ever would have considered calling Rhonda. The former Sue-Ella had shown herself to be manipulative, conniving, lazy and wanting someone to care for her. *We're bound to have interactions with both of us in Arkansas, but I'm glad she is going to Gurney. As mercurial as my sister is, she never stays one place for any length of time.* A smile played across her face. *Thank heavens.*

Sandra stared out the window. Now it was the unusual darkness of the early afternoon sky that reminded her of something. It had been nighttime when she ran away. She was fifteen years old. First Daddy was imprisoned for vehicular homicide while driving drunk. He had killed a couple and their infant. Unable to cope, her mother abandoned her children. Child Protection put Sandra's little sisters in one foster home and Sandra in another. Her foster home housed teen-agers, including two boys who constantly bullied her at school. She couldn't stand living in the same place as them. That's why she sneaked out as soon as everyone slept. The first thing she did on her way to the town's bus station was to change her name to Sandra Dee, after the movie star. Lewis replaced Jackson as her last name because of the television puppeteer Sherry Lewis, whose Lamb Chop character the little sisters loved. Sandra spent all the money in her piggy bank on a bus ticket that took her two-thirds of the way through Arkansas after which she hitched rides with kind people who sometimes bought her a meal. In Oklahoma a trucker with a friendly orange cat stopped for her and promised to take her to Dallas, Texas, where she'd told him relatives lived. That wasn't true about relatives. She wanted to go to Texas because she believed everyone there was rich, and Dallas was the only location she knew. As she rode to that destination, she loved holding the purring cat on her lap.

The driver didn't take her to Texas and even now she couldn't let herself think about that awful man who had been nice at first. Because of what he proposed that she do for him, she had jumped from the slow-moving truck as it entered a rest stop. She hurt her right ankle and limped to take refuge in the women's restroom, where she spent the night. The next morning, she saw kids boarding a school bus and joined them for a ride to the next town, Modell.

Sandra smiled broadly as she thought about that person in the town, Lurene, who had considerable influence on her young life.

The black clouds gave way to huge raindrops that pelted the windows. The sound awakened Rhonda.

"What are you grinning about?" asked Rhonda, yawning and stretching as much as she could in the confines of the bus seat. "Was I snoring?"

Sandra wanted to tell her half-sister that not everything was about Rhonda Collins but refrained. "I was thinking about the woman who became like a mother to me when I wound up in the Oklahoma panhandle." Sandra rummaged in her purse for the energy bar. "I bet you're starved. You missed the food stop but I bought this for you."

"Aren't you sweet, Sister," Rhonda commented between bites and then asked, "Could you tell me about her? I told you in Oklahoma about my string of stepmothers; now it's your turn."

Sandra brushed her bangs to the side and complied. "Lurene loved to tell anyone who'd listen that she had lots of experience with stray dogs and cats, but I was the first stray girl who came to Smokey's, her bar and grill. She took care of me right away, binding my sprained ankle and putting ointments on bruises and bug bites I'd gotten hitchhiking. She cooked a great big juicy hamburger for me and let me sleep on a cot in a little room behind the bar. I found out later this

21

is where her husband napped during the day when he became ill. She told me that she planned to send me back on the bus to my family; but once I told her why I'd left, she decided that would be too cruel. She let me move into her cozy home near the bar. She wanted me to go to high school, but I was too afraid. Lurene told me later that she was certain if she had pushed me I would have run away again. That's why when there were no customers she helped me study for my GED, and she threw a big graduation party for me when I aced all the tests. She told me, 'Sandra, as long as you work hard, you can be anything'."

Sandra paused a while before taking up her story as both looked out the window at the increasing rainfall. Resuming, the younger sister explained, "Lurene put away money for my college education, and she planned to adopt me legally when I turned eighteen. She told me she was going to change her will to insure that I, not her brother, would inherit Smokey's. She told me I could sell it, run it, whatever I wanted."

Rhonda interrupted, "I remember you told me you went to college and became a teacher."

Sandra remembered that conversation, too. She had told her half-sister, when Rhonda first visited her in Tulsa, that she had been a teacher, but she'd let her assume the bit about going to college. Having a college education had seemed to impress Rhonda, who now said, "Did she adopt you?"

"No." Sandra sounded deflated as she choked back tears. "She developed cancer. All the money she had saved for college went to medical bills. When she died, I met her brother at the funeral. He said his sister had never mentioned me. I knew he was lying. The first time I drove alone after I passed my driver's test was to the post office to mail the letter Lurene wrote to tell him. It said since he was well established and had shown no interest in Smokey's, I was to inherit it."

"And then you sold it, went to college, became a teacher, and then a hair stylist and bought your own shop."

Sandra let her half-sister think she had it all figured out. Tears again formed in her eyes as the rain fell harder and harder. Almost to herself Sandra whispered, "If Lurene hadn't died, I'd have been a better person."

Rhonda gave her a strange look. "Sweetie, I think you turned out just fine, a lot better than I did."

At that moment the bus swerved to miss an oncoming car from the opposing lane that had skidded on the wet pavement, crossed the yellow line and headed towards the bus. The driver over-corrected the steering. The bus shuddered. Passengers screamed as the big bus began to tip. For a time it seemed the driver's braking would put the bus back on all its wheels. The screaming that would seep into the ears of the passengers and intrude on their dreams grew as a louder and louder crescendo.

Chapter Five

Olive Branch

Later in the afternoon Stan stopped by Maria's cubicle. "Still in a snit?"

Maria beamed because she had figured out how she was going to progress without Belkin's help. "What snit? I wasn't in a snit."

"Could have fooled me. You missed a fantastic Whataburger lunch."

"You and your Whataburgers. I hope you take your wife someplace nicer when you go out."

"Who says I take her out? She's on the road all the time and appreciates a home-cooked meal when she's at home."

"Do you cook?" Maria sounded incredulous.

"Of course not. I'm sure she misses cooking. I let her cook anything I want."

Maria shook her head but continued smiling because she knew his theory was that it didn't cost any more to be sarcastic.

Stan cleared his throat, "Uh, Maria, I know this sounds inconsistent but there's something about this drug case that bothers me. The dealer said this was a one-man operation but I'm not sure."

Maria bit her tongue, refraining from saying anything about his questioning a closed case. "Why's that?"

"During surveillance, did you ever see more than one person in the dealer's car?"

"Not that I remember."

Stan Belkin spat out an expletive and continued, "I was hoping you'd say you saw an older guy in the car with the dealer."

"Maybe there was. Remember I was rather busy acting the part of a high school girl and didn't see as much as you did."

They both laughed as they remembered the undercover charade that ended in the arrest of the man selling drugs to

24

high school students. It started when Ortiz had sauntered into the officers' pod of cubicles and, in his usual brusque manner shouted for Belkin and Hernandez. "I'm getting complaints from the high school principal at Flour Bluff about a pusher who practically walks the halls pedaling his wares. I'm assigning you to surveillance. Catch the sucker for me and get the principal off my back."

The two detectives found no one pushing for several days, and then spotted a car with a man in a suit, looking like a dad picking up his kid. Only the kid didn't get in the car with "Dad". Just handed him something resembling currency and stuffed something "Dad" gave him into his backpack and walked away.

Maria commented, "He must have forgotten his permission slip for some after school event." Maria's unusual sarcasm made Stan roar with laughter.

The man in the car drove away, but not before they had his license number. They traced that to a Darrin Chapman of Sinton, Texas. Checking with the school, Maria found no parent at the school with that name. The two detectives hatched up a plan to catch the man in a transaction; the Chief gave his hearty approval.

The next day Maria, dressed in clothes borrowed from a high school cousin, entered the high school near the time of the last bell and departed among all the other students. She spotted "Dad" and walked up to his car and said, "My friends say you sell the good stuff."

"Dad" gave her his price but added, "Y'all are a pretty little thang. I'll give you a special price. Share this with your friends and if they like it, Ah could make you a seller and cut you in on the profits."

Maria smiled, handed him the "bargain price" of fifty-three dollars and he handed her a tiny bag of cocaine. Stan had appeared out of nowhere and snapped a photo of the transaction with his cell. He arrested the pusher before he knew what was happening. Cuffed and being walked blocks away the pusher asked, "Why are you picking on mc? What about that kid that just bought illegal drugs? Why not arrest her? She bought enough to sell, too?"

Maria had faded into the crowd. She called the station to have the pusher's car impounded and it yielded a large stash of drugs of many varieties from marijuana and prescriptive drugs to meth and cocaine. Maria hoped he would be identified as the same one who sold drugs to the young man she had gotten to know, which is what happened. Regardless the case was going to trial because the dealer secured an attorney who screamed "Entrapment", but Maria and Stan weren't worried. They were certain the judge would rule that what they did justified their means. After all, they had the approval of the Chief.

"We worked well together on that case. If you'd only cooperate with me now."

"Nope," he tossed over his shoulder as he sauntered out.

Maria still looked triumphant. Stan's visit probably was his way of offering her an olive branch, or maybe the Whataburgers improved his mood. She'd talk him into getting the case reopened eventually.

She had become very fond of her partner, but he sure wasn't of the generation of enlightened caring man like her Xavier. She couldn't wait to talk to her man about plans she'd made.

Chapter Six

Bus Crash

Continued screams of terror, prayers, and profanity accompanied airborne passengers from what had been the left side of the bus. They and carry-on luggage from overhead racks as well as purses, water bottles, computers, and books from laps flew downward towards passengers on the right side where the bus temporarily had landed. As the bus rolled, those on the left side where Rhonda and Sandra had been seated, landed on top of groaning passengers smashed against the right side of the bus. The bus continued to roll until it was upside down on a rise thirty yards from the two-lane highway. The passengers bled from lacerations inflicted by glass shards and suffered from pain due to broken limbs and internal injuries caused by collisions with the airborne missiles. Some lucky ones suffered only bumps and bruises while others were unconscious. Any fatalities yet unknown. All was chaos, and some passengers would be prone to endless nightmares of the rolling bus.

The stunned driver bashed out windows with emergency equipment while the riders untangled themselves from each other. The best possible break was that a cable truck equipped with ladders appeared first at the scene. Two passengers, including one who had boarded in Chicago and the man in the suit Sandra had noticed get on at the truck stop, aided the bus and cable truck workers in helping the less injured through windows and down ladders to the flat soggy ground where they wandered dazed and bleeding.

The auto driver who had gone into the slide drove as far as he could from the horrible scene but called 911, as had the bus driver and able passengers. Distant sirens became louder as emergency vehicles headed to the accident scene.

Once she descended the ladder into the rain, which mercifully had let up, Sandra returned to doctor mode. With the bus's expansive First Aid kit she bandaged and comforted scared, wet, bleeding passengers, including Rhonda who had a small cut on her arm. As Rhonda made a scene, Sandra reassured her sister that the cut was not life threatening. Rhonda watched her sister with amazement as she moved among the injured passengers rendering aid and soothing words.

Sandra noticed the man in the suit she thought she'd recognized earlier also comforted the scared and injured. Sandra kept as far from him as possible. As soon as EMS arrived she faded out of the action and helped Rhonda look for their luggage.

Everyone had survived the crash but fifteen were transported to the nearest hospital, which the bus had passed over an hour ago. "That means we're close to Harmon, but who knows when we'll be able to get there," Sandra told Rhonda, who moaned in response.

Pandemonium continued as police officers took names, addresses and telephone numbers of all passengers possible and told them they would receive accident forms to fill out. Both sisters gave Rhonda's dad's address in Gurney. Passengers whispered about a lawsuit from which they hoped to prosper. The driver said the bus company would receive copies of the information taken by the officers. "That way they can return our luggage," speculated one passenger, while another said, "No, this isn't like the airlines."

The driver had requested another Byways bus, which was forty-five miles away. As passengers waited, two school buses from Jugo, the emergency crew's town, arrived. Muddy, less severely injured passengers climbed into them with any baggage they were able to find. Emergency crewmembers had tossed all they could out of the overturned bus once the passengers had been rescued and treated. Some suitcases, including Sandra's classy new ones, were still in the crushed right-side cargo bin; but she was grateful that both she and Rhonda had their carry-ons. "Why can't this bus just take us where we're going?" whined Rhonda but cheered up when friendly volunteers from Jugo gave the passengers sandwiches and cookies and poured coffee from thermoses into Styrofoam cups.

A monster tow truck and the replacement commercial bus arrived at the same time. The sisters boarded close to the front since the new driver told them Harmon would be the next stop, which also was the destination for the man in the now mud-caked suit.

Though it seemed as if the mishap had lasted forever, the passengers on the replacement bus had been detained only two hours. The sisters sat in silence, each processing what they'd been through. Sandra was the first to speak and that was to comment on all the Harmon billboards miles before they were due to reach the town. Sandra could tell their no-count town had changed as they observed advertising for new businesses: motels, fast food places, as well as more than one bank and a car dealer.

"Are you planning to stay at a motel?" asked Rhonda

"Yes, I checked that out on the Internet," her sister answered,

Rhonda asked, "That reminds me, have you used the Internet to find our relatives? That's how I found you in Tulsa even though both of us had changed our names from our hick little girl names."

"I didn't have much luck with the Internet. I want to try the direct approach. Go back to where we lived and ask people who knew our family."

"Sounds good. You'll keep me in the loop, won't you? I'll be just an hour down the road."

"Is there a bus station in Gurney now?" asked Sandra.

"No. Usually the driver will let me out there, but I better go ask this one."

Rhonda made her way to the driver's seat and in her best flirty, eye batting way, asked if he would do her the favor of stopping the bus in Gurney. The driver said most emphatically not, it was against company rules, and he would not budge. Unabashed, Rhonda returned to her seat and told her sister, "I changed my mind about going to Gurney. I really want to stay with you a while and help you find the family."

Sandra, who was looking forward to some distance from her half-sister, asked, "But what about your visit to your father?"

"He doesn't know I'm coming. I wanted it to be a surprise. After we've found our family, I'll go see him."

In spite of her feelings toward her half-sister, Sandra warmed to the idea of not being alone in her quest. Dejectedly she thought that for all she knew Rhonda was the only family she had which meant she'd better value her more. "That sounds fine. We'll get a motel room together."

As they settled this, the bus approached the "WELCOME TO HARMON" sign with its same old slogan "Where Size Don't Matter".

Chapter Seven

Home at Last

The sun shone brightly in Harmon, surely a good sign. The driver directed them to the motel, within walking distance. As they brushed off dried mud from their clothes before entering the motel, they realized their grade school used to be where the Red Roof Inn now stood. No one was behind the desk. Rhonda rang the bell as both looked at a poster of a missing young woman, raven-haired and quite beautiful. She'd been last seen at an RV park on the far south side of Harmon on October 21, about two weeks earlier.

The desk clerk, a younger woman with a name tag introducing her as Mary Belle came on the run. Before her stood two women with expensive-looking, but soiled, clothing, and one had a bandaged arm. As she faced them she did a double take.

Noting her look, Rhonda explained, "We were in a bus accident."

"Oh, yeah! Heard about it on the radio. I'd been wondering why the bus was so late. You all right?"

"We're fine," Sandra answered. "We were among the lucky ones, but no wonder you were staring at us. We must be quite a sight."

"Sorry for staring but are you two twins?'

"Yes!" caroled Rhonda. "But two years apart." She chuckled at the clerk's confusion.

Sandra broke in, "We need a room for a couple nights."

The clerk took care of the transaction, and blurted out, "You two look exactly like someone I went to school with."

Both sisters bombarded the clerk "What's her name?" "Does she still live here?" "Does she have a sister?" "Does her mom still live here?"

"Not so fast! Her name is Rainey Butler and she works at the post office, but I don't know anything about her family…"

"Rainey is here!" Sandra hugged her sister, and then Rhonda inquired, "Is the post office still in the same place?"

"Yes, two blocks up from us, but you better hurry. It closes at 5:00."

Only this incredible news kept their minds off the crash. Without checking out their room and leaving their battered carry-on luggage in the lobby, the two disheveled women left in search of their sister. The desk clerk immediately was on the phone and before the sun set on Harmon, almost everyone in town knew of the sisters' arrival after surviving the bus crash.

The pair found Rainey, efficient in a postal uniform, behind the counter waiting on a long line of end-of-the day customers. Standing at the end of the line, the sisters watched the smiling, competent blonde postal clerk for some time. The line continued to grow. Rhonda nudged Sandra when she noticed a poster of the missing woman.

When they reached the front of the line, both broke into their own huge smiles until they noticed a long scar down the side of Rainey's face which otherwise looked like theirs with the same features and skin tone.

Rainey looked confused as she observed two excited women who looked like some sort of disaster victims. Finally recognizing them, she spoke with little emotion and a flat look in her eyes. "Ronnie Lee? Midge?"

"Yes, your sisters but . . ." Sandra looked at the people behind her who gawked at the trio of look-alikes and spoke quickly, "Could you meet us for dinner after you get off work and we will explain all this?"

Rainey nodded. Her voice lacked the warmth she'd shown customers. "Okay. I have to check in on my family. How about 7:00 at the Texas Roadhouse? It's new. On the main street."

Agreeing to that, the two sisters returned to the motel. A different desk clerk was on duty and Rhonda asked, pointing to the poster, "Have they found that girl yet?"

"No," answered the elderly clerk, a man stooped by age with thick glasses and without a nametag, "And I doubt they ever will."

"Why?"

"After she was reported missing, half the town, me included—I'm Chet, by the way—scoured every bit of the land around the RV Park. They even brought in dogs, but they couldn't pick up any scent and none of us volunteers found a trace of her."

"Do you think she just got tired of RV-ing and left on her own?" asked Rhonda.

This conversation made Sandra very uncomfortable. Beginning to feel sore from the accident, she spotted a young man and asked if he'd help them with their luggage. Rhonda noticed the good-looking man, also, and cut off conversation with the old desk clerk.

* * *

Both sisters fortunately had a change of clothing in their carry-ons. Each showered and dressed for the dinner with their sister. Rhonda put her thoughts into words, "Rainey didn't seem happy to see you, and she called me Midge. Wow, do I look that young?" She preened in front of the mirror over the desk in their room, and changing course asked, "How on earth did she get the scar? How terrible to have her beautiful face marred. That makes me think of that poor missing woman and what kidnappers could do to her."

Sandra ignored most of Rhonda's monologue and addressed the question about the scar. "It looks well-healed which means it must be an old injury." Then almost under her breath she murmured, "I'm afraid she blames me for her going to foster care, where she might have gotten the scar. Somehow I have to win her over."

"Sandra, while we wait, we should do something about clothes. We can't wear two outfits forever and I know there aren't any good clothing stores in either Gurney or Harmon. We should use the motel's computer for guests and order some to come overnight."

Her sister answered, "Great idea!" as Rhonda rummaged through her purse and howled, "My wallet must have fallen out of my purse during the crash. Now what will I do?"

After some discussion, Sandra agreed to put her sister's purchases on her card. They went downstairs to find a computer. Shopping occupied them until it was time to meet their sister, whose acceptance Sandra wanted more than anything.

Not to happen that night. The older sisters, well observed by Harmon diners, waited for some time in the restaurant for the third sister. Sandra sipped a Diet Coke while Rhonda had downed two dirty martinis by the time Rainey arrived. Looking very reserved, she apologized for her lateness but gave no reason. Sandra explained that the one she thought was Midge is Sue-Ellen, their half-sister. Rainey looked thoroughly confused but before she could ask, the waitress wanted their orders. Rainey and Rhonda opted for dinner salads while Sandra wanted a more substantial steak.

Sandra and Rhonda filled her in on the bus accident, and Rainey's eyes grew big. She felt somewhat drawn to her sisters who had gone through that ordeal in a quest to find their family and asked for assurance that both were okay.

Rhonda, tongue loosened by the drinks, was ready to move on from the bus accident. She babbled on about their relationship, talking about their Roy Lee who she thought was her father until her real father showed up her and moved her to another town, before Rainey and Midge were born. The rest of the evening evolved into a convoluted conversation about given names and current names and relationships.

Rainey said little to Sandra, but she warmed somewhat to Rhonda. "You're my sister and no ever told me about you. This is baffling." Rhonda took her sister's hand.

Sandra interrupted by asking about Midge. Rainey said with resignation in her voice, "When Mama didn't come back for us, a couple adopted her. I haven't seen her since. For a moment I thought one of you was Midge, which is silly because she was very dark-haired." Her voice trailed off.

"But what about you?" Sandra pried.

Rainey's voice turned icy. "I did just fine without any sisters or Mama. Please excuse me. I need to go home, need to help my daughter with her math homework."

"Oh, we're aunties!" Rhonda cooed.

"That's true. My husband and I have a son and daughter."

"We're sisters-in-law, too!" Rhonda's enthusiasm, fueled by a third dirty martini, was over the top.

As Rainey walked away, Sandra asked after her, "When may we meet your family?"

"We'll see." Rainey's indifference showed in her voice.

Back at the motel, Sandra felt depressed. "The Ice Princess. She doesn't care about us."

"Oh, give her a break, Sandra. You're too uptight. She never expected to see either of her sisters again let alone a new one. She was overcome."

"I sensed much hostility, and I didn't even get to ask her about Mama."

"Sorry to end this conversation but I need to get ready to meet Ray."

"Ray?" Sandra couldn't keep the surprise out of her voice. "Is he someone you knew before?"

"No, remember, he was that hunk with the curly black hair who helped us with our luggage after we came back from meeting Rainey?"

Sandra recalled that incident but except to tip him, she scarcely had looked at the man. Then she remembered. "Wasn't he a lot younger than us?"

Rhonda ignored the question. "He gets off at 11:00, and we're going somewhere for a nightcap."

Sandra shook her head. They'd been in town less than six hours and her sister had a date. *Oh, well, all I want is to soak in a hot bath. I hurt all over from being bounced around in that bus.*

First, she rinsed out her blouse. She was grateful for extra underwear she'd slipped in her purse and hoped the Internet purchases would arrive if not tomorrow, very soon.

Sandra had a nightmare of the bus crash, only Rainey also was on the bus. Rhonda dreamed of Ray.

Chapter Eight

Body in Paradise

Stan Belkin already had figured out Maria was up to something. Before he could question her, Chief Ortega summoned both of them.

"Something new for the 'Dynamite Duo' to investigate. There's a rash of boat thefts out on the Island. Apparently, someone with a truck equipped with a trailer hitch, trolls neighborhoods on Padre Island in broad daylight, looking for boats on trailers. If the hitch matches or can be adapted, he hooks up a trailer with a boat on board and drives off. Most have taken place on two streets, Coquina Bay, close to the National Seashore Park, and Captain Kidd, closer to where they're building that damnable water park."

Maria held her breath, fearing another diatribe about one of the chief's favorite topics, the folly of the new park that would be "a (expletive) nightmare of traffic and security problems for SCCPD". He had gone ballistic once about the troubles ahead for the SCCPD; everyone in the department believed their epithet spewing, red-faced chief was going to have a heart attack.

"How does boat stealing affect us? Isn't this a job for..." Detective Belkin wasn't allowed to finish as the volatile chief interrupted with a few choice words before shouting, "I say whose job is whose, and if you'd hear me out, you'd know this definitely is a job for two hotshot detectives."

Chagrined, Belkin and his partner, who also wondered why they would have to spend time looking for stolen boats with the trial looming, didn't say another word as the Chief gave them a withering look. "We got an anonymous tip, apparently from a boat thief with a conscience, to look on the Island Road for a boat christened 'Hole in My Pocket'. The boat he described fits the description of one of several reported stolen. Just last night the owners reported it as gone but failed to mention a body."

Interest guaranteed, the detectives said in unison, "A body!"

"Forensics is on the way there now. Thought you might want to check out the scene. It already is on one of the stupid pop stations that there's a strong possibility it's your Missing Doctor, and homicide is likely."

"We're on our way."

East on SPID, across the causeway and JFK Bridge, the two detectives drove straight to the Island and turned left on 361, recently renamed The Island Road that bisected a small jut of North Padre Island and all of Mustang Island. They received a call from headquarters saying that the church secretary of Island in the Son United Methodist church reported a boat that had been abandoned in the church parking lot. The name was the same, "Hole in My Pocket". They saw the church to their left and pulled in the lot. As soon as they saw the body, which had been partially unwrapped from a tarp, they knew it didn't belong to the missing Dr. Rhonda. They called headquarters for the address and sped away to find the owners of the boat.

Ed and Sally Post, residents of a North Padre neighborhood, sat at the breakfast table. They'd been sitting there a long time but except for a few sips of coffee, neither had touched the breakfast tacos Sally had prepared in hopes of cheering both of them. It hadn't worked.

Holding her head as if suffering from the empress of headaches, Sally moaned, "What are we going to do?"

Ed shook his head but grabbed for the phone in his pocket that has become like a body part for him as for millions of others. "I'm calling the cops again. I called last night, and I haven't heard a word, not a word. That's one expensive boat, and what are they doing to get it back?"

"Ed! How can you even worry about your stupid boat at a time like this with Daddy's death . . ." Sally burst into tears.

She and her husband had moved from Connecticut four years ago. Ed had gotten sick of northern winters and wanted a job in coastal Texas where he could buy a boat and spend his free time fishing. Sally's aging father had moved with them. He spent his days in the warmth of the South Texas sun as he fished off the dock of the canal house Ed and Sally bought on The Island.

Dean's health began to decline, but one Sunday when Dean seemed to be feeling better than he had in a long time, Ed and Sally took him for a ride in their new boat. Sally now fixated on her dad's last boat ride in the Gulf at sunset, which had been especially glorious. The doorbell startled her as it chimed a strain from "Margaritaville".

Ed jumped up, grumbling it was too early for visitors. Sally, thinking it was one of her church friends, gathered her robe around her. By the time she reached the door, the two detectives had introduced themselves.

"Did you find my boat?" demanded Ed while Sally flew at Belkin, clawing his jacket. Ed tried to stop her, but the bereaved guilt-ridden woman spilled all, "Was Daddy still in it? He was ninety and we took him for a ride in the boat late Sunday afternoon. We think he had a heart attack and we wrapped him in a tarp and tied rope around the tarp, and we left him in the boat because we wanted our kids to come down here for a burial at sea because he loved the Gulf, but Sunday night someone stole the boat."

Sally stopped for a breath while Ed shook his head, Belkin pried her off him, and Maria assured the stricken woman that her father had been found just as she described. Sally hugged Maria in gratitude as she sobbed, "I was petrified that the thieves would find him and on their way to Mexico—that's where they're selling all these boats they're stealing, you know–they'd dump him in the desert."

Stan asked if they could sit down. Defeated, Ed led them into their spacious living room with its exquisite pastel coastal décor. "I have to charge you with not reporting a death and there are specific regulations about 'burials at sea', but because the body was stolen before you reported the death, charges may be dropped. You will have to come to SCCPD headquarters to make a statement and to identify the body. Forensics will determine how your father died. If it's as

39

you said, no foul play, the body will be released to you in a few days. You probably will face a fine."

Both Ed and Sally nodded.

"You really should have mentioned the body when you called to report the boat missing."

Sal and Ed bowed their heads in shame. Finally, Ed asked," We're ready to go, but could you tell me where they found the boat?"

"The parking lot of the church on 361, on Mustang Island," replied Maria.

"That's my church!" Sally shrieked.

"You probably know the secretary," Maria added,

"Of course, Connie Harris."

"She was the first to spot the abandoned boat and called us; she said a lot of things had been abandoned on the church lot, including a dog, but this was the first boat. She pinpointed where to locate it."

"I feel much better that Daddy was by the church," Sally said simply.

"Come with us as soon as you can dress."

* * *

After viewing the body and making their statement, Sally and Ed received a ride home from a police officer. Ed wasted no time going to the church to hook up his boat, guarded by another police officer, who knew that he was coming but had to check his credentials. Sal rushed into the church office to talk Connie about a memorial service for her father.

* * *

Lost in their own thoughts about the peculiarities of their jobs, the detectives said little on the way home. They heard the police radio crackle and a news bulletin that there had been a bus wreck near Harmon, Arkansas. It would be a while for the name of the town to have any meaning for either.

Reaching SCCPD, Belkin said, "I do believe the couple is telling the truth. They'll get both the boat and Daddy back. They aren't criminals—just stupid. They may not be charged

40

for a crime, but they'll face a stiff fine for not reporting 'Daddy's' death."

"I agree. That has to be the easiest case we've ever cracked," Maria commented, but never giving up, added, "but it didn't lead us to the Missing Doctor. That case still isn't solved."

Chapter Nine

Back to Childhood

The following day Sandra led her reluctant sister from the motel on the lot where their school had been located along the familiar path to the trailer park. Their clothing order had arrived and both looked quite presentable.

Rhonda had balked. "Why do you want to go there? I'd rather find the little house where we lived." Then changing the subject she added, "I don't know if I want to walk around. What if we find that missing woman's body?"

"All I want to find is someone who knew our family. It's not far and well-traveled. I doubt we'll find a body. I walked this route every day from school, and you must have until your daddy came."

"I don't remember," Rhonda murmured.

The Bluebird Trailer Park looked even more run-down than they could have imagined. They walked past aging trailer homes with bedraggled yards, junk piled around each site; most, they noted, looked vacant. A few people sitting outside on sagging webbed lawn chairs looked at them with curiosity but didn't return the smiles and "good mornings" of the women. They found home site Number 14 with the trailer where they had lived. The former home listed to one side, leaning off the foundation, front door open, hanging from one hinge.

Sandra gasped. Not just at the state of the trailer but the auditory memory of the door as her father slammed it, the beginning of the end for the family she wanted desperately to reunite.

Both peeked inside and could see nothing but rotted paneling, broken furnishings. Vandals had trashed their home, anything of value gone long ago. No treasured items they could keep for the memories. Looking closely, they saw someone had used red paint to scrawl "Murderer" on the outside. The sun had faded it to palest pink.

None of this moved Sandra as did a yellow climbing rose, brave with the last blossoms of the season. Mama had planted it in front of the trailer and trained it to grow on a broken wooden trellis she bought at a garage sale. The trellis had rotted. A partial post to which it had been attached still stood, and the rose had wound itself around it. Sandra took out her phone and took a photo of the yellow roses that were her mother's pride. *Someday I'll show it to her, but I never want her to see the rest of this.*

"Let's go over to the rental office," Sandra suggested.

"Why?"

Sandra didn't respond as a trip to the rental office brought back a memory, the angry voice of the owner, demanding overdue rent. Sometimes her mother put her hands on the welfare check before her father cashed it to buy Jack Daniels. Sandra, imitating her mother with head held high, would march with her to the office to pay the rent even before it came due. *Then we'd go to the grocery store and have good meals. That was before Mama started drinking.*

Rhonda interrupted her sister's thoughts as she raised her voice. "For the second time, why do you want to go there?"

"Just to ask if anyone knows anything about Mama."

Under the now familiar poster of the missing dark-haired woman taped to the office window was a hand printed sign: CLOSED——BACK IN AN HOUR.

Who knew when the owner left? Five minutes or fifty-five minutes? Since that person could be back any time, Sandra convinced her sister that they should wait. Rhonda made it clear she wanted to leave this depressing place and kept up her moaning.

Sandra sat in one of two swings in a set that was all that was left of the trailer park playground. Rhonda joined her.

"Do you remember swinging here?"

"I really don't remember anything about here. It was such a short time before a strange man saying he was my daddy came to take me away. I didn't want to leave my family, but I was only six and had no choice. I hated Mama because she let me go without a fuss, but later I understood she knew I'd be better off."

A teasing voice derailed further conversations. "Aren't you girls a little old to be swinging? It's good you're both skinny because that rusty, old thing looks like it's about to collapse."

Both looked up to the bent, rusted pole to which the swing chains attached and then to the man unlocking the office door.

Jumping off the swings, Sandra asked if they could talk to him a minute. As she asked, she realized that he was the familiar-looking man on the bus, who helped passengers, the one in a suit who now wore beige cargo pants, a faded Mount Rushmore T-shirt and a baseball cap. Relief swept over her that he wasn't a police investigator trailing her. As she wondered if he was the owner's son, she almost missed what he said next.

"Sure can, but I hope you're not looking to rent a site because I have been bought out by a corporation. They're building a 'big box' store. I'm trying to relocate the few people left. A lot of folks just left their trailers and moved into subsidized housing."

Sandra stammered, "We definitely don't want to live here. I just wonder if anyone around her could tell me about the family that lived on Site 14, where the trailer has almost fallen over. Are you . . . (she took a deep breath and voiced an assumption because she'd just figured out he had looked familiar on the bus because he resembled the owner's little boy she used to know) . . . the owner's son?"

"I am. Always meant to clear site 14 because after such a long time, it didn't look like anyone planned to come back. Now the new owner will have the pleasure of bulldozing it."

Sandra repeated her question. "Do you or anyone know anything about the family who lived there?"

"I know the site but all I know about the family is from my ma, who owned this before I did. I wish she were here because she could help you, but she's in a nursing home in another town. Anyways she said there was a big scandal. The man was driving drunk and killed a family in a head-on. He went to prison—ten years for each one he killed—I think. The mom disappeared right after they sentenced him." The man's voice trailed off.

"Do you know where the mom went?" Sandra asked with urgency in her voice while

Rhonda appeared fascinated with her shoes.

"No, I don't, but the girls lived there alone for a while. My ma knew they were too young to live alone and, besides, they had no way of paying the rent. I think she turned them in to Child Protection. Or maybe she called the school and they did. I was in a world of my own back in junior high because I don't remember anything except the oldest girl ran away. Everyone in town made a big deal out of that."

"They did?" Sandra asked with surprise.

"They sure did. I knew her because we were in school together and I'd seen her here in the park. I'm sure she never noticed me, but I noticed her because she was pretty and had blonde hair. There was a big search for her and the police questioned all of us in her grade about her, if she'd told anyone where she was going, all that. Then the police called it off because they believed she was with her mother. The littler girls got adopted and moved away."

As he spoke Sandra remembered an under-sized kid with severe acne that received his share of bullying just as she had. She smiled and said, "I'm Ronnie Lee, the one who ran away and, as you talked, I remembered you. We had something in common because the bullies made our lives miserable."

The man's eyes brightened, "You're Ronnie Lee? No way! Didn't I see you on the bus that had the rollover?" As both women said "yes", he, looking at Sandra, continued, "I thought you were a nurse or maybe a doctor the way you took care of the passengers. But, what's more important, are you both okay after that crash?"

"We were among the lucky . . .'" began Sandra, but Rhonda interrupted, "We're fine, how about you?

"I had a goose egg, still here," he lifted his baseball cap to show them. "But no real damage. As I was saying," he continued, looking at Sandra, "You looked vaguely familiar, but in my memory, you were blonde."

Sandra, even more determined to grow back her natural color, apologized, "I'm sorry, I don't remember your name, but I remember you always sat in the back of the class."

"I'm Wayne Clark, and I did sit in the back. I was a runt with pimples."

Rhonda interrupted, "Well, you sure turned out to be a fine-looking man. Are you married?"

"Not at present. And who are you?"

"I'm Rhonda, a half-sister to Ronnie Lee, only now she's Sandra."

"Glad to meet you both."

"Wayne," implored Sandra, "are you sure you have no idea where our mother went?"

Wayne frowned. "I take it that you keep asking about your ma that you weren't with her."

"Right."

"I'm sorry. I don't think anyone knew where she was except maybe the police and I guess they didn't pursue looking for her and charging her with child abandonment."

"At least people did look for me." That thought made Sandra inordinately happy because ever since she ran away, she had wondered if anyone even bothered to look for the murderer's daughter.

"They certainly did."

"By the way, speaking of missing girls," interrupted Rhonda, "do you know anything about the woman who's missing?"

"Only that she has been missing for several weeks, and there has been no trace. It's real hush-hush but there are rumors the sheriff's department found evidence of a kidnapping or possibly a murder. Her name is Marjorie, I think."

Rhonda's eyes had gotten very big when Sandra broke in, "We won't take up any more of your time. Thank you, Wayne."

"Just a minute. One of the police officers told me that the reason we had to fill out papers after bus crash is because there could be a class action suit against the bus company."

Rhonda interjected, "We're staying at the Red Roof Inn if you'd like to get together with me some time, you know to discuss the accident and a settlement that will make us all rich."

As they walked away, Sandra poked her sister with her elbow and commented, "You're shameless."

"I don't want to live like my sister, Sister Sandra the Nun," Rhonda teased.

"Hey! You have Ray. Maybe I wanted Wayne. I did see him first, years ago."

They both laughed, and Sandra suggested that before returning to the motel they stop at a diner that she remembered because Daddy took them and Mama there on payday back when they owned their own home. Smiley's, known for his world-famous burgers, was in its third reincarnation. The place had gotten shabby but still had the best burgers in this part of the world, recently reinforced by a visit by Guy Fieri. A life-size cutout of the television star, connoisseur of "Diners, Drive-ins, and Dives," stood at the entrance.

Besides Guy's likeness, the missing woman stared down on the diner from posters displayed on the walls of each booth. As they enjoyed burgers and malts to commemorate their trip back to childhood, Rhonda looked very solemn. She stared at the poster and shuddered, "I hate the idea that beautiful girl was murdered."

Rhonda had seemed obsessed with the missing woman from the first time she saw the photo in their motel. Her eyes were glued to the photo and then shifted her eyes to her sister. "Sandra, was your dad really a murderer?"

"The court had another name for it. I can't remember it from when I was a kid, but today I assume it was criminal negligence or vehicular homicide." As she spoke both girls noted people in a booth across from them looking at them and talking in low voices.

47

"I bet that is what those people in the booth across from us are whispering about," Rhonda commented.

"Possibly," Sandra answered decisively, "but we just can't let it bother us."

Rhonda played with her straw and uncharacteristically was silent. At length, she confessed, "Sandra, there's something I need to tell you."

"What?"

"Let's wait until we get back to the motel. It's a long story."

"I thought we should stop at the police department and tell them who we are and ask if they know where Mama went."

"Wait until you've heard my story."

Sandra couldn't coax another word from her sister.

Chapter Ten

Sleuthing on the Sly

On Friday evening Maria and Xavier drove to the San Antonio airport. They had to wait for several hours to board their flight to Chicago. Xavier had no trouble sleeping in a hard, plastic chair but Maria stayed awake thinking about the secretive trip she had plotted after her non-productive conversations with Stan.

As soon as Stan had left her cubicle, she'd thought: *What I need to do is go to the last place Rhonda/Sandra was known to be, at the Cavendish home in Chicago. I know both Dr. Linda and I talked to the couple on the phone, but I want to talk to them in person. Mr. C. gave us a phony address, but I did find the correct one on the Internet. Chicago could be a nice little get-away for Xavier and me. I'll tell him tonight.*

That night the almost engaged couple met at Applebee's for their mid-week date. The crowded restaurant had a waiting list. They opted to sit at the bar even though Xavier had to help his petite gal climb up on the tall stool.

Maria asked if Xavier would consider a weekend trip to Chicago, "I have enough frequent traveler miles for both of us to fly on an airline from San Antonio."

"This isn't like that trip to San Antonio not too long ago that could have landed you in the unemployment line, is it?" asked Xavier with a sly wink.

Maria looked embarrassed and spoke rapidly, "Oh, no. This doesn't have anything to do with an ongoing case. I thought we could have a romantic getaway, do a little Christmas shopping…" Her voice dropped, "and …"

Xavier interrupted, "Sounds great up to the 'and'. What's up?"

"There is a little digging around I want to do, but it won't take long."

"I knew it! What are we getting into this time?"

Maria wanted to avoid another argument about her job, which her man considered much too dangerous for a woman.

The only reservation she had about marrying the smart, good-looking Xavier was the fear her job would be the cause of ongoing arguments. On this issue, he wasn't sensitive of her needs like most men of their generation. Playing up to him, she replied, "I just want you to go with me as back-up to a guy's place to ask him a couple questions. I'll call and make an appointment for early Saturday. That way we won't waste any of our time together." Maria ended by leaning sidewise to give him a persuasive kiss and almost falling off the barstool.

After he finished laughing, her fiancé-to-be agreed, "How can I resist?"

They picked a date, the second Friday of the month, and Maria made plane reservations for late Friday night. The night arrived. Their flight was delayed.

When they finally boarded the flight, Xavier Valdez asked Maria to tell him about the "Chicago thug" with whom she had scheduled a visit.

"I wouldn't call him a thug, more of a 'white-collar criminal'. I think he's part of an extensive network of people who produce false documents, everything from driver's licenses and birth certificates to college credentials."

"Is there a big market for all that?" Xavier was incredulous.

"Unfortunately, it's huge, but let's talk about something else. Like getting engaged."

"Oh, is this a proposal?" Xavier teased.

"Come, on! Do I have to remind you that you proposed weeks ago and that we agreed at Christmastime we'd announce it.

"Oh, sure, I remember! I got down on one knee with only that monster cat of your as a witness. How old is he anyway?"

"Big Boy is six. Why?"

"How long do cats live?"

Maria didn't like the tone of this conversation. "Why do you ask?'

"Ma is deathly afraid of cats."

"That's okay. I don't intend to include him in the wedding party."

"You know what I mean, when Ma comes to visit us."

"I'm not even sure Big Boy will live with us. Sydney and I share custody of him." *But I love cats and always expected to have a cat for a pet. Maybe I can help my future mother-in-law overcome her fear.*

Xavier had his own thoughts. *I guess this is as good a time as any* since *I brought up that overbearing cat I only pretend to like. Maybe I'll have to bribe Sydney to keep him. I could give her a good trade-in on her old car.* He finally broke the uncomfortable silence "Speaking of my mother, Sweetheart, I wanted to tell you something. I thought we'd shop for rings in Chicago…"

Maria's eyes lit up, and she clapped her hands.

"But when I told Ma, she had a different plan. She wants me to give you my great-grandma's ring. She says it's really beautiful and a family heirloom."

Maria had met Xavier's mother and liked the sweet, though stereotyped traditional Hispanic woman completely different from her mother. Mrs. Gonzalez was a contemporary working mom while Señora Valdez had always stayed home to care for a large family of children, cleaned endlessly, and cooked incredible Mexican meals. Now Maria wondered how much power her future mother-in-law had over her only son. Not wanting to make a fuss over a ring she hadn't even seen, she responded with mustered enthusiasm, "I can't wait to see it!"

"It won't be long until Christmas."

They both slept.

The pilot asked the passengers and attendants to prepare for landing.

* * *

After securing a rental car and a checking-in at the hotel where Maria had made reservations, the couple left to find the address for Brian Cavendish.

51

"I can see why you wanted me to come along," Xavier boasted. "This isn't the best neighborhood."

Maria let him think what he wanted. This neighborhood wasn't that bad. She'd been called to considerably worse in Corpus Christi, especially during her second case when they tracked down the kids from the worst parts of the city, kids who had tagged beautiful Corpus Christi homes with gang graffiti on Woolridge near Rodd Road.

As they reached an apartment complex, Maria checked for the right apartment number in the bright red notebook she always carried instead of the black one supplied by the PD, just to show her independence. She rang the doorbell. A tall man with a baby resting on his shoulder opened the door. Baby gear filled the room behind him.

For a second Maria gazed at the darling baby and thought of the ones she and Xavier would have someday, but got down to business immediately

"I'm Detective Maria Gonzalez from Corpus Christi, and this is my assistant, Xavier Valdez. Maria showed him her badge and asked, "Are you Brian Cavendish?"

"I am, and this is Sadie. How can we help you? He moved a basket of infant laundry he had been folding from the couch and invited them to sit down. He handed the baby to Xavier, who reacted as if he had been given an explosive device, while Brian scooted a chair over for himself. Retrieving his child, who promptly fell asleep, Brian explained, "My wife is grocery shopping. It's just Sadie and me." (He didn't say, *Actually I arranged a day-out for Gracie because I didn't know how this will last and what it might be about since I haven't discussed my former career with her.)*

"Please, can you tell me what this is about?"

"Do you know Sandra Lewis?"

"Sandra? Of course, she has been a friend forever."

"Do you know where she is now?"

Brian looked thoughtful. "She came to Chicago in September and we saw her a few times. She left after Sadie was born in October. She planned to return to Corpus Christi and go to college winter term."

Another clue made Maria smile. *I'll check that out when I get back. I know from Dr. Hernandez that she has put the Missing Doctor's townhouse up for sale but who knows where she's living?*

The smile gone, Maria answered, "There's something I have to ask. Did you create medical credentials for Sandra Lewis?"

Brian put on a quizzical look. "Medical credentials? I don't know what you mean by that, but I certainly did not." And then he thought, *At least I can be truthful about that. I gave those credentials to her sister and not her..*

"Do you know Dr. Rhonda Collins?"

"Funny you should ask. Someone from Corpus Christi called me a while ago and asked if I knew a Dr. Rhonda. Don't remember the last name and I said 'no'. Then it occurred to me. Sandra has a sister in Corpus Christi, a physician. I never met her, but Sandra showed me a photo and they look enough alike to be twins."

Shock registered in Maria's eyes. There really were two women involved in the crime she'd solved. *But only one DNA for Rhonda and her 'sister'? No! Impossible. Sandra and Rhonda are the same person. That's what we figured out. I'm determined to find her.* Maria thanked Brian for his time and commented on his cute daughter who just woke up to give everyone a smile.

"Sandra isn't in any sort of trouble, is she?"

"She's not the person of interest. We're trying to find the person who is manufacturing false credentials."

Brian gave no indication he knew anything about such nefarious matters or about the investigation he now faced in Illinois.

Maria thanked Mr. Cavendish and indicated to Xavier that they were leaving.

"He sure didn't seem like the hard-core criminal type with all that baby stuff," commented Xavier as they walked to their rental car.

Maria nodded but she had different thoughts. "Cavendish wasn't honest with us. He acted too cool about

53

everything. He pretended not to understand what I talked about, but I think he's knows a lot more than he let on."

"I sure wouldn't brand him a criminal."

"That's why I'm the detective and you're not."

Xavier scowled. "Only until we have our own baby and then you will stay home where you belong."

This made Maria angry, but she ignored it, because she didn't want a fight. "My love, work's done. Let's go have fun!!"

Chapter Eleven

Putting on a Show

Rhonda took a deep breath. "Okay, Sandra, here's what I've been keeping from you. I've seen Mama. I know where she is."

Sandra's eyes flashed anger as she lost the cool, polite demeanor she had perfected as Dr. Rhonda. She stood over her sister who'd flopped down on her bed and barked, "What? You know where she is? Why haven't you told me?"

Rhonda sat up. "Settle down, Sis. It's complicated."

"How long have you known? Did you know when we were in Oklahoma?"

"I've known for a few years, but not until after you left Tulsa. Sit down and I'll tell you all about it."

Both sisters sat on the edge of one bed. Rhonda had plan how she would tell her sister about Mama from the time they met on the bus. This was a chance to show off her acting ability, which for years had fueled her greatest desire of being an actress in Hollywood.

Rhonda jumped up and stood at the end of the bed in front of the dresser, topped by the television. "This is what happened to Mama. I pieced this together from several sources, but I will tell it just as she might have told it. When I say 'I', that's Mama talking."

Sandra gave her a look of resentful acceptance; her sister, the drama queen, was now Mama. Changing identities obviously ran in the family.

Rhonda clasped her hands to her chest and began in a soft, trembling voice, "This first part I don't remember but people have told me there was a trial in my hometown. When the judge handed down the sentence, I went nuts. They say my husband was given 30 years for three counts of death while driving drunk because he had a long, drunk driving record. But the part about him being my husband is wrong because I never married. What I remember is all I wanted to do was get as far away from Harmon as possible. I hitchhiked from one town to another. Finally, I wound up in a town about a hundred miles from home."

Sandra interrupted her sister's dramatic recitation, "And she didn't think about the little girls and me at all?"

"No, apparently not," Rhonda said in her own voice. Noting the sadness in Sandra's eyes, she amended, "If she had been in her right mind, she never would have left you, but she had a total psychotic break-down when she heard the sentence."

In a stern voice she admonished, "Now please, don't interrupt me again."

Sandra mused. *How she's enjoying this. All those trips to California when we were in Tulsa had to do with my sister pursuing an acting career.*

"Mama's" voice returned stronger and more confident. She held her hands, palms up high like an evangelical preacher. "The police found me drunk on a street in the town of Homer. I didn't know my name or where I came from. They put me in detox. Afterwards I joined AA and have been sober ever since, but I suffer from a sort of amnesia. I don't remember big chunks of my life. All I remember is that at sixteen I got pregnant and had a daughter out of wedlock. She looked just like me. I named her Sue-Ella. Somehow I knew that when I left Harmon she was safe with her daddy."

Sandra stood up, challenging her sister, "Why doesn't she remember the rest of us?"

"I asked my Tulsa therapist that and she said what she had done, abandoning three children, horrified her to the extent that she blocked it out. The same for the husband, who beat her and wound up in prison. She's forgotten that, too. Now, let me finish her story."

Rhonda obviously enjoyed telling the story more than Sandra endured listening to it while she wondered how much improvising her half-sister was doing. With a defeated look Sandra sat down again while "Mama" continued proudly. "With help I found a studio apartment and a job with a tailoring shop. I was there until I retired a few years ago. Then I decided I wanted to see my daughter and her daddy. I took a bus to Gurney. B.J., Sue-Ella's daddy, took me in and I've been there ever since." Rhonda smiled and gave a little bow. "The end."

"Why didn't you tell me sooner, Rhonda?"

"One reason is selfish. You and Mama had all those years together. I enjoyed being her only daughter. Even when I found out you were in Texas, I made no effort to find you and tell you."

"That doesn't surprise me," Sandra snapped, unable to suppress anger towards her sister.

Ignoring the outburst, Rhonda continued in a soft, please-believe-me tone, "There's another reason. As we became reacquainted on the bus, I wanted to tell you, but I didn't want you to be hurt. Now you're hurt and probably hate me."

Sandra said nothing as she considered if her sister was as sincere as she sounded.

Rhonda looked imploringly at her sister, waiting for her forgiveness.

"We're renting a car and going there tomorrow."

"Sis, I don't think it's a good idea."

"Why? Did you make up this whole thing?"

Rhonda backed away from the always-composed Sandra who looked as if she might slap her. "No, Sandra. I'm sorry you believe I'd lie about our mother. I just want to protect you from more hurt."

"Don't worry about that. I'm going tomorrow. You can come or stay here."

"Tomorrow's Sunday, and Ray has it off. We were going on an autumn picnic. Can we postpone the trip?"

"NO. I repeat: I am going tomorrow with or without you."

* * *

Later, when both were in bed, Sandra asked, 'Have you ever considered acting?'

57

The woman who thrived on any compliment, first excitedly answered with a question, "Did you think I did a good imitation of Mama?"

"Yes, you change voices very well."

"Oh, thank you, Sandra. I've quit counting all the auditions I've gone to in Hollywood, but I've never had a speaking part. I'm always the out-of-focus blonde with a ponytail in a background scene of some commercial."

"That's a start," Sandra responded.

"The most important thing that has happened to me is I met Eva Longoria on a set. She is gorgeous and really nice."

"Did you know she's from Corpus Christi?" Sandra asked, yawning.

That really excited Rhonda. "Where you lived? If I'd known that then, maybe she could have pulled strings and gotten me a part. Right, Sis?"

Sandra feigned sleep to avoid answering.

Chapter Twelve

The Missing Doctor

It was an unreasonably hot November day in Corpus Christi. Residents lived for the time of year when temperatures changed and tourists disappeared up north, presumably to peek at leaves. Maintenance had taken advantage of cooler temperatures the previous week to turn off the AC in police headquarters, and Stan noticed it seemed as hot inside as out when he entered the police department.

Immediately the desk sergeant Angie, shouted at him, "Do you know, Stan, how many calls we still get on the tip line regarding the Missing Doctor?"

"Only because you tell me every day." Belkin's tone bordered on surly. He walked away after his comment but turned back as Angie continued.

"Obviously the public isn't satisfied that that particular story didn't have an ending, especially a happy ending since they adore the Missing Doctor."

"Nothing we could do when no charges were made against her."

"But people want more. There still are sightings of her and the public doesn't think we did enough to find her."

Belkin shrugged as Maria drifted in with a big smile on her face.

"Whose canary did you swallow, Gonzalez?"

"Let's go in your office."

"I think I have found a positive link between our Missing Doctor and a man in Chicago."

"You, too? Angie was giving me a bad time this morning because of all the calls we still are receiving on the tip line about the Missing Doctor. I keep telling you that ship has sailed."

"True, but we may be able to pin the forgeries on Brian Cavendish of Chicago."

"A bit out of our jurisdiction, partner."

"I know that, but if we link him to it, maybe that will smoke out Dr. Rhonda. Then, at least, we can charge her with the fraudulent will even though the clinic is paranoid about bad P.R. they'll never charge her with impersonation."

"A long shot, and frankly not worth the effort. Forget it, Gonzalez." Stan knew full well she wouldn't.

"By the way, I did pay a visit to Brian Cavendish in Chicago over the weekend. He just lied about everything, but we can't let him get by with it."

Stan shook his head. He should have guessed.

Maria returned to her cubicle. Oblivious to the heat and humidity that caused perspiration beading up on her concentration-creased brow, Maria compiled information from Internet research. Her notes showed that it was relatively easy to obtain documents like I.D. and Social Security cards but much more difficult to secure those like Dr. Rhonda's that included med school, internship and residency records. Basically, it was a matter of finding the persons who could provide what they needed.

The young detective had proved such credentials that enabled Rhonda Collins to practice as a physician were not authentic, but she wouldn't rest until she nailed the person who had provided them. If they could find and arrest the Missing Doctor, who called herself Doctor Rhonda Collins but whose real name was Sandra Lewis, perhaps they could plea bargain to have her provide the identity of the person who aided her. *Or, if I could prove the guilt of the man in Chicago, maybe they could bargain with him to help find Sandra Lewis.*

Her partner said they didn't have jurisdiction over someone in Chicago but if what he did affected a case in Texas, he could be extradited. Somehow, she still had to convince Stan the case merited being reopened, and possibly something she learned in Chicago would give her just the leverage she needed to I.D. the man who had aided Dr. Rhonda.

Maria had a dreamy look and said under her breath. *Someday I will crack this case, with or without Stan's help. I love my job! Nothing will keep me from giving it my all.*

Chapter Thirteen

Not My Daughter

Early Saturday morning, Sandra asked the clerk at the desk, Mary Belle, about car rentals companies. "There still might be one on the main street. It's supposed to close soon, but go ahead and use my phone to find out for sure."

The number had been disconnected.

"Doesn't surprise me," Mary Belle commented, "Even with the new places they've been building, it's a dying town. Wait a minute; maybe the car dealer a few blocks from us rents cars."

Sandra walked half a mile to the car dealer. Posters of the missing woman with a different photo were plastered all over the dealership. It disturbed Sandra whenever she saw these posters throughout the town. From her Internet research, when on the run, she had learned through newspaper photos and televised blurbs that her friends, co-workers, patients, and even strangers had saturated the Coastal Bend with such posters. They even held a vigil for her. It distressed her that she had caused such heartache for so many people. But that wasn't her problem today.

The owner, Jock Paisley, smiled widely when Sandra entered the showroom. His smile disappeared quickly as he refused to rent a loaner to someone from out-of-town even if she had been born in Harmon. As Sandy started to walk away, he smiled big again. "Now, Honey, don't go away mad. I have some unbelievable deals on pre-owned cars."

I might as well buy a car, Sandra thought... *I can walk any place in town but to see Mama and find Midge, I'll need one.* "Anything but a gray Taurus," Sandra murmured.

The cheapest car on the lot was a ten-year old over-sized white van with low mileage as its only virtue. Ugly described it. The dealer didn't point out the van as he showed Sandra several much more expensive too-good-to-be-true bargains, but Sandra spotted it. She took it for a test drive and found it handled well for its size. The man again was filled with smiles and "God Bless You-s" as he accepted Sandra's cash and did the requisite paperwork. "My friend Bucky sells insurance; you're going to need it. Here's his card, and don't forget to transfer the title come Monday and get plates. God Bless you again and just because you're such a sweetheart, I'll put in some gas."

She pondered the purchase on the way to the motel. *I still have quite a bit left in the Chicago account, but it won't last forever.* Back in their room she dragged her sister out of bed and opened the drapes to show her the new chariot.

Rhonda laughed and joked about the "rental" and laughed even harder when Sandra told her she owned it.

"Sorry, they were out of sports cars." There was sarcasm in Sandra's voice, and Rhonda ceased joking but admonished, "Remember I told you this trip isn't a good idea. I hate to see you disappointed."

"It's worth it to me. I want to see Mama again. Who knows, seeing me might be a breakthrough? Please, hurry. I'm ready to go."

While she waited on Rhonda, who took forever, Sandra called the national company that insured her BMW. She gave her Texas address and had the van added to her policy, all done in minutes with a credit card made out to Rhonda Collins. *I didn't do anything to disclose my location,* Sandra assured herself.

With the temporary permit and insurance, the van was road ready before Rhonda. At last they were on the road. Neither said much during the hour-long trip except they agreed they wouldn't tell the parents about the bus catastrophe. Surprisingly, neither had experienced more than one nightmare about the bus incident; but perhaps that was because it was just one more dramatic event in the Jackson sisters' histrionic lives.

An open-air craft stand beside the road, near Gurney, caught Rhonda's eye and she asked her sister to stop. They examined the exquisite handcrafted items the crafter had made. Rhonda bought a patchwork hobo bag for herself, and Sandra found a sweet baby sock doll in a gingham dress and straw hat with tiny flowers. She planned to give it to her mother. They returned to the van enthusiastic about their purchases.

Reaching Gurney, Rhonda gave directions to the home where she grew up after her real father took her from the only family she knew. It still stung that Mama didn't protest at all about giving up her first child to the man whose child she carried when she married Sandra's father. Her life growing up wasn't perfect because of her dad's stream of girlfriends, two of whom he married. Regardless, life was a lot better than it would have been staying with the Jacksons. That life caused Sandra to run away.

Rhonda's dad answered the door and joked while hugging his daughter, "Ma, look what the cat drug in!"

"Sue-Ella, what a wonderful surprise!" Her mother peeked out of the kitchen and then darted back, explaining she needed to take something out of the oven. Calling over her shoulder, "You're just in time for Sunday dinner."

"Dad, this is my sister. She used to be Ronnie Lee."

Sticking out his hand, he welcomed her but said, "I remember you, Honey, but I hope my daughter told you that your ma, she doesn't remember any of her children except her first."

"I hoped seeing me…"

"Well, maybe. She's had a good spell, but some things set her off." He explained she'd had a brain trauma.

The girls' mother returned and stopped when she saw Sandra. "Well, if you're not a beauty. What's your friend's name, Sue-Ella?"

"Mama, I'm Ronnie Lee. I'm your daughter, too."

Mama rotated her right index finger outside her right ear and whispered to Sue-Ella, "Your friend's a bit daft but tell her to stay for dinner. I just took chicken and dumplings out of the oven."

Though prepared, Sandra found this incredibly difficult. She handed her mother the little doll as she wondered about showing her the photo of the roses on her phone. The woman accepted it with a show of gratitude by hugging the guest,

"Well, aren't you sweet. No gal is too old for a dolly. Just look at those bitsy flowers on that hat." She put down the doll, saying. "I was so busy admiring her I almost forgot to say it's time to eat, everyone."

Sandra took a helping of biscuits with the gravy, while avoiding the chicken she couldn't bring herself to eat. Throughout the delicious meal, Sandra tried to catch her mother's eye to see if there was any recognition. Nothing. The main conversation centered on the young woman missing from the RV Park.

"Now I heard," said Rhonda's dad, "and it's true because I heard it from Billy John, whose brother is the sheriff, that they think she was kidnapped from the restroom because they found all her clothes and towel there, and her family said she had gone to take a shower after everyone else went to bed."

"The Missing Woman" had become Rhonda's favorite topic of conversation, much to Sandra's discomfort, and what her dad reported excited her. "Does that mean that her family didn't miss her until they woke up the next morning?"

"Naw, her husband woke up a couple hours after she went to the shower and he realized she hadn't come back; he went looking for her. He found her belongings and, get this, they found a rope on the floor and the shower still was running."

"Well, then everyone I've been talking to is wrong because they say she might have taken off with a lover and doesn't want to be found."

"You two," Mama said. "I don't think that is fit dinnertime conversation." Looking at Sandra, "Don't you agree, Honey? Now what did you say your name is?"

Rhonda diverted her mother's attention from Sandra. "I need to tell you that you might be receiving some mail addressed to Sandra and me."

"How's that again?" asked B.J.

Not wanting to go into the crash that would upset her parents, Rhonda explained without detail that she and her sister didn't have a permanent address after they both recently moved and for that reason had given her parents' address.

That satisfied her dad, who thought that was just fine as they earlier told him that they now stayed at a motel in Harmon. "Yup, lot safer to have mail sent here than to a motel, where they can't be trusted not to open up important things."

"Excuse me," Mama spoke in her loudest voice. "You two interrupted me. I was asking this gal her name."

* * *

Sighing, Sandra crawled behind the wheel for the trip back to Harmon. She tried to keep the bitterness from her voice as she commented, "This must be a fairy tale come true for you, Rhonda, with both of your parents together."

"Something like that." Both women's eyes filled with tears as Rhonda added with true compassion, "I just wish she could have accepted you as part of that fairy tale."

Sandra quickly controlled her emotions and said, "I wonder if Rainey knows her mom is nearby? I also wonder if Mama would have a breakthrough if she saw all four of us together. We have to find Midge."

"Sandra, what if the missing woman is Midge?"

"Please, don't go there."

Chapter Fourteen

Making a Case

Maria almost staggered under the weight of books checked out at the Corpus Christi library. Sydney couldn't help laughing at the little gal with the heavy load. "What's this all about? Wait, I know. It's about a case and you can't tell me a thing; I withdraw my question."

Turning to look at her housemate, Maria laughed, "I've taught you well. You've learned that my cases are the only thing I can't share with you. I'd rather visit with you, but I've planned a quiet evening at home perusing these books in order to solve another case, in my quest to be become Super Woman Detective." She pounded her chest.

Sydney laughed and said, "I thought today everyone uses Google to do research."

"Oh I learned tons on the Internet, but a couple sites referred me to all these source books for more information."

"It will take you eons to get through those. I'm sorry you're stuck here. I planned to ask you to go to a movie I'm seeing with a couple friends, but I won't because I won't mess with your plans, Super Detective. But are you interested in supper? I have carry-out and they gave me way more than I can eat."

Maria inhaled deeply, "Thai food! My fav. Of course, I'll help you out."

The two housemates seldom had the same schedule, but they always enjoyed what time they had together. Maria already had asked Syd to be her maid of honor, and they talked a little about the wedding as well as "comparing notes" about the approaching Thanksgiving weekend.

Afterwards Maria in PJs and red fuzzy rope holed up in her room with Big Boy trying to weasel in between her and whatever book she held. Automatically she'd push him away, and he'd be right back. Maria tried to concentrate on the "manufacture and issuance of false documentation", but she had to stop to pet the demanding cat until he fell asleep.

The biggest "bogus doc rings", she read, currently had to do with passports and travel papers for immigrants, for which they paid enormous amounts of cash. This problem wasn't limited to the US; there were huge rings in Europe, the Middle East and China. The profession of creating "false papers" seemed to date back to the beginning of the written word. *Maybe*, Maria conjectured facetiously, *Prehistoric men lugged around slabs of rocks with false info in drawings.* She learned that International and US Federal agencies as well as states had laws and sentences for those who manufactured and issued such bogus papers and for those who used them.

She found out about "diploma mills" that offered false educational credentials. She learned that forging driver's licenses had become more difficult because of magnetic strips and chips recently embedded in such forms of identification.

Some forgers could supply people with complete new identities with I.D. cards, birth certificates, high school and college credentials, and anything else a person could need. This could be done legally for those in the Witness Protection Program and was done far more often illegally by small-time operators throughout the world.

The problem was bigger than Maria had realized. Like busting a drug dealer, anything she accomplished with false documentation would be small potatoes. She sighed. Then sitting tall, she looked determined. *That's no reason for not trying.* "Big Boy, tomorrow I'm calling the Chicago Police."

The cat woke up with a start and gave her a look she interpreted as encouragement.

* * *

The next morning Maria called the central Chicago PD, gave her name and position and told Desk Sergeant Bailey, who answered, that a Chicago resident might be in the business of manufacturing and issuing false credentials. She finished by stating, "I don't believe he's a member of a ring. I think he works independently and has nothing to do with the major industry of false immigration papers, including passports."

68

The officious desk sergeant thanked her. "Leave your number and we'll call if we need more information."

She wrote it down on the post-it note where she had taken down the facts of the Corpus Christi detective's call, balled it up, and threw it into the trash receptacle. She had a change of heart, dug it out of the receptacle, typed up all the info and put it on a detective's desk.

Chapter Fifteen

Serial Headaches

Returning to the motel, Rhonda immediately called Ray. They arranged to go out for an early supper. Rhonda half-heartedly asked Sandra if she wanted to go along, but Sandra assured her that she had eaten too much of Mama's Sunday dinner and wouldn't need supper.

All I need is a nap to escape life for a while thought Sandra, asleep before her sister finished primping for her date. It was dark when Sandra awakened with a raging headache. She took two Tylenol, which dulled the pain in her head but not in her heart. Being abandoned by her mother a second time when she didn't acknowledge her today was too painful to think about. Her thoughts turned instead to the unsettling state of her finances due to the van purchase. When her sister returned, they needed to have a serious discussion about money. *As if it is possible to have a serious conversation with my flakey sister.*

The headache was back but Sandra decided to ignore it and call Rainey to ask if she knew about their mom. She realized Rainey hadn't given them a number. *One headache after another.* She looked in the phone directory in the bedside table, grateful the small town still put phone books in motel rooms. Not being able to find the number she needed, she decided, *I'll walk up to the post office tomorrow to see her. In the meantime, I want to see what I can do to find Midge.*

She went downstairs to the lobby and used the computer to begin an Internet search for Midge Jackson in Arkansas. She widened the search to the entire USA. She found nothing and conceded: *My head hurts too much to concentrate. My only hope if, no, when, we find her, she reacts better than Rainey. I loved on that baby girl all the time when we were all together.*

Rhonda returned, in no shape to discuss finances. "Sandra, he's the nicest guy," she slurred. "We went out to

70

eat and had a few drinks, and then——well, let's say it's not hard to get a room when a guy has all the motel keys and knows which rooms aren't rented!"

Sandra chose to ignore all that. "Tomorrow we need to have a serious discussion."

"About what?"

"Finances for one thing, and exactly what our plans are from here out."

Rhonda sobered up, afraid her sister wanted her to move out. "That's easy. I like this little town, especially after meeting Ray. I want to stay here a while with you, Sis." *This works for me because she's so generous. I like having her in charge of finances,* she thought without guilt

Sandra had similar thoughts: *She wants to stay and let me pay all the expenses like Tulsa,* but said, "I'm not opposed to staying, I want to get to know Rainey better."

"Me, too, though she seemed a little judge-y. Probably wouldn't approve of me and Ray."

"We'll talk more tomorrow, Sis." Sandra switched off her lamp to end the conversation though she knew sleep would evade her. She kept thinking how she really did want Rhonda to stay; the more she was around her the more she liked her sister's carefree attitude towards life. She really was a sweet person; but with her dwindling account, she couldn't afford to support both of them,

At last the insomnia gremlins released her and she slept, only to be awakened at 2:00 AM by her cell phone. It showed the call was from Brian.

Sandra glanced at her sister, who slept on, and answered, "Brian, are you all right? Gracie? Baby Sadie?"

"We're fine. Sorry to call in the middle of the night but Sandra, I need to warn you and your sister about something. I have to talk fast because I don't want Grace to hear any of this if she should wake up. "

"Go on, I'm listening."

"A detective from Corpus Christi paid me a visit, and that worries me because I'm already in big trouble. I've helped lots of strangers but only one of my friends, besides you and your sister whom I really know only through you. I agreed to help him transform into attorney. He was fired because of false credentials and he ratted me out. I learned this week I'm being investigated. I know you won't betray me but is there any chance your sister would talk? Then I won't be able to plead it happened only once, which I plan to do since except for this guy, you and your sister, I didn't know any of the other people I helped and they didn't know me. I'm just worried about your sister. . ."

Sandra interrupted, "I can assure you that my sister won't say a word." *How could she when nothing but her borrowed name was involved?* "I'm sorry this happened to you after you've gone straight and have a family."

"Just don't mention this to your sister then, and Gracie just can't know."

"Don't worry. You know I wouldn't do anything to expose you," Sandra promised, but he'd already hung up. The call disturbed her. She's always feared if Brian went down, she would, too; she brushed the thought away. She needed more sleep for something else she had on her mind for today, talking to Rainey.

Chapter Sixteen

Problem Parents

Before Rhonda awakened, Sandra wandered down to the post office. Rainey gave her a tentative smile when she saw her. Sandra asked if she has any breaks when they could have coffee. Rainey said she wouldn't be free until lunch.

Sandra returned to the motel. Following the advice she had given many patients who suffered stress-caused headaches, she meditated and did relaxation exercises. When Rhonda finally awakened, Sandra invited her to come for lunch, but she decided to stay at the motel to catch up on her favorite soap, Days of Our Lives.

As soon as the waitress at Louise's Lunches took their salad orders, Sandra began, "Rainey, there's something I need to tell you. Yesterday Rhonda and I drove to her dad's place in Gurney and Mama is there."

Rainey's usual cool demeanor turned to excitement she couldn't contain. "Mama's alive!" She added, "Praise the Lord!" After a moment her expression of joy left as she asked, "Has she been there all the time?"

"No, she's been in Gurney only a couple years." Sandra watched anger leave her sister's eyes. "Here's the condensed version, and it isn't all good. After Daddy was sent to prison, she had a complete psychotic breakdown. Currently she doesn't remember being married to him or having you, Midge, or me, only Sue-Ella, I mean Rhonda."

Rainey shrugged, waiting for Sandra to continue.

"She hitchhiked to another town west of here right after the trial. She was arrested, went through rehab for her drinking and worked in a tailoring shop there until she retired. She came to Gurney to find Rhonda's daddy, and they've been together ever since."

Rainey grasped her forehead, closing her eyes. "It makes sense why she never has been in touch with Daddy."

"You mean you have?"

"He's not that far away either. I try to go to the prison every month. I'm off Thursday and I'm going then. Would you like to go along?"

It was Sandra's turned to be stunned, "I'll have to think about that. I didn't know if he was out by now, or still alive, for that matter. I guess I didn't even care."

"Let me know. I'll give you my number."

Rainey sounded as if Sandra's coming didn't matter one way or another to her. Sandra felt another headache coming on and began taking deep breaths as Rainey recited the number to put on her phone. With her usual lack of warmth Rainey stated she had to get back to work and left money for her share of lunch.

Sandra sat there a while longer, thinking and doing breathing exercises. She had never wanted to see her father again. Her images of him, a drunk beating his wife while Sandra tried to divert her little sisters with games, still haunted her. *I guess I should go. Car trips always are a way to get to know people better. Rainey has set up boundaries and I want to get past them and be closer to her. If I just can't go through with visiting Daddy, it's not a wasted trip for her because she planned to go anyway.*

Later she called her sister to say she would be happy to go with her on Thursday.

Rainey picked her up at 9:00 sharp and seemed friendlier than she had been on the other occasions they'd been together. "It's about a three-hour drive. We can stop for lunch when we arrive and then go to the prison."

"That sounds fine with me, though I don't know yet if I'm ready to see him."

"The first time is hard, but I've gotten used to it and know how he looks forward to my visits." Anticipating her sister's next question, Rainey continued, "I started visiting about eight years ago when I decided he was the only family I had left."

"How much do you remember about him when you were little?"

"Not much. I remember Mama, you, and Midge much better. What I remember about Daddy is all that I heard whispered by kids at school and in the foster home: he was a drunk and he went to prison because of driving drunk. Later I learned that he had killed three people, including a little baby."

Sandra sighed, "I blame myself for not fighting to keep us together after Mama left, Rainey."

"I heard from kids at school that you ran away. Everyone was talking about the missing girl. The police looked for you, and they finally decided you were with Mama they quit looking for you. They were busy with a new arson case and I guess that's why they didn't look for Mama—all her kids were safe. That's what I heard eavesdropping on my foster mom."

"I was with Mama? Did you think that, too?"

"Yes, and I wanted to cry myself to sleep at night because Mama didn't take Midge and me, too; now I was the big sister and had to try to take care of Midge, who cried for her mama all the time."

"You poor kid."

Rainey lowered her voice. "In spite of my religious beliefs, I hated you up until I heard what you told me about Mama Tuesday."

"Some time I will tell you what happened to me after I ran away from the foster home I was in, and I want you to know I never stopped thinking about you and Midge and how different things could have been if I had stood up to the judge and told him I had been taking good care of you for weeks and I wanted to keep us together."

"You were too young. Even I understood that." Both sisters were near tears, but Rainey got a hold of herself.

"My heart broke again when Midge was adopted. She was cute and sweet while I got ganglier and homelier and became unadoptable."

"Homely? Never!"

"It turned out okay. I stayed in the foster home until I graduated; they treated me like one of their own. They took me to church and that has stayed with me all my life. They supported my participation in school activities, and they were so proud when I was voted Homecoming Queen."

"Good for you, Sister. You and I both are survivors, and that brings me to something personal. It's hardly noticeable but I see you have a scar. How did that happen?"

"Hardly noticeable, ha!" Rainey laugh was filled with bitterness.

"It's okay if you don't want to talk about it."

"It's fine. I went to junior college and I fell in love. We were in a car crash; I suffered several facial wounds but the others weren't as serious. It really didn't matter. He died."

Sandra tried to touch her sister's shoulder, but she flinched. "I've tried not to dwell on it, but you're not only one carrying a load of guilt. The crash happened because he was speeding to get me home because Papa, my foster dad, had a heart attack. He never was well after that. When he died, Clara, my foster mom, moved back to her hometown in Iowa. We still correspond, but I haven't seen her since Papa's funeral."

Sandra had tears in her eyes as she listened to her sister finish her story.

"It was a hard time but I finished junior college, took the Civil Service Exam and have worked for the Post Office ever since. I didn't think any man would want me with my scars, but one did. We married and I became a mom."

"In spite of everything, your adult life has been a lot more   conventional than I've had, or for that matter Rhonda has had."

"Maybe my life seems more conventional than either of yours, but right now I am feeling anything but 'conventional' with a father in prison, two sisters that show up from out of nowhere, and a mother living an hour away that doesn't claim me. I have you and Rhonda but my nightmare of losing people continues, and what can I do about it?"

"I understand, but don't give up. Somehow there has to be a way we can get Mama to recognize us."

The sisters were silent for a long time until they reached their destination. After a light lunch, they went to the prison. Rainey knew all the protocol, which made things easier for Sandra, who had decided she was up to visiting the one person she never had been able to forgive.

When Roy Lee Jackson appeared at the window in the small partitioned visiting section, Sandra, standing back behind her sister, didn't recognize him. He seemed smaller than she remembered. The anger that always showed on his face had been replaced with a kicked-dog look. His thick head of black hair had thinned and grayed. He looked meek in the prison uniform that hung on him, not like the mean drunk she remembered. This poor man didn't look as if he'd swat houseflies.

Rainey sat down first and grabbed the phone, "Hi, Dad. You're looking good."

"Maybe for a prisoner," he said softly. "Not that being in prison all these years will bring back the family I killed. I deserve to be here," he finished dejectedly.

Rainey had heard that statement of remorse many times before and ignored it, "Daddy, I have a big surprise for you today."

"Did you bring one of my grandkids?"

"Not this time. It's another one of your daughters, who," she lied, "is anxious to see you." She beckoned to Sandra, who traded places.

"Hi, Daddy. It's Ronnie Lee."

Her father's eyes filled with tears. "I heard you ran away and I never expected to see you again."

"It took a long time, but I came back. Do you think you can get used to calling me 'Sandra'? That's what I go by now."

"Sandra? Always thought that was a pretty name. Might even have named you that but your mama demanded to be the one who did the naming of our girls. Have you seen her?"

"Yes."

"How is she?"

"She seems happy."

"She never comes to visit me and all the letters I sent her got returned. I don't blame her. I was mean to her and she didn't deserve it. I loved that woman to death, but it was the alcohol that made me mean. I haven't touched a drop since I've been here and, believe me, there's plenty of booze that makes its way in here."

Sandra didn't know what else to say but finally said, "Good for you."

"Daughter, would you tell your mother I never quit loving her?"

"Sure, Dad," seemed like the easiest response. "I guess I should give Rainey a chance to talk."

"Will you come see me again?"

Sandra swallowed. "I will," and she handed the phone back to Rainey while she found a restroom and sobbed for all the lives her daddy had wrecked besides those killed by drunken driving. *But I have to forgive him.*

She splashed water on her face and pasted on a smile for the trip back but after visiting her dad the possibility of both Brian and her going to prison would haunt her more than ever.

Chapter Seventeen

Lunch with Mama

"Rhonda, there's something I need to discuss with you. I want to take Rainey to meet our mother."

"Why? I know it hurt you. Why hurt her, too?"

"I just keep hoping for a breakthrough and one question is, do you want to go?"

"Sure, but when? I don't want it to interfere with another date with Ray."

"You seem quite taken with him."

"Not really. He's just available until someone better comes along."

Sandra didn't respond immediately to that but explained, "Rainey doesn't have to work this Saturday; and on the way back from seeing Daddy, I talked to her about going to see Mama then."

"But Ray has Saturday off, too, and we sort of had plans."

Sandra showed her irritation. "Rhonda, I think taking Rainey to see her mother is more important than 'sort of plans' you have with someone who you're stringing along until 'someone better comes along'. We could take Mama out for an early lunch, and you will have the rest of the day with 'Mr. Available'. Maybe Mama will recognize Rainey."

Sandra usually wasn't unkind and her words stung, but Rhonda rebounded from the thought of arguing. "Okay, okay, I'll go."

"Could you call your dad and make the arrangements?"

Rhonda agreed merrily, "Sure and then I'll call Ray to let him know I can fit him in my busy social calendar later in the day."

After calling her dad, Rhonda told Sandra that her dad said each had a letter from the bus company and there was even a crushed suitcase with Sandra's name. "You have all the luck, sis," Rhonda sniped, trying to get back at her sister for the earlier comments about her relationship with Ray.

The three sisters left for Gurney the next morning. Today they showed similar tastes in clothing with Rhonda taking a clue from Sandra. They wore pants in fall colors and light sweaters with simple jewelry, appropriate for Caleb's Local Diner. Mama had dressed in her finest, a shimmery blue suit, pink striped scarf, oversized earrings, clunky necklace and a jeweled pin in the shape of a turkey.

Rhonda's dad had decided he didn't want to "partake of a hen party". He was content because Mae had put together his favorite ham and cheese sandwich to eat in front of the History Channel.

"Why, Sue-Ella, this time you brought two friends, and they look almost like twins!"

"We'll talk about it at lunch, Mama."

The waitress did a double take when she saw the three nicely dressed women who had to be sisters and the over-dressed but still pretty older woman, obviously their mother. "Why look at you. This must be a family reunion."

Mama laughed. "Not really. This one's my daughter and the other two are her friends."

The waitress raised her eyebrows as she went to get the sweet tea Mama ordered for everyone.

"Mama, remember Sue-Ella brought me to visit."

"Sure, you said you were Ronnie Lee, and who are you?" she asked Rainey.

"Mama, I'm your daughter Lorraine, but you called me Rainey. Ronnie Lee is your daughter, too."

Mama looked obstinate but remained polite. "No, ladies, I just had one child, Miss Sue-Ella, and let me tell you a secret, her daddy and I never got around to getting married. And that's not the worst thing I've ever done..." All three girls held their collective breaths, as Mama paused and finished, "...but I don't remember what it was."

"Mama, but you did marry another man. Remember Roy Lee Jackson or Daddy Jack as Sue-Ella called him?"

Mama closed her eyes and looked as if she was trying hard to remember someone by those names.

80

"I'm sorry, but I don't know anyone with those names."

The waitress returned with the tea and asked for their orders. All ordered a cup of soup and a salad. When the waitress left, Sandra/Ronnie Lee said, "Mama, I saw my daddy, your husband yesterday. He's in prison and he told me to tell you that he's sorry and that he loves you very much."

Mama stuck to her story. "Well, you can tell your daddy, I never knew him but it's nice of him to say he loves me."

Later, as they finished eating, Mama asked, "Why's your daddy in prison anyway?"

Answering honestly in hopes this might trigger a memory, Sandra forged ahead, "He was drunk and had a car accident that killed the people in the other car."

"Oh, my land. That's what a person gets for drinking. I never drink."

"You used to drink a lot, Mama," Rainey said softly.

"Maybe you're right but I haven't for a long time. And I wish you two would stop calling me Mama."

"But, Mama," Sue-Ella/Rhonda chimed in, "All three of us are your daughters and we look just like you."

"Now, Sue-Ella. You're sounding like these other girls. Let's order the banana cream pie for dessert, forget all this crazy talk."

When the sisters dropped off the mother who acknowledged only one of them, Rhonda's dad met them at the door with the letters and badly damaged suitcase. He looked quite proud of himself because he had figured out Rhonda and Sandra had been in the bus crash he'd seen a while back on the news.

"I've been most interested in those envelopes. Like are they settlement checks from the bus accident you didn't even tell us about?"

"We didn't want to worry you," explained Sandra and they both opened the envelopes to find forms saying there might be a class action suit if the driver was convicted of wrongdoing.

Back at the motel Sandra found much of her clothing had escaped from the suitcase but she was happy to find one

81

new outfit she's purchased in Chicago, plus her favorite tan pants and a silk blouse she had purchased to replace one she'd stained with sauce from a burrito on the day she stopped being Dr. Rhonda.

Chapter Eighteen

Apartment Hunting

A few days after the lunch with Mama, Sandra, having paid for the motel for another week, told her sister, "Quite frankly, I'm running low on money. If we want to stay in Harmon, it would be cheaper to rent than stay in a motel."

Rhonda tried to change the subject to the missing woman, but Sandra cut her off.

"Do you want to stay in Harmon?"

"Yes, I want to stay and I really like this motel."

Sure, as long as I pay. "I realize that but unless you'd like to pay for it we need some place cheaper where we can cook meals instead of eating out all the time."

"Do you think we could find a decent place?"

"I checked the newspaper ads and I've made appointments at a couple. Do you think you could afford half the rent on a reasonably-priced apartment?"

Rhonda assured her sister it wouldn't be a problem. "I told you in Tulsa my third husband was rich." She added, "I don't want to live in any place crummy."

The first apartment the sisters viewed definitely fit Rhonda's description of "crummy". The second one, considerably better, required a reference. The sisters stopped at the post office to ask Rainey to write the reference; she promised to do that during her break.

Rainey met them at the town's coffee shop. She knew the woman renting the apartment from church and called her––the apartment was theirs.

"No smoking and no pets," the landlady, Ruby Smith, warned as she took their deposit and handed them the key.

"I was afraid Ruby was going to say no men visitors and booze, too," Rhonda quipped as she looked around the cheerless but sound two-bedroom flat on the upper floor.

Sandra paid no attention to her sister as she thought about how they could make a home out of the place. Rainey had offered some furniture, and Sandra had found some good pieces at an estate sale and a second-hand store, on hold for her. She stopped by the trailer park to ask Wayne if he knew any painters to repaint their four rooms and bath. Taken with his old schoolmate, he volunteered to help do that. Not to be outdone, Rhonda asked Ray if he'd help.

Over the weekend the two men with buddies Ray rounded up gave all the walls in the small apartment two coats of semi-gloss in Sandra's preferred muted southwestern hues. Sunday evening they and the two new residents sat on the floor and ate the pizza and beer Sandra had purchased. Sandra winked at her sister, who understood what she meant about not violating any of the landlady's rules.

Sandra talked the men into helping move the furniture she'd purchased: two beds, two dressers, a loveseat and a table and chairs. They proved willing to do anything for the two charming sisters. "The best thing that happened to me in a long time," said Brad, a muscular, swarthy complexioned man recruited by Ray. Bart, with such a pale complexion there was teasing that this was the first time he's been outside in decades, asked, "Are there any more like you?"

"Actually, there are two more; but they're both married," Sandra answered, ending the discussion.

In the next few days the place had begun to take shape. Sandra had scoured a local thrift store and dollar store for cooking utensils and dishes. Rainey loaned her a sewing machine to make curtains. Rainey also gave them their spare television. Thinking ahead, Sandra dreamed of making a trip after Christmas back to Corpus Christi to obtain some of the artwork, lamps, and occasional furniture from her townhouse. Rhonda suggested that they throw a Christmas party to thank all who helped them, and that meant another trip for Sandra to the dollar store to buy inexpensive decorations.

The older sister thought she should contribute to their new place. The day after they moved in, Rhonda brought home a neglected looking gray cat she'd seen several times skulking around the garbage cans in the alley. She'd lured him to the apartment with kitty treats she'd purchased when she'd bought cat food and a litter pan. She decided to forget to mention that she had removed a plain collar with no tags from the cat because she knew Sandra would insist they find the owner. Rhonda already had figured out the cat had a family once, but as skinny as he was, they must not have looked for him very hard. He was theirs now.

"But, our lease says 'No Pets'," reminded Sandra, reaching out to stroke the cat ensconced in her sister's arms.

"He's not a pet; he's a family member. Besides the clause about pets, I think just refers to big, barking dogs. By the way, I named him George and we need to get him a bag of litter. I was afraid I'd break a nail if I tried to carry a bag by myself."

Sandra couldn't help herself. She laughed at her impossible but loveable sister.

Chapter Nineteen

Thanksgiving Dinners

In Corpus Christi the Hernandez family sat down to their Thanksgiving dinner. The youngest son looked around and began to cry. "Aunt Rhonda didn't come!"

"I know, sweetie, but remember she moved far away," his mother explained without a trace of the betrayal she still felt.

"When will she come back to visit?" asked another son.

Dave, speaking for himself, cautioned, "Hey, guys, this is the day to count our blessings, not whine about what we don't have. Now who wants a piece of this delicious turkey our favorite grocery store, HEB, cooked for us?"

* * *

In Harmon, Sandra and Rhonda stood in line for their Thanksgiving meal at the United Methodist church. Sandra had seen a sign for the free community meal and decided that made more sense than preparing a feast for the two of them, especially since she didn't eat turkey. Actually, both had hoped that there might be an invitation from Rainey, but she seemed opposed to having them meet her family.

Rhonda wore a red turtleneck after Sandra told her she didn't think the tight, low-cut blouse she had chosen was right for a church affair. Sandra's half-sister complained about her neck itching all the time they waited in line, but Sandra ignored her as she smiled and spoke to everyone who greeted them.

When they reached the serving table with all of its huge stainless-steel containers of turkey and sides, they discovered Rainey dishing out mashed potatoes.

"Hey, Sis," called Rhonda.

The man, serving gravy next to her, looked perplexed while Rainey was very flustered. "Dan, these are two of my long-lost sisters, Sandra and Rhonda, who have moved back. This is my husband, Dan."

"Good to meet you two! I know Rainey has been looking for her sisters for years, but she didn't tell me that she found you. We're glad you came to the community dinner, but you're family, which means you two must come to our own dinner tonight. You can't beat two Thanksgiving dinners in a day. Besides my wife is a terrific cook."

Seeing how uncomfortable Rainey looked, Sandra jumped in before Rhonda could accept, "Thank you, but we just moved into our new place and we have much work to do."

"Okay, but definitely spend Christmas with us, and you're welcome to come to the church any time." Dan turned to the young girl next to him, who neglected her job of putting a roll on each plate because she was busy texting. In an irritated but low voice, Dan admonished his daughter, "Andrea, you have a job. This is the last time I'm going to remind you to put your phone in your pocket and leave it there. Give these special ladies their rolls because they are your aunts."

Andrea rolled her eyes and showed no interest in the aunts. Dan again reprimanded her, "Have you forgotten your manners? These are your mom's sisters."

Barely looking at the two women, Andrea muttered, "Pleased to meet you", and remembering to put on plastic gloves, plopped the homemade rolls on their plates.

The sisters smiled and thanked their niece but made no attempt at conversation as several people waited behind for their own mashed potatoes, gravy and rolls. Later, Rhonda asked her sister why she turned down the turkey.

"I'll tell you later."

* * *

Back in Corpus Christi, Maria's family asked her to bring Xavier for Thanksgiving but when she asked he said, "Maybe after we're married, but Mama expects all of us to be together, and you are welcome to come."

Maria wondered if being married would make any difference to the woman who seemed adept at running her children's lives. "Maybe since we aren't officially engaged, we should both should be with our own families."

"Okay, just as long I get to see what I'm most thankful for in the evening." Xavier winked.

"It's a date," Maria agreed, leaning in for a kiss.

They both had a good time at their own family dinners though constantly thinking of each other.

Across town Diana Belkin, who had voted to go out for Thanksgiving dinner, prepared dinner at their home for Stan, his daughter, husband, and two sons. She kept it simple. Roasted the turkey stuffed with the dressing made from Stan's mom recipe, fixed yams and cranberry relish and served rolls and pumpkin pie bought from a famed local church sale.

* * *

In Chicago two police officers, one tall and thin, the other just the opposite, came to the Cavendish apartment as the little family had their own Thanksgiving dinner that Grace had delighted in preparing for her husband.

"Is this a joke?" asked Brian, in a jocular manner. "Please don't tell me you're hauling me off before I finish my pumpkin pie?"

"Bad timing, but no joke," answered the heavy-set officer, who practically drooled at the sight of the pie in front of the man they'd come to arrest.

Always the hostess, Grace, who felt certain this was a mistake, invited the men to join them for pie. "I have pumpkin or pecan."

"Thanks, ma'am, but we can't."

"Sure looks good," added the burly one.

"May I ask why I'm being arrested?" asked Brian, all seriousness now.

The tall officer looked at the warrant. "For participating in the manufacture and distribution of false documentation."

"What?" Brian and Grace chorused.

As the officers slipped on the cuffs, Brian asked Grace to call their attorney, Jack Cox, and asked him to come to the police precinct whose number and address the tall officer gave her.

Both Grace and baby Sadie wailed as Brian left. Gaining control, Grace made the call.

* * *

Sandra thought Brian called to wish her "Happy Thanksgiving" but instead his voice held a mixture of panic and accusation. "I'm in jail. They traced me to your sister, I think, in Corpus Christi and implicated me in a crime ring of people who manufacture and issue false documents, primarily passports and travel papers."

"Brian, I'm sorry. You know I had nothing to do with this and neither did my sister."

"I'm glad to hear it, but it isn't just reassurance I need. Sandra, I need bail money."

"Did you tell Grace about everything?"

"I meant to, but the time never was right. I gave her a "Mom's Day Out" when the detectives came from Corpus Christi a while back."

"What exactly happened then?"

"They asked about you and if I knew where you went. I told them you planned to go to the University of Texas the last I'd heard. I conveniently forgot you went to Arkansas. Then they asked if I knew a Rhonda in Corpus Christi. I told them she's your sister and a physician, even showed them a photo. It's obvious they put it all together. I thought I was helping you, but I think they were after me then."

"Maybe your attorney could get you out on a technicality. Probably they are looking for links to organized crime. You were never a part of that. You always were a non-traceable independent."

"My attorney is here, and he told me to arrange for the bail money. Then we'll talk. I'm supposed to be interviewed soon, but if I need it, can you help me with the bail?" He told her the amount.

Sandra searched through her last statement from the bank in Chicago. "Brian, I'm not in good shape financially,

89

but I think I have enough to pay ten per cent. I hope they'll accept a money order."

"I'll pay you back, Sandra. You know I will."

"I know you will and you'll get it back if you don't need it. I'll take care of it first thing tomorrow." *Appropriate to spend a lot of money on Black Friday.*

"Sandra, could I ask you another favor? Could you call Grace and explain it's all a mistake."

"You know I will do anything to help you." The conversation ended.

Rhonda who had been listening in and was very curious "What was that all about?"

"A friend in need. I can't do anything about it until tomorrow when the post office is open. I'll think I'll take a walk. I still feel stuffed from all that good church food."

"I want to watch *Planes, Trains and Automobiles*. My last husband and I always watched that on Thanksgiving."

"You don't have a date?"

"No, Ray went to his mom's, some little town in Illinois. Salem, I think."

Sandra bundled up and walked the streets of her old hometown as she called Grace, who between sobs, showed amazement when she heard Sandra's voice, "Sandy, how did you know to call? The police came to take Brian. It has to be a mistake."

"It has to be, and he'll probably be home soon."

"I know you're right. I called our attorney. The cops said they arrested him because of being part of some ring that manufactures false documents, and I know that isn't true because he works for an international banking company. He makes good money. He wouldn't need to be involved in some crime ring."

Sandra never would be able to tell this sweet trusting woman the truth of her husband's previous occupation as she continued to try to comfort and reassure Brian's clueless wife. Sometime later after they hung up, all the fears Sandra had experienced when she fled Corpus Christi came back with a vengeance. *I know the police found out about my bogus credentials, but how did they associate me with Brian? Will they find out I'm here? I know Brian wouldn't betray my location, but I bet the police still are trying to find me and charge me with all I've done. Sometimes I think I should go back, confess and get it over. Would I implicate Brian if I did that?*

* * *

In a police station in Chicago, officers began questioning Brian. He honestly answered "no" to every question about the organization and his part in it. Officers brought in two other men in handcuffs, and asked Brian if he recognized either of them. He truthfully answered that he knew neither. Both swore neither seen Brian before and didn't recognize this name. There was a lot of conversation about helping illegal immigrants and the document syndicate that Brian didn't understand.

His attorney explained, "My client's name might have come to your attention because of a federal investigation initiated because of a debarred attorney in Michigan, who accused my client of providing false credentials for him. Absolutely no evidence has been found linking my client to that case. Unfortunately, that case must be why you wrongly arrested my client."

This statement and the lack of recognition of the other two suspects, who had admitted they knew each other but not the third man, was enough to release Brian. The officers said the Feds still might want to talk with him, but he was a free man now. The attorney dropped him off at home, where he found his wife talking to Sandra.

Grace put down the phone to hug him and then told him to say hello to Sandra. Brian spoke in generalities to keep Grace from knowing about his previous call to Sandra. "I had quite a scary encounter with the Chicago PD, but everything is fine now. They let me go. I didn't even have to pay bond money. They're sure the Feds will drop the case."

Sandra felt great relief. She couldn't turn down her former lover's request for money after all he had done for her, but it would have almost wiped out her account. Any crisis could break her.

Chapter Twenty

Choices

Sandra had covered the table with paperwork. She checked the balance in her Chicago bank account and found all the bills she's paid for the townhouse, including taxes and insurance—household, FEMA and Texas Windstorm Insurance—had cleared. She didn't like the balance.

George, well-adjusted to his new home sprawled all over some of the papers. He had made such a good adjustment to living inside that Sandra felt certain he had belonged to someone. Rhonda protested this. At least, the cat looked a lot better now with regular meals and brushing.

Her greeting to her sister, arising at her usual late-morning time, was, "The December rent's due in a couple days. Do you have your share?"

"I do, but I have a problem."

"What now?" Sandra had decided to be firm with Rhonda.

"I'm miserable, simply miserable. A toothache kept me awake all night, and all I could do was think about that poor lost woman." As her tooth throbbed, she whined, "Oh, it hurts. It hurts" Putting her hand to her jaw, she looked wretched as she conceded, "Now I'm going to have to see a dentist. I don't think I have enough money for both."

"You're in luck." She held up a copy of the weekly newspaper, **The Harmon Bugle.** There's an article about a coalition of volunteer dentists coming to underserved towns in Arkansas, including ours, the first week of December to provide free dental care for those who need it. They'll be here tomorrow."

"I saw an article in that same paper about the missing woman. I read that her name is Marjorie Daniels and . . ."

Sandra cut her off. "Pay attention. I said there's a free dental clinic here tomorrow."

"A free clinic? But I can pay. I just won't be able to pay my share of the rent."

"No. You will pay the rent and go to the clinic or pay the rent and suffer with your tooth until you can afford to go to the dentist in Gurney. I'll see you in a bit; I need to run to the grocery store."

While her sister was gone, Rhonda called her stepson. Sandra had forgotten some store coupons, came back, and overheard her sister. "Just once I wish I didn't have to call to remind you to send me my check."

After a pause she responded evenly, "I know you don't see your sister every day, but you see her often enough that both of you can sign my check a few days before the end of the month." She then protested, "I sent you my new address."

Then she sounded angry, "I'm sick of you calling me a widowed gold digger. I loved your father. Also, you don't have to tell me again that the payments stop when I remarry. I haven't remarried and I'm tired of you lecturing me every month and making me beg for what is rightfully mine."

Sandra, quite enlightened about her sister's financial woes, left again without being seen.

Rhonda indulged in some soul-searching accompanied by tooth throbbing. She knew she shouldn't keep taking advantage of her sister. She had to make Sandra understand how difficult it was to fight with her adult stepchildren to obtain her monthly allotments from their father's estate. *I shouldn't have to call to beg each month, but that's the way it is, and it's hard for me to admit that to my sister after talking about how rich he was. when we were in Tulsa.*

Besides when I receive my share, I have bills to pay, too. I'm nice enough not to ask my sister, the professional, to do my hair and nails. I go to a salon, which is pricey. Then I have the pay-per-view movies I like and clothes I need and order on-line, which means I have big payments on my credit cards. I've almost maxed out one of them, and that's why I told Sandra I thought I lost it in the crash and now I owe her money for clothes I ordered on her card. Besides, I'm generous. I put money in every bucket I see to help with finding that poor missing woman.

She sighed. *It was embarrassing enough to stand in line for the Thanksgiving meal but to be a charity dental patient is too much. Thinking about Thanksgiving dinner, Sandra never told me why she didn't eat the turkey. I hope she didn't know something about it I didn't. I've felt queasy ever since Thanksgiving. What if I got a flesh-eating disease from that turkey? Maybe the people at the Dental clinic can tell me.*

Later in the day Rhonda forked over the rent money and remembered to ask Sandra why she hadn't eaten the turkey. Sandra understood her sister had come up with the rent money because of the pressure Sandra had put on her. For a moment Sandra felt guilty and wanted to tell Rhonda to go to Gurney to the dentist but her sister's question put her on another course. "I've had my share of humbling experiences, too. One of my first jobs was working in a poultry house where they sold both eggs and chickens they killed." Rhonda made a disgusted face and a gagging sound as Sandra talked on. "I've never gotten over the smell of bloody death and wet feathers, and I can't bring myself to eat chicken or turkey, any poultry."

Feeling instantly healthy now she knew it had nothing to do with the Thanksgiving turkey, Rhonda also felt very benevolent towards Sandra who handed her a small bag, saying," I bought a tube of over-the-counter medication at the drug store that might help the pain until the dentist can look at your tooth tomorrow."

The next day Rhonda came back from the armory where the mobile dental clinic had been held. Sandra hesitated to ask how it had gone. Before she had a chance to ask, her sister bubbled over about the fine experience it had been. "There were two dentists. While I waited I crossed my fingers to have the young, good-looking one, and I did. His name is Dr. Jon Nash, and he was really nice. I confessed I hadn't been to a dentist for a while and he said I am lucky to have strong teeth and that I've taken good care of them with brushing and flossing." Rhonda looked pleased with herself.

Sandra realized how much a little praise meant to her sister. She listened as Rhonda continued, "He's from Duluth.

95

Isn't that close to the Arctic Circle where they have a lot of snow?"

Sandra didn't think her sister was dumb, but she lacked some basic knowledge. "Actually, it's in this country, Minnesota, next to the Canadian border. You're right. They do have cold, snowy winters."

"Oh, well, he told me how beautiful Duluth is, even in the winter. The town is right on the shore of some big lake."

Sandra interrupted, "Lake Superior, one of the Great Lakes."

"Hmm, I think he said that."

This prompted a memory for Sandra. "There are five of them; I used to tell my third-graders how to remember them by the word 'HOMES'—Huron, Ontario, Michigan, Erie and Superior."

Rhonda ignored the mnemonic help and babbled on, "He said that it is a small scenic city built on hills with a lot going on like hiking, biking, sail boating, fishing and just as much music, cultural things. And actual ships come into the Duluth Harbor. I don't like snow, but he made me want to visit there."

Sandra almost gave herself away as a former doctor by commenting that she once met someone where she worked who lived in Duluth but came to Texas for winters. The patient also talked about what a great place Duluth is, though she preferred to skip the harsh winters and became a Winter Texan

"Anyway," Rhonda chirped on, "After he filled a cavity in my tooth, I didn't think it would hurt to ask him if he had plans for dinner. He made it clear that he's married and has a little boy, and he and the other dentist already planned to go to Texas Roadhouse."

Thinking, *It's nice to hear her talk about something but the missing woman,* Sandra said, "It sounds as if you had a very good experience."

"Definitely. He was the best dentist who ever has worked on me. He's a good man, too, because he said that the free clinic is a mission project for his church."

"I'm glad for you, Sis, and I thought maybe your mouth would be sore and that's why I'm making corn chowder for supper."

Rhonda put her arms around her sister, "You're always good to me."

This wasn't the time, Sandra decided, to suggest they both find jobs.

Chapter Twenty-one

Missing People

"Every month we get data on every missing person in the US, around 1000 missing on any given day," announced Stan as if Maria didn't know that. "I hope our Missing Doctor didn't come to the same end as this woman did in Arkansas,"

"What's that?" asked Maria, already wondering if there could be any link to the Missing Doctor.

"She and her family were at an RV Park some place in northern Arkansas. In October she left their motor home to take a late-night shower and there hadn't been any trace of her since that time. She is presumed kidnapped or dead."

"Just like everyone thought about the Missing Doctor," Maria reminded him. Could she have just taken off?"

"Not according to this report because her street clothes, pajamas, towel, shampoo, all were left behind. They should have found her right away. Not hard to spot a missing naked lady hitchhiking."

Maria smiled in spite of herself, "You are terrible, Detective Belkin. Besides, she could have set it up and brought hitchhiking clothes to the shower room. And maybe she didn't hitchhike. Maybe she'd arranged for a lover to pick her up and they're living it up in Wyoming."

"Do you suppose that is what our good doctor did?

Maria gave his a "who knows?" shrug of her shoulders and asked, "Where did this happen again?"

"Near some little town called Harmon."

"Harmon? Isn't that near where we heard about a bus crash?"

"You're right. Some place we've never heard of and then twice in a matter of weeks."

* * *

That evening, Maria's roommate dropped the only bomb she hoped she ever had to drop. "I've decided to join the Air Force."

"Syd, that's great. I know you have been interested but now you've decided, what about me? I'll be all alone."

At that moment Big Boy entered the room on cat-like feet, which because of his size sounded more like boot stomping.

"I mean alone, except for you, Big Boy."

Sydney looked down and twisted a bracelet on her right arm, her words showing she'd anticipated Maria's questions. "Your getting married is a factor. I didn't want to be alone here either, but I don't know yet if I'll be accepted and exactly when I'd go to San Antonio for basic. You may not be alone very long before your wedding, and I guess I have to give you full custody of Big Boy. Xavier likes him, doesn't he?"

"He says he isn't crazy about cats but there is something about Big Boy he really admires. The only problem is Xav's mother is afraid of cats, and he doesn't think we should keep Big Boy."

"What? You aren't planning to live with her, are you?"

"No, of course not."

"Sounds like his mother is used to running his life."

Maria didn't say anything but looked downcast.

Changing the subject, Sydney asked, "Have you decided where you will live after you're married?"

"We aren't even officially engaged. The answer is no, and here could be a good option. Actually, anything could be a good option as long as it's not with his folks."

Sydney laughed at her spunky roommate's answer and added, "I'm going to get my hair cut tomorrow to see how I'll like an Air Force cut."

"I think I will, too," announced Maria.

Chapter Twenty-two

Bad Beginning, Happy Ending

Sandra awakened with a start. Late fall rain hammered the roof and perhaps that sound had triggered the awful dream she hadn't had for years. In it her parents were arguing, and she could hear her father slap her mother. Then he threw open the door to where she and her sisters huddled and started throwing their toys all around the room. She pulled the covers over her little sisters' heads and awakened as, in real life, one of her dad's boots came flying towards her.

She suppressed that memory but then the rain reminded her of the bus crash. A miracle Rhonda, Wayne, and she weren't seriously injured. The local paper had an article about the accident and some people did suffer life-threatening injuries. Rhonda checked with her dad frequently to see if the mail regarding a settlement had arrived, but they sure couldn't count on provisions from that to help out with their financial difficulties now.

With all this swirling around her head, Sandra couldn't get back to sleep and left her bed before dawn. This delighted George, happy to have someone feed him. A pang of sadness hit her heart as the cat wove pretzels around her legs and made her think of her little dog, Poppy, always running around her feet. She didn't want to condemn herself by thinking this was going to be a bad day, but it sure had gotten off to a less than auspicious start. The phone rang. It was Wayne. Sweet reality eased the feelings from the dream and current concerns from her mind.

"I'm sorry to call this early, but I'm going to be busy all day and I wanted to ask you to dinner this evening."

Sandra didn't hesitate, "I'd love to."

They agreed on a time. Wayne commented he would look forward to it all day. Sandra felt giddy. She couldn't remember the last time she'd been on a date. Probably back in the Oklahoma panhandle with Brian, shortly after they met.

Yes, that was it. He asked her to drive to the next own to go to a movie if Lurene was all right with that. Sandra asked; and from her bed Lurene said, "Honey, you deserve a break but watch that Brian. I don't think he's completely honorable. Don't let him talk you into anything."

With embarrassment Sandra remembered that Lurene's advice had come too late. They had put the cart before the horse the first time they were alone on the day they met, and their first date ended the same way.

She and Dave Hernandez never had a date. They couldn't be seen in public; he came to her place. Sandra visualized her beautiful townhouse with its tasteful furnishings and collection of Mexican art. Dave loved to come to this peaceful love nest, the opposite of his home with three noisy boys.

Sandra saw herself during the time she was Dr. Rhonda in a lavish negligee, opening the door to the man whose company she enjoyed too much. She had a gourmet stew simmering on the stove, fresh bread kept warm in the oven. They ate, went to her bedroom and stayed in each other's arms until guilt about Linda, his wife and her best friend drove them apart. Until the next time.

Sandra had missed dressing up every day in her designer wardrobe for work or out to dinner or cultural events with Linda. I've let myself go since I've been Sandra, and I'm just not going to let that happen. I want to keep all I can of my Dr. Rhonda persona.

She carefully chose an outfit from her Internet shopping spree even though they were going to the Texas Roadhouse. Her hair was growing out, brown hair with long blonde roots, quite the opposite of what she usually had worked on in her own salon. She treated herself to a visit to the local hairdresser to have her hair trimmed and processed to restore the original color. *Would I want to be a stylist again? I probably could pass the Arkansas cosmetologist exam, but…*

Rhonda noticed her sister's hair right away and gave her approval as she commented, "You'd think you have a date."

"I do." Sandra tried to sound casual but there was a tinge of excitement in her voice.

"That's great. Ray's off tonight and we're going out, too. We'll compare notes later."

Wayne brought Sandra a bouquet, yellow, gold and orange chrysanthemums with sprigs of autumn leaves. Sandra stood admiring them and remembered how Dave always brought her flowers from the airport floral shop. She had insisted, after enjoying the lavish arrangements all evening, that he bring them home to his wife. Wayne's bouquet brought her no guilt, and Sandra kissed him on the cheek. After a quick tour to show all she'd done to make the apartment cozy since the painting party, they went out to the town's "hot spot".

They compared notes about the bus incident and quickly went on to other topics. Drawn together in conversation by the similarities they'd shared by being "trailer trash" kids bullied by their tormentors, they talked easily. Wayne admitted he really had her on a pedestal for running away because it was something he had thought about doing, but he was too chicken. He told her how the teachers had drilled into them the dangers that awaited run-aways after Ronnie Lee took off. He quoted one, "It's impossible to run away from your problems because the ones you encounter may be worse."

Sandra thought about the two times she had run and found the truth in what the teacher had said. Yet, the first time also had brought wonderful experiences, living first with Lurene and then Brian. Her escape from Texas, which she thought she had planned remarkably well, had been one scary misadventure after another. Looking at the kind man across from her, she decided things had turned out pretty well. She found she enjoyed life in her small hometown, and she was relatively content to be with her sisters while she tried to figure out how to find the youngest and to help her mother remember all of them.

Wayne requested a penny for her thoughts. "I could use that penny," Sandra said with a laugh. "I need to find a job. I

102

thought places would be hiring for Christmas, but I had no luck at shops downtown, and there is nothing in the want ads except heavy machinery operators and welders. I don't have the qualifications for either."

Wayne laughed. "What are your qualifications?"

"I've worked with children."

"My former girlfriend," Wayne said, while knowing Thelma would be surprised to hear she had become 'former', "has a childcare center, and I know she always needs teachers. If you said you did clerical work, I would have told you about a temporary job at the City and County office. It would pay a lot better."

"I can do clerical work. Maybe I should try for that. Even though it's temporary, I know those things can lead to permanent jobs. I adore kids but it's appalling how little teachers make and how little respect they receive."

Wayne nodded at everything Sandra said. "Another idea. You could go into business with me, but I haven't decided what that will be. I will get a good price for the land, but I don't know yet how I will invest it."

"This town needs more affordable housing," Sandra stated emphatically.

"That's true. I don't know where I'm going to live after the land deal is settled. Maybe I should buy some old buildings and with your taste in decorating, we could rehab them into affordable apartments."

They chatted about those possibilities for a while and then Wayne said, "I have a confession to make."

Sandra cocked her head. "Yes?"

"Remember the first day I met you and Rhonda, and she asked if I was married, and I gave her an answer that would lead you to believe that I had been married but currently am not. The truth is I have never married. Until recently, I had a long-term girlfriend."

Sandra confessed, "I've never married but I did live with a guy for a while." *What if I confess everything about myself to him like being a fugitive from Texas because of impersonation and fraud?* Because she had deleted a phone

103

call without listening while waiting for the ill-fated bus headed for Arkansas, she had no idea that charges against her had been dropped. She also didn't know that all her assets had been frozen. Sandra thought better of telling this appealing man anything unnecessary.

They continued to enjoy each other's company until a waitress indicated the restaurant's closing time was near. At the door of the apartment Wayne gave Sandra a chaste kiss. She embraced him and gave him a more encouraging one but didn't invite him to come in. He promised to call.

As she prepared for bed Sandra's heart filled with hope that this relationship might work out. She focused on his comment that until recently he'd had a girlfriend. *Is that because of me that he broke it off? Good I don't want to work at her childcare center. I definitely will take his suggestion to apply at the City and County*

Rhonda came home much later. She tapped on Sandra's door and was welcomed. She sat on the bed, and the two chatted about their dates like a couple of teen-agers.

Chapter Twenty,-three

Girl Talk

Linda and Maria met for lunch and to exchange small Christmas gifts. Linda raved about Maria's very short haircut. Maria beamed and then jumped right to her burning question, "Do you ever wonder if the Dr. Rhonda case really is over?"

Linda paused before answering. "Most of the time I am glad she is out of our lives. My marriage is on solid ground, and I've pretty much reconciled myself to the fact the woman who meant the world to me was only a fabrication."

"Then you are satisfied with the outcome?"

"I guess I am. Dr. Ron will never change his mind about filing charges and create bad publicity for the clinic. It's over, but at times I worry that Dr. Rhonda could be practicing in another state and jeopardizing someone's life. Then I remember how good she was at what she did."

"The way I see it, there are two criminals here, the doctor and the one who made her a doctor on paper. I would like both of them to pay the debt they own society."

"You're right. There are two halves to the situation, but I never thought much about the one who made it possible for Dr. Rhonda to become a physician. Do you think the man in Chicago had any part?"

"I have no evidence, but I keep thinking he could be the one. Xav and I went to Chicago, and I interviewed the man. I'm convinced he's guilty, but I don't have proof."

"How are things going with Xavier?"

"Great! We're becoming engaged the day after Christmas, and I sure would like you and your family to come to the party Xavier's 'mo-ther' is throwing for us."

The way Maria pronounced "mother" and rolled her eyes amused Linda. "Problems with the matriarch already?"

"Not really. She's really has been sweet to me, BUT…"

"Do you want to talk about it?"

"Yes! I need to vent about my future m-in-l! She's one bossy old bird. She has made it clear that my cat Big Boy can't live with us because she is deathly afraid of—not allergic to—cats. I thought maybe I could help her get over this, but I know it's not worth trying because we don't even get to pick out the engagement ring. Instead she insists I wear her grandma's heritage ring."

Linda shook her head about the mandated ring and thinking about the cat said, "I'm sad about your pet. Thanks to having Rhoda's little Chihuahua, I've gone from not caring about pets to wondering how I ever lived without one. What I'd do is keep Big Boy and give Mama the boot."

Maria laughed.

"As for the ring, heirloom rings can be gorgeous."

"I'm sure it is. It's just that Xavier and I didn't have the opportunity to choose my own ring."

"I understand. Our only way to get even with our mothers-in-laws is to dominate our sons in the old time Mexican way and drive their sweethearts crazy!"

Both women laughed at the expense of Maria's future mother-in-law.

"What about a dress?" Linda asked.

"I always dreamed about going to Mexico to buy a traditional lace-covered dress, but with all the drug problems Mexico is having it has become too dangerous for tourists."

"I agree. Too many tourists have had their cars stolen or worse have been kidnapped or killed."

As their time together came to an end, Maria added, "I shouldn't have been nasty about Zavier's mom. She really isn't as terrible as I have described her. Zavier says she goes to Mass every day to pray for her family and does lots of volunteer work at the church. He said she works hard and is a spectacular cook."

* * *

Back at headquarters Stan asked Maria why she felt certain that the Missing Doctor received her medical credentials from the guy in Chicago.

"It's a just a hunch, but isn't it hunches that solve cases?"

"Spoken as a true detective, but they have to be backed up with," said Belkin squeezing his left thumb and forefinger together, "a pinch of evidence to assure the judge won't throw it out."

Maria raised her eyebrows and then explained her hunch. "We know Dr. Rhonda went to Chicago when she fled Texas. Isn't it logical she might go to the man who had not done such a good job of producing records for her?"

"Maybe, but I doubt Ortega will open the case on that basis, and we know the clinic will never press charges."

"I talked to Dr. Linda today and she confirmed that, but…" Maria lowered her voice to a confidential tone… "I watched Brian Cavendish's eyes. He tried to break eye contact with me more than once. He lied to me. Wouldn't it be something if the Missing Doctor case led to a much bigger fish, like smashing an underground crime ring dedicated to the manufacture of false documents of all kinds?"

"Delusions of grandeur, Detective. This is one for the Feds."

"I suppose, but if people didn't make these documents available no one could purchase them, and in the case of physicians, wouldn't jeopardize the health of patients."

"Luckily, not in the case of our Missing Doctor. She 'did no harm'; in fact, didn't she win a big award?"

Maria's voice had risen. "True. She is an exception and, if she hadn't been exposed, she could have run out of luck and prescribed the wrong medicine for a child. What if she is practicing someplace else? For all we know she could be compromising a patient's health right this moment."

"Most likely completely out of this jurisdiction just like her provider in Chicago."

"Maybe not. He said she was coming back to Corpus Christi."

"To go to college." Stan harrumphed. "Have you checked that out?"

"I haven't been able to prove she's registered for Winter Quarter yet."

"The way I see this, all you have is a hunch." More than ready to end the useless conversation, Belkin pulled a dime out of his pocket, "Shall we flip a coin to see who has the honor of a court appearance in the drug pusher case?"

Maria lost the toss but helped win the case. The judge might have thrown it out because of entrapment, but he was impressed with the witness whom Maria provided. Austin's testimony about buying drugs from the accused and nearly dying from an overdose convinced the judge to prosecute the drug dealer.

Chapter Twenty-four

Family Connections

Sandra applied for the job at the City and County building to replace a woman on maternity leave. Lily Hanson, the city/county supervisor, told Sandra all she had to do was pass the Civil Service exam and the job was hers. Sandra, who never had needed to prove anything to obtain a job, worried herself silly about passing the battery of tests, which were scheduled for the second Saturday of each month, only days away.

She was ecstatic when she received the call saying she had passed and would begin work on Monday. What a great break!

Rhonda couldn't understand how her sister could be excited about a job as a flunky in an office. As for Rhonda, she had something to be excited about, a prospective new boyfriend, someone classier than Ray, this time the UPS man.

"I met him when he brought my cosmetic order today, and he said next time I have an order he'll deliver it last and we can go out afterwards,"

"Do you have a date tonight?"

"No." Rhonda answered with resignation.

"Good. I propose we go to Smiley's to celebrate my new job,"

There was a chill in the air. The women took the van the few blocks to the café. It wasn't busy; they had their pick of booths. A poster of the missing woman still loomed over each booth, and Rhonda studied it intently. After ordering, Rhonda looked again at the photo and said insistently, "Doesn't she look like she could be me, with dark hair?"

Sandra stared at the photo and replied, "No, I don't think there's a resemblance to either of us."

"Really? Look at the high cheek bones, the wide-set eyes, the nose."

Sandra felt her stomach knot. Maybe there were some similarities, but she didn't want her sister's "missing woman" obsession to ruin the evening. Rhonda persisted. "You and Rainey have talked about Midge having dark hair. Sandra, that could be Midge."

"Oh, Rhonda, I doubt that." Sandra dismissed Rhonda's fears with less assurance than she felt.

Rhonda started to weep. "Our own sister and nobody knows where she is. I have spent hours and hours on the Internet trying to find her and nothing."

Both sisters had lost their appetites. They asked the waitress if there were any more of the posters lying around. She found one in the back.

They took the poster home and studied it under a bright light. Rhonda conceded that she was wrong because the woman's complexion looked too dark while Sandra tried to bury any thought this was her baby sister. She couldn't. She had to find out more about Midge to banish any possibility of her being the missing woman; but, now she needed to concentrate on her new job.

* * *

As the first person the public saw at the City and County building, Sandra made a wonderful impression with her radiant smile and the warm personality developed as Dr. Rhonda. She efficiently waited on each person who came to the City and County offices. She asked questions of the other employees to learn the answers to the many questions she received each day. Like her former jobs, she became popular with her co-workers and customers. She and Marsha Brown, native of Harmon, who worked in the records department, became friends. Marsha remembered the Jackson's tragedy and how Ronnie Lee ran away, and that Rainey became Homecoming Queen and someone adopted the youngest girl.

Sandra made the most of working where she did to aid in her search for Midge. With Marsha's help she learned how to access public records and found all she could about Midge. It wasn't much. Her birth certificate that confirmed her age, thirty this month; another birth certificate with the same birth date and names of Edward and Patricia Brown listed as her parents, which had to be the finalized adoption certificate.

Naturally Sandra asked Marsha if she knew these people with the same surname. She answered encouragingly, "They could be relatives of my husband, and it would be great if we are related to them and you and your sisters can find her immediately. I'll call him on my break."

Sandra couldn't have been more excited, but when Marsha called her husband, Fred, he said he vaguely remembered an Aunt Patty and Uncle Eddie who lived in Harmon but moved away. He didn't remember anything about an adoption, but he'd call his mom. Another wait.

Fred called back and said his mom confirmed their relatives adopted a little girl from the Jackson family before the Browns moved to Scottsbluff, Nebraska. Fred's mom said they had exchanged Christmas cards for years with her husband's brother and wife, but they hadn't heard from them for a long time.

Undeterred, Sandra spent her lunch hour at the utility company, which kept meticulous records. She found the Browns' local address and learned they had received their initial deposit when they moved, shortly after the adoption. The company had their forwarding address in Scottsbluff, Nebraska and their phone number.

Sandra immediately called the number, but it had been disconnected. She wrote to the Browns at the forwarding address, and without telling her sisters, waited nervously for a response. The current occupants returned the letter with a scrawled "Moved". No one at the post office was able to help her with a more recent address.

On her own Marsha went to the home where the Browns had lived and asked if anyone knew where they lived now. The present owners, who had been in the house only a year, knew nothing about them. She checked with an older couple next door, who not only remembered the Browns but had been good friends who had corresponded with them until a few years ago when she didn't receive a Christmas card.

Marsha didn't even bother to tell her friend Sandra about this. She planned to wait until she had an address for Midge. Though she would fail, Marsha was determined to find some member of her husband's extended family who knew what had become of the family who once adopted a little girl, the youngest little Jackson girl, the one with the dark hair who had to be about thirty.

Chapter Twenty-five

Party On

The Saturday before Christmas Wayne invited Sandra to look at some of the buildings he considered purchasing. That fed a dream she had of going into business with him. She kept the possibility of a partnership alive when they went out for lunch by offering to contribute capital to the endeavor. She explained she had to contact her bank in Corpus Christi to access funds. Wayne said there was no rush if she really wanted to do that. She found herself quite attracted to the man she wouldn't have given a second glance in junior high.

On Monday Sandra called the bank for her account balances.

"I'm sorry, Ma'am, those accounts have been closed," the Corpus Christi clerk in charge of accounts explained when Sandra asked for a transfer of funds to the bank in Harmon.

"Impossible, I'm the owner of the accounts and never authorized that," Sandra countered with false confidence.

"Let me check again."

Sandra waited as her stomach knotted with fear and annoyance not eased by recorded tinny brass music that tortured her ear.

"Sorry that took forever. This is what I found out. The accounts were made unavailable to the owner by a Nueces County Court order."

"Thank you. That sounds preposterous, but I will contact them and get back to you."

"Have a nice …" Sandra pushed the end button on the phone before the voice finished. *I think I understand what happened. My accounts were closed there and probably at the Credit Union by the court because I'm a fugitive. Unbidden, a thought struck Sandra. I have to have my sister "Sandra" claim that I died and demand the funds as the beneficiary to my will. I have to figure this out. All I need is a death certificate, probably can find one on-line, and Rhonda, parading as Sandra, my beneficiary, could claim the money for me. This should work. I could appeal to Rhonda's "acting ability".*

A plan had started to form, but right now Sandra was busy getting ready for their Christmas party. They had invited Rainey and her husband, who had declined. "That's the same night as the postal party," Rainey had explained though they sensed she was happy she had a conflict. She mentioned to Dan it was rare to have two parties in one night, and he thought they should attend both when he found out one was at the sisters' home, but she refused saying, "No. I don't think it is a good idea to get too close to those two" and he reminded her, "They're family, and I have invited them for Christmas."

Their other relatives declined the invitation. They'd asked Mama and Rhonda's father, but B.J. complained, "Too durned fur to drive at night but your mama and I; we'll come over in the daytime to see your place." They considered inviting Ruby, the landlady, but feared George might make an ill-timed appearance. That left Ray, Wayne, and one of the friends who had helped them paint, Bart, Marsha, Sandra's friend from work, and her husband Fred, and Ben, the UPS guy.

Rhonda's idea of decorating was attaching plastic mistletoe all over the acoustical tile ceiling. Though not inclined to cook, she surprised Sandra with the array of hors d'oeuvres she could create, something she said she had learned from the chef who catered parties when she was married to her third husband. Together the sisters achieved an impressive spread of stuffed mushrooms, miniature pigs in blankets, freshly made salsa and tortilla chips, a cheese ball with crackers, and ham and cheese pinwheels. They found a cookie-press at the thrift store and made Christmas cookies just like their mother once made for them. They had enjoyed themselves preparing the food together.

With sparse furnishings they had room for a large tree, decorated with an assortment of ornaments, some antique, which Sandra also had found at the thrift store. Each time she had entered that store she conceded how her shopping habits

114

had changed since her time as the affluent Dr. Rhonda. She congratulated herself a bit. *I am nothing if not adaptable, and I do have Dr. Rhonda's superior taste, which allows me to recognize the very best in a second-hand store.*

The sisters made a festive punch with a raspberry puree and Prosecco. The men, with the exception of Wayne, and Ben, preferred the beer Sandra had purchased, just in case some would want it. Christmas music played on a radio from Goodwill, assuredly a comedown from the Bose music system Sandra had enjoyed in her townhouse, but cheery.

Marsha and Wayne commented on all the homemade delicacies. The rest of the guests wolfed them down. All the men but Wayne and Fred took advantage of the mistletoe, guaranteeing a great time for Rhonda and probably the reason the UPS man left early. Wayne waited until the party ended, took Sandra in his arms and made certain they were under a mistletoe sprig, many having drifted down from the ceiling during the evening. He kissed her and whispered, "You are the best thing to happen in a long time. Please save New Year's Eve for me.

The sisters hugged and congratulated themselves on the success of their first party.

Chapter Twenty-six

Merry Christmas

A few days before Christmas Rhonda and Sandra drove to Gurney to take gifts to B.J. and their mom, who promised to visit soon, which they never did. as B.J. died the following June.

Sandra had turned down Rainey's invitation to go to the prison two days before Christmas, but she sent a card and gift for her father from the approved list Rainey had given her, a book and candy. Both would receive strict scrutiny to make certain no contraband lurked between pages or in brown fluted paper cups.

Rhonda and Sandra shopped together for gifts for Rainey and family. For the two children they didn't know, they bought iTunes gift cards, for Dan, a wall calendar featuring Arkansas nature scenes, and a sweater for Rainey, whose size they knew from their own.

Together the sisters baked and decorated Christmas cookies to take to the family dinner. Sandra convinced Rhonda to accompany her to the Christmas Eve service at Rainey and Dan's church. Rainey had tears in her eyes when she saw them.

Christmas morning Rhonda and Sandra arrived at the Butler's home, a modest rambler exquisitely decorated for Christmas, with many of the decorations crafted by Rainey. Sandra and Rhonda raved about the beautiful Christmas décor, and Rainey showed more warmth than they ever had seen. She accepted their offer to help prepare dishes for the oven, and the three and Dan talked as if they did this together every year.

The two kids, Andrea, 12, and Jake, 9, hung out in the kitchen, saying little. They seemed well behaved though Andrea received a scolding for texting her best friend "Holly". She argued it was her friend's birthday after all, and she was allowed to go to her room for a brief call.

There was a break when there was nothing left to do in the kitchen, Dan announced it was a good time to open the gifts the aunts had brought. Both kids thanked their aunts profusely for the gift cards. Dan said the calendar was just what he needed for his office and said, "Rainey must have told you I work for the Chamber of Commerce." She hadn't. Rainey raved about her sweater, which received high praise because her almost teen daughter liked it, too.

Rainey used festive Christmas dishes for a feast of crown roast with stuffing, sweet potatoes, corn pudding, cranberry sauce, green bean casserole and homemade dinner rolls. *No poultry!* cheered Sandra inwardly.

Under the tree Sandra and Rhonda found a big box for both of them, a set of brightly colored cookware. The gift that meant even more to Sandra came in the form of a compliment Rainey relayed as Sandra helped her load the dishwasher. "My friend, Lily, who works at City and County, say they really are pleased with your work and she told me a secret. They may have something for you after the one you're replacing comes back."

After the kitchen clean-up, the six of them played board games, which Andrea called "bored–to--death" games. For dessert Dan brought out an ice cream filled chocolate "Yule Log" he'd made to eat with the decorated cookies brought by the aunts.

As Sandra looked around at her family, faces illuminated by candles that Rainey lit at dusk, she couldn't remember when she had felt happier.

117

Chapter Twenty-seven

Celebrate, Corpus Christi-style

Xavier's mom, along with her two sisters, four daughters and a cousin, had been working for weeks preparing food for a party to be held the day after Christmas, a party to celebrate the engagement. It was a lot for Josephina Valdez to accomplish with her volunteer work at the church during the busy Holy season and the family food preparations for Christmas and in a few days Epiphany; but as she said, she would do anything for her son.

She was a traditional Mexican cook, and she loved having big parties; but this one she admitted was bittersweet. She finally understood her own mother, who prized her brother more than her and her sisters. Like her mama she had only one son, and she loved him with all of her heart. With tears in her eyes, she would tell anyone who would listen how hard it was to lose her only son. All tried to distract her with comments about the wonderful food.

The whole family dressed in Mexican costumes. The men's clothing was similar to the familiar dress of Mariachi Bands with black pants and embroidered vests over white shirts and matching sombreros except the men's vests were scarlet. The women wore white blouses with exquisite embroidered woven shawls in dark colors and full skirts in bright shades of red, yellow and green. Maria looked beautiful in an outfit like theirs, which came from a trunk at her family's home.

The Valdez family had hired a Mariachi Band, which played throughout the affair, and a bartender who made traditional Margaritas and served a selection of Mexican beers including Dos Equis, Corona with lime slices, and Carta Blanca, as well as the Coast's ever-popular choice, Bud Light.

Added to the crowd's delight, five little cousins, Folklorica students, performed costumed dances three times during the afternoon. Linda and Dave's sons were quite taken

118

with the cute little girls in their fancy dresses and traditional hairstyle, knotted high on their heads.

At the time deemed appropriate, Xavier, in tight toreador pants, got down on one knee and asked Maria to marry him. She said "yes" and he put his Great-Grandma's ring on her finger. It was breathtaking, a marquis emerald surrounded by tiny diamonds in a silver filigree setting. Mama made her way to the couple as she crossed herself and looked heavenward, "My mama gave me that ring that belonged to her Mama. It seemed only right to give it to my only beloved son." She dissolved in tears, and one of her sisters rushed up to comfort her and lead her away. Xavier laughed nervously while Maria felt decidedly uncomfortable.

Señor Valdez, Used Car Czar and head of the family, took advantage of the awkward pause to give a lengthy toast to his son and his beautiful señorita and explained the responsibility of the husband to be a strong head of the family and the expectation of the wife to be submissive to her husband. Xavier puffed out his chest while Maria looked helplessly at her family.

Mama, recovered from her crocodile tears, crossed herself and proposed her own toast to her oldest son. She wept again and expressed the pain of losing him.

One relative whispered to another, "He's getting married, not off to fight in the Middle East."

Maria proposed a toast to her future mother-in-law, the thought of which made Linda Hernandez giggle into a napkin.

"Mama, don't worry about losing Xavier. You are gaining me, and the way you cook, we'll be at your house every night for dinner!"

Linda was proud of her friend rising to the occasion. Mama smiled through her tears as everyone laughed at the plucky daughter-in-law-to-be. Xavier proposed his own toast to the two most important women in his life and received cheers and stomping of feet when he urged everyone to refill their plates.

Someone shouted, "When's the wedding?"

Before either of the couple could respond, Mama shouted, "It won't be for a long time. The bride has to let her hair grow out or the wedding guests will think she's a boy."

Linda watched for a reaction from poor Maria with her new darling short cut. Though she tried hard not to show it, Maria felt fury rising within her. Everyone else had loved her haircut. How could Mrs. Valdez be that cruel? She also fought being overwhelmed by meeting all those who would become her relatives and frustrated by having only minutes to greet her own family and friends. A slim stylish woman in her late 40s tapped Maria's shoulder and said. "Don't listen to a THING his mother says."

Maria smiled in gratitude as she recognized Diana Belkin. Her own completely Americanized Mexican mother grabbed a chance to hug her and said, half-seriously, "I hope there isn't too great a cultural difference between our family and the one you're marrying into."

The partygoers turned their heads toward the bride-to-be and her mother, who shared a hearty laugh.

Chapter Twenty-eight

Greeting the New Year

A week later, on New Year's Eve, Sandra and Wayne went to a dance at the VFW with Rhonda and a new man, Gene, she had met in line at the post office. Wayne told Sandra that he had put a down payment on the former movie theatre and buildings on either side. He was negotiating to buy other buildings on the same side of the street.

Wayne told Sandra about his trip to visit his mother. "She remembered you. She said you were a tough little girl who always came with your mom to pay the rent." He didn't tell her how his mother had lamented the downfall of the family but added, "She also talked about what pretty little girls the Jackson sisters were." Raising his glass, he added, "Pretty little girls who grew up to be beautiful women."

At midnight, everyone toasted Wayne and Sandra's partnership. As they danced the last dance, Wayne admitted he had fallen in love with his partner. Sandra, swept off her feet, told Wayne that he was the reason she had never married before. "You're the man I've waited for all my life."

* * *

On New Year's Day, Brian called Sandra. They exchanged greetings of the season. Brian didn't sound happy. Heart pounding, Sandra asked him what was wrong.

"The Feds dropped all charges because there was no evidence that I had provided false documentation to my friend. They did investigate me but found nothing in our home or on my computer to implicate me. They have no reason to believe I am part of any national ring of those involved in fraudulent documentation, just like I was cleared in the Chicago ring."

"Then you should be very happy. But you sure don't sound it."

"I'm not. I decided another year wouldn't come and go without telling Grace about my past. Finally, a couple days after Christmas I told her everything."

"About me, too?"

"No, I didn't tell her about your involvement, and it wouldn't have changed anything."

"What do you mean?"

"She took Sadie and left me."

"Oh, Brian, she'll come back. She loves you."

"I'm not sure. She feels hurt, angry, betrayed. She's the one who was here alone when the Feds came. She was an innocent in all of this; she even offered the Chicago police officers pie when they arrested me on Thanksgiving. She was angriest about my making a fool of her. I'm stupid. I should have told her when we were dating."

Sandra, who had worried all day about the same thing of telling Wayne after his declaration last night, didn't know what to say. Brian filled the silence by saying, "I should have married you, Sandra. We're two of a kind, while Gracie is sweet, trusting."

Though she should have been insulted Sandra knew Brian was right, and his statement fanned a flame in her heart. In spite of what she had told Wayne last night, she still loved Brian. In her heart she knew his marriage to Grace wasn't over, and she had no right to him. She ended the conversation by saying, "It may take time, but she will forgive you, and you will have your family back."

Chapter Twenty-nine

Wicked Web of Lies

Wayne stopped to see Sandra almost every evening and discussed progress in converting the block he now owned. Sandra enjoyed his company and could imagine being married to him. Still the possibility of being with Brian enticed her. *Maybe if I tell Wayne the truth, it will be over between us, and I will pursue Brian.*

This particular evening Rhonda plunked herself on Wayne's lap to look at blueprints. Wayne told her that he was in an exclusive relationship and asked her politely to move.

She pouted, "I just wanted to see if there was anything I could do to help with the project."

"I'm sure there will be," Wayne assured her as Rhonda, like a sulky child, flounced to her room. Wayne shrugged and gave Sandra a "what a piece of work" look.

"She hates to be excluded from anything," Sandra explained, standing up for the sister who drove her crazy most to of the time. "I'm sure it goes back to our childhood when the stranger who was her real father took her away from our family. I'm afraid all of us have abandonment issues."

Wayne embraced her and promised that he never would abandon her. Sandra looked apprehensive but decided to go ahead and tell him the truth. His reaction might remove him from the "competition" tonight. She spoke softly, "That might not be true when I tell you what you need to know about me."

He looked perplexed as she began, "When I was nineteen I met a man in Oklahoma while I was tending bar for my foster mother. It was love at first sight for me; and when Lurene died, he and I moved in together."

Interrupting, Wayne put his hand over her mouth. "Sweetheart, you don't have to tell me about your past loves."

Sandra pushed away his hand and shushed him, "That's not it. This man's job was providing false credentials for people wanting jobs without going through the necessary steps to achieve them. It made sense to me. I wanted to be a teacher but there was no money for me to go to college. My friend gave me teaching credentials without the expense and bother of college. He had an Internet business called "Dreams Come True".

Wayne heard nothing but "dreams come true" because for him that's what happened that day at the trailer park when he saw Sandra, the girl he was certain he had loved all his life. From Wayne's reaction, she could see that hadn't fazed him. *But she was young, alone. This guy swept her off her feet, talked her into doing something illegal.*

Sandra droned on, her voice flat. "Teaching is the hardest possible job. I loved the kids, but the administration had too many regulations. I had to spend every moment out of school learning about the things I needed to teach, correcting papers. I admire teachers, like your friend, who works hard at the childcare for little pay."

Wayne raised his eyebrows and looked stunned as what she had told him sunk in. "I only taught a year, and then I then I asked my lover to manufacture the credentials and a license needed to make me a hairdresser. I had many fans among my clients at the shop where I worked. It followed that in time I owned my own salon. A couple years later Brian left me because I wouldn't give up my successful business while he moved someplace else with more opportunities for his trade."

Continuing to listen, Wayne felt the color drain from his face.

"What a jerk," he murmured.

Defending Brian, she continued, "Then I wanted to be a physician, but my friend refused. He'd gone straight and wanted me to do the same. However, I tricked him into providing all the necessary documentation by asking him to do it for my sister, Rhonda. We had been in touch but weren't at that time, and she knows nothing of this. I, as Dr. Rhonda Collins, found a position as a GP at family clinic in Corpus Christi, and for eight years I led a happy, productive life."

She paused, wondering how much more she had to tell Wayne, whose look Sandra couldn't interpret. In a voice without emotion, he asked, "And then what happened?"

Leaving out her flight from the Sparkling City by the Bay, Sandra explained, "I discovered that what I really wanted more than anything was finding my family."

Shaking his head, Wayne didn't know what to say. Sandra waited and said what she was sure he was thinking, "Now that you know about my past and the lies I've lived, I wouldn't blame you for ending the partnership and our relationship now."

Wayne didn't need to say anything. His look had turned to disappointment. After a long pause, he stood up and in a hoarse voice muttered, "I need to think about all this. Part of me says, 'What difference does it make now? It's all in the past,' but part of me realizes that I don't know you at all. I think I'd better go."

Sandra didn't realize how much she cared for Wayne until she understood she had just destroyed their relationship. *And I haven't even told him the worst part of my story.*

She had to lie down as more questions swirled in her brain. *Will Wayne think it's over and decide my past doesn't matter? Or should I just forget about him and concentrate on the one man who doesn't judge me? Will I always be haunted by my past?*

Sandra made a decision. She cared for Wayne, but Brian still was the love of her life. She could be packed and back to Chicago in hours. She always had liked Grace, and Brian and Sandra never acted on their feelings during his marriage. If the marriage had ended, this was what was meant to be. She called Brian.

Brian's cell rang and rang. When he finally answered, he sounded depressed.

"Brian, I keep thinking about what you said to me the other night."

"I have more to tell you now. In fact, I planned to call you."

"First, Brian, there is something I have to know. I never have gotten over you. Were you serious about us being together if your marriage is over?"

"I was upset, Sandra. I could have said anything." Quickly he added, "Of course I still care for you." Speaking carefully, he didn't say what Sandra had expected or wanted to hear. "There is no future for us. The only thing I really want is to save my marriage, be the husband my Grace deserves, the man she thought I was. I want to be a good father to my little girl. There's only one way that I can do that."

Sandra's voice turned cold. "What do you mean?"

"I'm going to turn myself in, confess how I made my living for all those years."

"No, Brian, no." Her voice sounded as frantic as she felt. "That doesn't make sense. There's no evidence; you've been cleared. You don't have to do this and I'm sorry to ask this, but will this incriminate me?"

"I told you I care for you. I will try my best to make certain that doesn't happen. Not that there isn't a possibility someone will find out."

"But, Brian, you'll serve time. Unless you plea bargain by sharing the names of us who used your services."

"I told you I wouldn't do that. The whole idea is to prove to Grace that I am atoning for my wrongs. After I'm out of prison, we'll make a fresh start. I'll make amends with my family and Sadie will have two sets of adoring grandparents."

"It could be years!" Sandra sounded more and more out of control.

"I know but I will do anything to regain my wife and daughter."

"There has to be another way."

"Sandra, if you still care at all for me, you'll support me in this. Be a friend to Gracie, be an aunt to Sadie."

Sandra could think of nothing more to say to the man who had broken her heart for the second time. She hit "end" on her phone and did something Dr. Rhonda never would have done, threw her cell across the room. That frightened George, who had been napping on the bed. He yowled as despair leaked from Sandra's eyes.

* * *

Wayne returned to the motel where he'd been staying since he moved from the soon-to-be demolished mobile home park.

He had dated a little but never expected to marry. Then he met the beautiful, charming Sandra, who empathized with his childhood and had inspired him to plan something important for his community. In the brief time he had known her, she'd helped make the loser guy whose folks owned the trailer park into someone respected in his hometown. Sandra was smart and a good business partner. The life she had led before was wrong, but hadn't she left all that behind when she moved back to her hometown? At least, she had told him. But, did he want someone that deceitful as a business partner? Could he marry a woman like that?

He hated lying from the time when he was a kid when he figured out his dad lied when he said he was coming home and bringing his son a new bike. How many times did he hear those words from his dad's mouth before he agreed with his mom that his dad was nothing but a dirty liar?

Chapter Thirty

Never Give Up

Maria couldn't give up on the Dr. Rhonda case. She opened the page on her computer where she had found information about Brian Cavendish to see if she had missed anything. She spotted a new link to a current article. An attorney had filed suit against Brian Cavendish because he said he had bought false credentials from him and had been disbarred because of a malpractice suit. Her eyes wide, Maria read: "After months of interviews and checking Cavendish's home and computers, the court could find no evidence that the defendant had provided such documents. The manufacture of any kind of documentation is punishable by 10 to 20 years in federal prison.

She printed out the article and took it to Stan. "I think this says it. The Missing Doctor's friend made her a doctor."

"Weak! There's nothing to go on."

They'd had this conversation about evidence many times before. Steamed, Maria raised her voice, "This IS something to go on. We could have him extradited from Chicago."

"The Chief would never go for that. I keep telling you, you'd have to have hard evidence. The only way is to procure a confession from The Missing Doctor alias Sandra Lewis that he provided her false credentials, and I doubt she would snitch on him." Then Stan added with sarcasm, "Oh, yes, and first you'll have to find her."

"I wish I could. I've checked every institution of higher learning in the entire Coastal Bend and she is not registered as a student. I've checked social media, newspaper archives. I Googled her and there are many women named Sandra Lewis but the most promising one is from Oklahoma. All I found out is that one used to own a salon in Tulsa but doesn't now. If you recall, Felicia Ritter, the aunt of the clinic owner's wife lives in Tulsa and when she saw Dr. Rhonda at the clinic, she insisted she used to go to salon once owned by the same woman, only she called herself Sandra Lewis. And further, it seems that when Mrs. Ritter kept calling her 'Sandra', Dr. Rhonda left the clinic and never returned."

"Hearsay."

"I **hear** what you **say**, Stan. I know there's **no hard evidence.** I've learned through my research that once a transaction is completed the one who creates documents destroys any connection by trashing his computer. It never existed, hence the evidence doesn't exist.   Regardless, it makes sense that Sandra went to Chicago after she left Texas. She'd lost her job and needed another. Naturally she asked her friend to make her into something else."

"If we knew that was true and we could find her, we'd have a case. Personally, I think there is a possibility she is hanging out some place right before our eyes trying to reclaim some of her assets."

Maria ignored that possibility and continued, "I wonder if I talked to the aunt who knows Sandra, the one who had the stroke who is better now, I'd find out what we need?"

"On your own time, Gonzalez."

"Hmmm. Maybe I could talk Xavier into another weekend trip."

"And speaking of him, let me say that sure was a spread at your party." Then looking a little embarrassed Stan lowered his voice and made the only reference he'd ever made to his good-looking partner's appearance. "And by the way, my wife and I like your new hair-cut."

Chapter Thirty-one

Hurting

Sandra, her distinctive green eyes focused on a pile of papers, sat at the kitchen table paying bills. Her job just covered food and household expenses for Rhonda and her with extra when her sister came up with the rent money. What a contrast to the income she had earned as a physician. She liked the job she now held, mainly because she had gotten it on her own merits. It wasn't stressful and she liked meeting people who came to the City and County offices with their varied requests.

Seldom did Sandra think about her life as Rhonda, but comparing paychecks brought back the lifestyle she had enjoyed. She doubted she'd ever make a salary that would provide all the luxuries she had taken for granted such as designer clothing, symphony tickets (*not that this little burg had a symphony*), trips, buying art pieces she liked. *Besides wealth I grew intellectually and emotionally working with other physicians and patients. I want to hang on to all of that.*

Pushing her fast-growing hair out of her eyes, she stared into space. Perhaps the real estate venture with Wayne would be a financial boost, or could have been. The man to whom she had become attracted hadn't called or stopped by all week. He's said he wanted to think about what she'd shared about her job history. Today she felt confident he was in love with her and in time would see that she had changed and was living a life free of speculation.

As the days passed without Wayne, Sandra missed him and regretted telling him anything about her past while knowing that secrets have a way of surfacing. She sighed. *Better for him to find out now rather than betrayed years later as Gracie had been. But, not better for our relationship apparently,*

Rhonda had noticed Wayne's absence and mentioned it repeatedly. Trying to act unconcerned, Sandra said he had become incredibly busy with the project. Her sister gave her a pitying look and changed the subject to the latest gossip about the woman missing from the RV Park.

Sandra admitted only to herself that she missed Wayne. This morning she pondered calling him to apologize, ask his forgiveness. Then she'd have to make a full confession. No, she wished she could think of another reason to call him. Some significant idea she'd had about the converted buildings. She couldn't think of a thing.

The only decision made was to try again to check with the credit union in Corpus Christi to determine if her assets were available there. Then she could offer definite financial support to the project, a good reason to call.

Neither a call to the credit union nor to Rhonda's attorney, pretending she was the sister named as beneficiary, brought good news. The attorney said a death certificate would be necessary for Sandra to have access to any benefits awarded her in Rhonda's will. The clerk she spoke with at the credit union said the account had been placed in escrow to make house payments.

I need a death certificate to obtain my hard-earned money. I mean Sandra needs a death certificate to obtain Dr. Rhonda's money. I knew that bit, just hadn't considered it.

Without her realizing it, the seed of a plan took root in Sandra's brain.

* * *

Wayne had been miserable all week. How could he have been impossibly wrong about the woman with whom he'd fallen in love? He never expected to meet anyone like her. Before she came into his life, he had just existed, doing as little as possible with the trailer park he ran for his mother because for years there had been rumors of a corporation buying it. Then it happened.

She brought out the best in this lazy cur. I had no idea of what to do with the money I would gain but Sandra gave me such a great idea, to do something important for this town, providing affordable housing, especially since the money I've gained displaced many folks.

131

Maybe he should still consider working with Sandra. She would be such an asset to the company he had begun to form. Not as a partner, but as an employee, who could share her discriminating taste in decorating? He could keep an eye on her, and if she proved she had changed, he might be able to forget her confession.

* * *

Agonizing over the catastrophic news from the credit union on top of Brian's and Wayne's rejection, Sandra had an incoming call. Her heart skipped a beat when she saw Wayne's number. She tried to keep her voice neutral as she answered.

"Wayne, how's it going?"

"I've been busy. The construction company has begun knocking down walls in the buildings."

"Wow! You have made progress." Sandra's enthusiasm didn't reflect her doubtful feelings. Was this talk of business a prelude to his reconsidering their relationship? She crossed her long fingers.

"I have run into a snag and thought you might be able to help me." He explained how he had tired of living at the motel and considered retaining one area of the top floor for "emergency housing for me". The purpose of his call was to ask if Sandra was interested in helping him design what would be the first apartment where he would live as the others were built.

"I'm not an architect," Sandra said.

Thinking with bitterness that maybe her old beau could create some false credentials, Wayne answered, "I understand but I would like to hire you to help with designing the apartment."

He obviously has given up the idea of a partnership, which is good since I have no money to invest. But at least I could see him. "I'll have to think about it. I have heard the City and County may keep me on."

"No problem. You could continue to work there and just help me in odd hours."

132

"Why don't you come for supper tonight, and we can discuss it."

Wayne sounded cagey. "I have plans tonight."

"Perhaps tomorrow."

Chapter Thirty-two

The Big Plan

Like Maria Gonzalez, the detective who pursued her, Sandra never gave up. She had spent days outlining her latest plan before telling Rhonda. It sounded easy, maybe too many.

"Sis, I need to talk to you."

"Sure." Rhonda settled on the loveseat with the cat in her lap, resignation in her expression, expecting another lecture on finances or worse.

"Don't look like I'm about to tell you the world's ending."

"I figured I'm not paying my fair share and you're kicking me to the curb."

"Rhonda, that's not it at all except because you have trouble paying for expenses, I need to get my hands on the money I have in Texas. I know you said you'd like to see Corpus Christi. I thought we'd take a trip."

"That's great! You made it sound wonderful. I'd love to see it, meet some new guys."

"I'm glad, but it's a bit complicated."

"Spill!" Rhonda had mentally packed her bags.

"I have been denied access to my bank accounts. The only one who can gain access to them is the beneficiary to my will."

"And?"

Sandra spoke with sincerity she hoped didn't sound fake, "You have shown me your incredible acting abilities and I want you to play the part of the beneficiary."

Rhonda furrowed her brow. "Just who is your beneficiary?"

"Actually, I am."

"What-the-? How can you be . . .?"

"This is the way it works: you will have to pose as Sandra Lewis and bring a death certificate to the bank and credit union. Then they will release my funds. There will be enough for us to live on for quite a while. I also own a townhouse that you can sell."

"I don't understand . . ."

"I said it's complicated, and I have to tell you the whole story…." *Almost.*

"Okay what?"

"When I moved to Texas, I wanted a fresh start. I gave myself a new name, nothing unusual for us, right?"

Rhonda grinned. "Sure, just like when I was looking for you, I changed my name to Rhonda to honor you"

"You might say I did the same thing. I changed my name back to a grown-up version of Ronnie Lee, the same as yours, Rhonda Collins. I was known as Dr. Rhonda Collins all the time I was in Corpus Christi.

The real Rhonda looked confused. Sandra tilted her head back and closed her eyes. "This isn't easy to explain but I knew at some point I would have to leave Texas, to disappear. Then I could pretend to be Sandra and be beneficiary of my own will and retain all my assets. After all, I worked hard to achieve them."

"This is too complicated for me. You're giving me a headache."

"I will make it as simple as possible. We'll go to Texas, but I will go into hiding because I have to pretend I'm dead. You will become Sandra Lewis and collect all that belongs to me, and I will share it."

"I don't see how it will work."

"It will work. I used the public computer at the library and found a sample death certificate on the Internet. All you'll have to do is exactly what I tell you, and I know you can pull it off because you are such a good actress. You just can't tell anyone here that we are doing anything but going on a little vacation. It will work perfectly, and then we won't be plagued with money worries. Besides we will have a great time in Texas."

Rhonda loved everything her sister had explained, especially the part about her acting ability. "When do we leave?"

135

"I found out my job ends the end of February. I could continue working there but I want to move on; we'll be able to go any time after that."

Rhonda hugged Sandra. "I'm overjoyed you're not kicking me out."

Chapter Thirty-three
Happy Birthday

February 16, Sandra's birthday. Rhonda had arranged a little party for her at a small Mexican restaurant that had big plans to move to one of the largest storefront spaces under Wayne's low-cost housing units. Rhonda had invited Wayne though she doubted that it was a good idea since recently he and Sandra seemed on the outs. At least Rainey and Dan promised to be there with their kids, but it was the landlady's church night and Rhonda didn't know how to reach Sandra's friend Marsha without spoiling the surprise. For her own date she had invited Ben. She'd asked Ray, first, but he had been promoted to desk clerk and had to work. Gene hadn't worked out.

Another year older. Sandra peered into the mirror as she put on make-up. Closer to forty, and what on earth had she accomplished? She'd held several jobs and had been unlucky in love. Brian no longer was a possibility, never had been after he met Grace. Wayne was smart enough to stay away from her. She had accumulated a pile of assets that weren't within her reach and her plan to obtain them was rife with difficulties. She lived with her goofy sister and for fun could visit her mother, who didn't recognize her, or her father, in prison. She hadn't come any closer to finding Midge than when she first moved here. *I've had every bad break possible.* Sandra had the birthday blues.

Get over it. At least now I can celebrate my birthday. I ignored it for eight years in Texas because it was not the same as the birth certificate Brian created to match the birth date on all my other documents. My sweet sister wants to take me to the town's only Mexican restaurant for supper. I don't have the heart to tell her that I got pretty spoiled when it comes to authentic Mexican food. I doubt Ark-Mex will measure up. She broke into laughter and chided herself for being an ingrate when Rhonda was being uncharacteristically generous.

When they walked into the restaurant and Sandra saw her family, Wayne and the UPS man, she beamed and hugged her sister. The party lifted her spirits. Wayne was very solicitous. For everyone Rhonda had ordered family-style platters of tacos, Mexican rice and refried beans. After two Mexican beers, Rhonda blabbed about the plans to go to Corpus Christi.

The guest of honor quickly gave Rhonda a look and explained before Rhonda could tell the details of her "acting job" that they were going to Corpus, where Sandra could take care of some unfinished business. "I own a town home there I should sell; I'd like to ship some of the furniture and other things here."

"When are you going?" asked Rainey.

I finish my job at the county, for sure, at the end of February. I could have stayed on in another position but I'm looking for something more significant." She looked meaningfully at Wayne. "We can go in March The weather is mild then, not as hot and humid as it is later in spring."

"Andrea and Jake have Spring Break in March. Dan and Jake are going on a male-bonding trip to Alaska, aren't you, Dan?" As her husband smiled 'Yes', Rainey explained, "I was thinking about something special for Andrea and me to do. If you go the second week of March, could we tag along?" Before her sisters answered, Rainey sat back, clearly embarrassed, and apologized, "I sure am brazen asking to horn in on your trip."

Sandra thought how this could complicate her already convoluted plans but smiled while Rhonda clapped her hands with glee and in a voice everyone in the restaurant could hear, "A sister road trip! What fun! That settles it. We'll go the second week in March, less than a month away."

The men laughed and talked about the Alaskan trip. Andrea rolled her eyes. Jake blew the paper off his straw across the table.

Wayne gave Sandra a ride home. He kissed her on the cheek, "I am happy to be back in your life."

Chapter Thirty-four
Death Certificates

Sandra had a week left to work at the City and County Offices when a good break fell right into her lap. With her usual pleasantness she had waited on two of a long line of customers before the supervisor, Lily, pushed her way up to the counter. Oblivious to customers Sandra served, she handed the clerk a large envelope. "This is my bad. We always send Francks, the funeral parlor on Second Street, a supply of these forms soon after the first of the year. Today someone called to say they ran out and I wondered if during your break, you'd mind dropping these by?"

"What are they?" asked Sandra.

Stated in a stage whisper that could be heard through the facility, the supervisor said, "Death certificates."

As soon as break time came, Sandra took the envelope to a stall in the restroom. There were several pages, each with six copies of the certificate to be filled out by the funeral director These, she knew, were returned to her office for an official stamp and filed until the time a member of the deceased family asked for copies, for which they paid a nominal fee.

What a stroke of luck! She had worried that she no longer had the skills Brian had taught her alter the sample she had found on the Internet to make it look legitimate. All she had to do was remove one page before delivering them to Francks place. She folded one carefully and put it in her purse, planning to fill out each of the six certificates at home. Tomorrow she'd bring them back for the stamp. She'd forge Mr. Franck's signature.

Sandra grabbed her coat and took a brisk three-block walk to the funeral home.

Wayne drove by in his truck, backed up and called out the window, "Are you AWOL from your job?"

"No, on an errand for the boss."

"Want a ride? It's a bit nippy."

"Thanks, but it's only a block away." She waved good-bye and full of guilt, her heart sunk as she thought about what she planned to do with the purloined certificates. The conversation they had a couple nights after her birthday came back to her, word by word.

"Sandra, it's plain and simple. I love you and I've thought constantly about what you told me. I've concluded that who am I to judge you for things you've done in the past?"

He had tried to take her in his arms but she stiffened. "But can you ever trust me?"

"I'm willing to try."

"I can't promise it'll be easy. There are other things I haven't told you."

Wayne put his hand gently across Sandra's mouth. "I don't want to hear any more. I want to forget your past. I just want to start over with complete honesty between us from this time forward."

Before Sandra could protest that she might not be able to live up to this, he kissed her. For the first time they wound up in her bed.

With the memory of that, Sandra loosened the buttons on her coat. I still love Brian. Maybe no one ever stops caring about that very first love, but I want to start over and it is time to forget about Brian. Wayne and I could have a wonderful marriage and partnership here, our mutual birthplace, the place where I belong, not Tulsa, Corpus Christi, Chicago. If only my plan goes well I could feather a nest nicely with furnishings and paintings from my place in Texas.

She had reached Francks place.

Chapter Thirty-five

Let it Snow

February had ended without a clue about Harmon's missing woman. March, unexpectedly had arrived like a snow-white lamb.

The Wednesday before school recessed for Spring Break the School Superintendent closed the school an extra day because two and three quarters inches of snow had fallen overnight.

Not only school kids but the entire population of Harmon shared in the special excitement of this uncommon event. Children found their snow saucers, and men debated whether they should shovel or wait until the sun melted it. Most shoveled just for the novelty of moving the fluffy white stuff.

Rhonda seemed to be the only Grinch in Harmon. She and Sandra were eating breakfast listening to the local radio broadcaster extolling the beauty of the town blanketed in white and reporting fender-benders caused by slick streets. "I hate that cold, wet, miserable stuff," Rhonda complained, "I wish we were going to Corpus Christi today. I bet it never snows there."

"Only one more day until we leave, sis. As for snow in Corpus Christi, it's rare, but it snowed once while I lived there. It was on Christmas Eve in 2004 and people called it the 'Christmas Miracle'. People have published books of photos taken of snow-covered palm trees and familiar locations all over Corpus Christi. Parents told me that when their little ones awakened they didn't even want to look to see what Santa brought them. All they wanted to do was play in the snow."

That brought a dubious look from her sister. Both turned their attention to the radio, where they heard breaking news form the tiny local broadcasting station. "A Harmon driver hit an icy patch and skidded into the ditch right outside the city limits and as he dug out the front wheels, he uncovered a body."

"A body?" was the reaction from both sisters.

The newscaster continued, "The station has been flooded with calls asking if it is the body of Marjorie Daniels, the woman who was staying at our RV Park. Until tests are done by forensics experts coming from St. Louis, the identity is unknown."

"This is turning out to be a terrible day," moaned Rhonda. "I'm going back to bed."

Here everyone but Rhonda wanted to be out in the snow or go someplace to talk about it with their friends and neighbors. Now they had the added mystery of the body after months of speculation as to what had happened to the woman staying at the RV Park.

The recovery of the body brought back too many bad memories to Sandra of the time not long ago when she was the missing person. Using motel computers, she had read newspapers and watched televised excerpts from newscasts, all showing the Corpus Christi citizens' widespread concern for the missing Dr. Rhonda. "Not deserved," Rhonda began out loud and then added under her breath, "And I am sorry I caused those good people unnecessary anguish in their lives."

A much worse thought was the possibility the body could be that of her sister. This hadn't seemed to occur to Rhonda, who seemed to have lost all interest in the missing woman.

I have to get out of here or I will drive myself crazy with memories I can't share and fears I don't want to face. Sandra put on her heaviest jacket and a pair of high-topped shoes and headed towards the coffee shop. Residents of the small town packed the welcoming place that tickled the olfactory nerves with the grinding of beans and the brewing of exotic blends. Rhonda knew many people through her now former job, both customers and other employees. Someone from work snagged a solitary chair and dragged it to their table for Sandra.

Instead of "Good morning" the standard greeting was "What you think of the snow?" or, "Did you hear about the body?"

Drinking their favorite coffee drink, while warming their hands on the mugs, most voiced the opinion that the body belonged to that poor missing woman. The other half insisted they'd heard it was the body of a man, an obese older woman who barely fit in the ditch, or just a skeleton with a few strands of blonde hair. Whom to believe?

Sandra wondered why this idea hadn't occurred to her before. *I'm going to the sheriff to express my concerns about the body belonging to my sister.* She tramped through fast-melting snow to the sheriff's office. The clerk told her the sheriff refused to speak with anyone about the body until the next day at 10 AM when he would give a public briefing.

Chapter Thirty-six

Maria on the Move

The weekend Maria had scheduled their trip to Tulsa, Xavier told her he had to work due to a big anniversary car sale. Maria didn't let her disappointment prevent her from carrying out her plans to see the woman Linda had called "the formidable Miss Felicity".

A few days earlier, Stan had called Maria into his office. "We just got a bulletin about an unidentified recovered body that might be of interest to you. It's from that same little town in Arkansas."

"Harmon!"

"You got it, and here's a photo that accompanied the bulletin, the woman missing from there."

Maria peered at a black and white photo. "I know what you're saying. Her hair is longer but otherwise she bears a strong resemblance to the Missing Doctor. Of course, by now her hair could be longer and if she kept coloring it, it could stay dark like this."

Stan elaborated, "The bulletin says they found a body in the same town, but they aren't saying if it is the body of the woman in the photo."

"Does it say how the victim died?"

"No. Report incomplete."

"That town of Harmon keeps seeking our attention. Maybe somehow it is leading us to our Missing Doctor."

Stan wasn't buying that and began to lecture his partner about not putting faith in coincidences.

Not really listening to Stan, Maria closed her eyes and clasped her hands in front of her. Soon with eyes wide with excitement, she stated, "If the Harmon body is the missing Dr. R., then the case would be officially closed." She thought a moment. "I could postpone my trip to Tulsa and we could go to Arkansas together."

"Nope. You're the traveler, Gonzalez. Be my guest. Go to Tulsa and then on to Arkansas. You'll have to ask the assistant chief because, as you've probably heard, Ortega is taking off some 'mental health' days prior to the beginning of Spring Break."

Maria had no trouble gaining clearance, but the assistant chief warned her that she must be back for Spring Break. Had she known what Spring Break had in store for her, she never would have returned to Corpus Christi.

* * *

Maria flew to Tulsa, rented a car and found the senior care residence where Felicity had lived since having a stroke. Once again Maria went over the things she knew about the woman. She was the aunt of Melanie Brooks, wife of Ronyl Brooks, owner of the clinic where Dr. Rhonda worked. When she visited the clinic with her niece, she spotted Dr. Rhonda Collins and loudly insisted she'd been her hairdresser in Tulsa, which all the doctor's friends found most unlikely. Not only that but the aunt maintained both once had lived in the same little town in the Oklahoma panhandle.

At an information desk near the entrance Maria asked where she could find Mrs. Ritter, and the smiling volunteer directed her to the common room.

Maria found a beautifully appointed room, antique furniture, framed Currier and Ives prints, a floor to ceiling twittering aviary. Residents sat in wheelchairs or chairs with walkers in front of them. Some chatted with others while others had conversations with themselves or others unseen. She spotted Felicity right away from a photo Linda had borrowed from Melanie.

Felicity with her sculptured gray hair presided over a small group of malcontents. With her foghorn voice, Felicity was telling these people they must overthrow the bosses of this place to get decent food and better bingo prizes. Maria couldn't help being amused but surprisingly intimidated about trying to interview her.

She approached the group, "Hello, Mrs. Ritter."

"Hello, yourself," retorted the peppery woman. Dressed in a conservative skirt and blouse, Maria didn't look like a

145

police officer and she didn't intend to tell Felicity she was one, as the woman looked her up and down.

"I need your help, Ma'am."

"Why would I help you? I don't even know you."

"You're correct, Miss Felicity, but you and I both know someone I'm trying to find."

"Your mother? You look like the illegal that kept house for my friend Eileen."

Maria ignored the woman's racist crack. "No, not my mother. A woman named Sandra Lewis."

"Of course, I remember her. That stroke I had didn't hurt my brain and I really don't need to be here with all these nuts but my kids insisted. Well, what do you want to know about Sandra? The last time I heard the police were chasing after her."

Marie asked. "When is the last time you saw her?"

"Right here in Tulsa. She had a beauty salon. I went to her because I knew her from a little town where we both lived. Then one day I came to her shop for my weekly appointment, and there was a 'For Sale' sign on her shop, leaving all us customers high and dry. Thank goodness my friend Lurene never knew about what Sandra did."

Hopeful she'd found another contact, Maria questioned, "Who is Lurene?"

"I told you. She's my best friend."

"Can you tell me more about your friend?"

"She's dead. Practically everyone I know is dead."

"Could you tell me about her when she was alive?"

"Who?"

"Your best friend, Lurene."

"You sure are nosy but I'll tell you Lurene was the salt of the earth. She ran Smokey's all by herself after her husband died and one day this scrawny run-away kid showed up at her door, and she kept her, and that kid was Sandra Lewis. Then Lurene got the cancer and died. And I wound up in this awful place."

"I'm sorry about your friend, Miss Felicity, and sorry you don't like this lovely place."

146

"Lovely, my foot! They won't let me keep my parakeet here because they said he's too noisy. I just opened the window and let Timmy fly away."

Maria looked dubious and changed the subject. "Do you remember seeing the woman you were sure was Sandra Lewis when you were in Corpus Christi?"

Felicity looked confused. "I have a niece in Corpus Christi, but I haven't been there in years."

"But, Miss Felicity, I'm sure I heard you visited your niece a few months ago and she took you to visit her husband's clinic."

"Now, where did you hear a thing like that? You shouldn't believe everything you hear, girlie."

Maria sighed and gave it one last shot, "It's been nice visiting with you Miss Felicity. I'm sorry I asked all these questions. I'm trying to find Sandra Lewis and I thought perhaps you know where she is."

"Sure, I know. She closed her shop and went running off to Chicago after that good-for-nothing boyfriend of hers."

Maria had started to stand but sat down again. "You knew her boyfriend?"

"Of course I did. That fast-talking no-good showed up at the bar and swept our little Sandra off her feet. They hardly knew each other when my best friend Lurene died but they started shacking up and then one day, poof, they were gone."

"Could you tell me more about Lurene?" Maria hoped that Lurene might have a relative with whom Sandra kept in contact.

"I told you she ran Smokey's. Clemmie and I used to go there every Saturday night. Lurene cooked the best brisket." Felicity closed her eyes and smacked her lips. "The food here tastes like pig slop."

"Miss Felicity, you were telling me that you think Sandra went to Chicago after she closed her shop."

"I'm sure of it. You see, she was crazy for him. One day she up and closed her shop and didn't even tell me. Can you believe that? I was her best customer and . . ."

An employee entered the room and said, "Happy Hour!"

147

Felicity grabbed her walker and joined the stampede of residents moving wheelchairs and walkers as fast as they could to the dining room for what must be the high point of the week. Maria would have that scene imprinted on her mind forever.

She barely made her flight to Arkansas. On the plane she had plenty of time to think of her visit with Miss Felicity *Waste of time and money. She doesn't seem to remember anything about the stroke or what happened just before it. My instincts about the boyfriend being in Chicago were affirmed, but I went there and came back empty handed. He's lying, but how can I prove it?*

Chapter Thirty-seven

Law Enforcement Gals

After flying to Little Rock, Maria had rented a car and drove hours to Harmon where the missing woman had been found. It fascinated her to see bits of snow stuck in the grass beside the roadside. She'd missed seeing the Christmas snow in Corpus Christi because her family had gone to Mexico to spend the holidays with her grandparents.

Arriving, she saw a vacancy sign at the Red Roof Inn. She noticed law enforcement vehicles from various states in the parking lot. The body obviously had drawn many inspectors looking for a missing person. Maria hoped someone hadn't forgotten to change the vacancy sign.

No problem. The desk clerk, a dark-haired good-looking young man, found her a room, ironically the same one not along ago occupied by Dr. Rhonda aka Sandra Lewis, Maria's obsession. The clerk had turned flirty as he asked if he could carry Maria's small bag. "Thank you, I can manage," Maria responded between gritted teeth.

"Okay, but my shift ends soon. You look like a lady who could use a drink. My name, by the way, is Ray and I know a nice place where we could have a night cap."

Maria wished she had worn her engagement ring; more she wished Xavier was with her. When she had told him why she was going to Arkansas after the visit to the Tulsa nursing home, he'd replied as she expected, "Maria, you already know how I feel about your job. These stupid trips make it worse. I don't like my little woman putting herself into danger." He finished with a demand, "Find someone else to go."

Recalling the tone Xavier had used, she took it out on Ray, saying icily, "The only thing this woman needs is sleep. May I please have the key card?"

* * *

The motel provided a continental breakfast. When Maria, wearing her SCCPD uniform, entered the room, it was abuzz with others drawn to the case. One of the law enforcement officers announced to the group, "The sheriff here says he will hold an informational meeting, 10:00 this morning at his office, north of town past the Flying J truck stop."

Several men made room at their little tables for Maria, but she declined politely and found a seat next to two women officers, both from Missouri but different towns. They chuckled about all three having been hit on by Ray. Their conversation veered from Ray to the harassment women in law enforcement continued to receive including a continued lack of acceptance by some, who disliked seeing more and more women in the field.

Maria responded, "My fiancé sure has that attitude. He constantly talks about how dangerous it is, and how he wishes I'd make another career choice."

"I get even more of that now," commented one of the Missouri gals, patting her baby bump.

The other Missouri officer, a cute redhead, added, "I divorced my husband because he insisted I quit my job." She looked directly at Maria, and spoke sternly, "You'd better work things out before marriage, believe me."

The women's conversation ceased as they all listened in on other loud conversations: "It is highly unusual for a person to be missing over a year but if this is one we're looking for, then it will be just a little under a year."

"The one we're looking for disappeared just a few weeks ago, and sure looks like the woman on the poster here."

"This could be it for us. A family from our district was on vacation when the wife disappeared . . ."

Someone interrupted, "Now listen to me. Everyone is assuming the victim is the woman in their poster, but we won't know until the sheriff gives us more information."

The women finished their breakfast. Being professionals, they shared nothing about their own cases. They decided to take a walk around the town. until the sheriff's info session.

They passed the City and County Building where until recently Maria's "Missing Doctor" had worked. When they passed a residential district, all Maria would have had to do was look up and she could have seen the previous "Dr. Rhonda Collins" silhouetted in the window of the second-story of a duplex. When they reached the sheriff's meeting, that woman on the second floor already was there.

The sheriff considered himself quite a celebrity surrounded by "alligators with their toothy grins, wantin me to do all their work for them". There were too many to cram in his office. Too darned bad they had to stand in the cold.

A shower of questions assailed him. *Worse than a press conference* thought Sheriff Carney, though he never had experienced one in a one-reporter town, and in spite of his carping, he loved this, his first time to be a "Big Deal".

His answer to all questions: "No comment, until next of kin gits here," delivered with a superior air.

"Sir, since this is an information meeting, can't you give us any info?" piped up Maria.

"Sorry," grinned the sheriff, "All you git fer now is what was in the bulletin we was required to send. A body was found Wednesday in a snow-filled ditch, which you probably find hard to believe because the snow, like the person, disappeared without a trace."

He laughed heartily at his own joke.

One of the women officers asked, "Sir, when do you expect the family?"

The sheriff noted the one who asked was a good-looking redhead. The other gal who'd asked a question was good-looking, too, but he wasn't interested in gals of other races. "Well, honey," he offered as all three women stiffened, "I don't rightly know for certain but they're on their way now. I also need the forensics report. Don't know when that will be back from Little Rock since they probably don't work on Saturdays."

He wanted to ask the redhead to step in his office but decided better of it. "Give me your cellular number, Red. I'll let you know when I know more and then you can tell the others."

"Most of us are staying at the Red Roof. Just leave a message there," the officer snapped back.

"And 'that's all she wrote'," concluded the sheriff, going inside.

The sheriff had done nothing but cause widespread frustration. The crowd dispersed, with the inspectors leaving as they carped about how long they would have to stay on in this pathetic little town while waiting to find out more, at least the age and gender of the body.

Maria had checked out of the motel before what she and other inspectors called "the Non-Information meeting". She said good-bye to her new female colleagues, who promised to call her if they learned anything worthwhile.

Chapter Thirty-eight

The Newspaper Office

Sandra, disgusted as anyone else about the sheriff's lack of information, pondered what to do next. Again wondering why it hadn't occurred to her before, she decided to go to the local newspaper office to see if she might learn anything about what had happened in the case before she and Rhonda had arrived in Harmon. She knew in her heart that she had been avoiding doing anything before because of what she might learn about Midge. Now, she just had to know.

The office of the <u>Harmon Weekly Bugle</u> office was next to the City and County offices. Sandra walked instead of taking the van, which was to have its repercussions especially when she arrived home and didn't notice the van not in its assigned parking spot behind the duplex.

A friendly woman about her age sat at the reception desk of the newspaper. "May I help you, ma'am?"

"I hope you can. I have been looking for my younger sister for some time. I have seen the photograph of the missing woman on posters many times, and there is a family resemblance. I wonder if she could be my sister."

"How long has she been missing, ma'am?"

"We were separated as children; I haven't seen her since she was four."

"Could I have your name, please?"

Sandra thought quickly. "Ronnie Lee Jackson. Her name is …"

The receptionist broke in, "Ronnie Lee! I kept looking at you and knew you looked familiar. You and I went to school together. Remember me, Rosie Phillips?"

Sandra looked closely and what she remembered was that the only birthday party she had attended as a kid was Rosie's. "I do. Once you invited me to your birthday party."

"What I remember best is you ran away, and the teachers told us to pray for you because bad things could happen. But look at you! You are one classy woman. You have the look of success. I'd say things must have turned out pretty darned well."

"Thank you, they have; but I moved back here because I wanted to be with my family. I found one sister who lives here and a half-sister who is visiting. Now I want to find my baby sister."

"Hey, Lowell," Rosie hollered to the back room. "Come meet one of our old school chums." To Ronnie Lee, she said, "He did a feature on the missing woman. Maybe he'll be able to help you."

A twitchy man with thick dark-rimmed glasses, who looked much older than the two women, came forward and his eyebrows rose above his glasses in recognition. "I never expected to see you again. Our teachers had you eaten by cougars by the second night you went missing. Glad to see you outran them." He smiled, showing a broken front tooth.

Rose asked, "You know that piece you wrote on the missing woman?"

"Marjorie Daniels, of course." Sadness came to his eyes. "Why?"

Well, Ronnie Lee hasn't seen her little sister since Ronnie Lee ran away and she thinks she might be the missing woman."

Sandra added, "Yes, her name was Midge but that is a nickname for Marjorie. That could be the name she uses as an adult."

"Hmm, Missing Times Two. I could do something with that, but from what I've squeezed out of the sheriff since the body was found, Marjorie no longer is missing, but they're waiting for positive identification." Seeing Ronnie Lee shudder, he added, "I hope for your sake the missing woman isn't your sister."

Composing herself, Sandra asked. "Could I ask you some questions?"

Lowell told her the information used in the feature came from the husband. He'd gotten his phone number from the sheriff on a good day.

154

The pair talked for half an hour and Sandra learned that the woman was the same age as Midge and that she had lived in Harmon. At one point, as he told all he knew about the woman, Lowell shut the door to his office. He had heard someone outside, that someone being Detective Maria Gonzalez, reading back issues of the paper to find out all she could about the missing woman.

* * *

Maria's flight back to Texas wasn't until 11:30 PM, which gave her plenty of time before driving back to Little Rock. She felt tempted to hang out with the Missouri detectives, but instead set out to do some detective work on her own. *I can't shake the feeling that Dr. Rhonda could be the missing person here, but I have nothing to link her to this town. Once I asked Linda if Dr. Rhonda had ever talked about her hometown, and Linda assured her that she never gave her any info about her past. The newspaper office, if they have one, would be a good place to start.*

Maria cruised the small downtown area. She saw one block that apparently was a project of renovation with a sign announcing "Future Affordable Housing". In the next block she passed the City and County Offices and almost missed a small sign next door indicating the home of the HARMON WEEKLY BUGLE.

She asked the friendly clerk for permission to check the archives for the past few months, and the woman smiled broadly and led her to actual copies of the newspapers. As she read all she could about the missing person, she could hear two people, a woman and a man, talking in the next room. She couldn't hear every word, but she determined the man was a reporter, and it sounded as if he was interviewing the woman. It had something to do with the missing woman. She strained to listen as someone shut the door to the adjoining room and all she could hear was too muffled to make out. The missing Dr. Rhonda and the detective who sought her, had been in the same crowd at the sheriff's

155

headquarters and currently were separated by a thin interior wall at the Harmon newspaper office.

* * *

After Lowell shut the door, Sandra asked, "Do you know anything about her family?"

"Let me look." Lowell checked his computer. "I don't remember half the facts in my own pieces. Let's see: a farming community called Republic, in Kansas, over in the northwestern part of the state, almost in Nebraska. The family went back there two weeks after she disappeared, and the husband has kept in touch with me and the sheriff's department, and I know there have were no leads until the body was found, and nothing is sure about that. The only thing new is the husband remembered something: he looked every place in his wife's bags and pockets of clothing and all over the RV, but he couldn't find her wristwatch. It was an expensive one she'd inherited. She seldom looked at it for the time because she carried a cell phone, but she always wore it."

"Did her husband ever say anything about her being adopted?"

"No, never came up."

"Thank you. I appreciate all you've told me."

"Let me think about it, Ronnie Lee. I have to wait for the results from forensics, but I just might be able to do your story. People in town might read it and help you find your sister."

"I'm leaving town for a vacation with my sisters tomorrow. Could you wait until we return before you write anything?"

"Sure enough." Lowell shook Sandra's proffered hand. "Have a good vacation."

As she left, she saw the back of a petite woman in a police uniform sitting at a large table studying newspapers. *No doubt one of the out-of-town law officers as disappointed in Sheriff Carney's talk as I was.*

Sandra walked home to finish packing for the trip. *I just can't let myself believe that body belongs to my sister; but with the information Lowell gave me, I plan to contact the husband of the missing woman. Now I need to concentrate on the trip and why I'm taking it.*

* * *

As Sandra left, Maria continued to take notes on what she learned: A young woman and her family, husband, and two preschool-age children, had registered for one night at the Bluestone RV Park outside the town in mid-September. After the children were in bed, the woman, identified as Marjorie Daniels, told her husband she was going to take a shower. She left for the public restroom/shower building at the other end of the park. Her husband fell asleep in front of the television but awakened at 1:00 and realized his wife wasn't back. He went to the shower room and found the clothing she had been wearing as well as her robe and towel on hooks in a private shower cubicle. A personal bag filled with toiletries and nightclothes had been placed on a chair. The water ran cold in the shower.

The husband called 911, a sheriff's deputy responded, and a massive hunt, involving citizens throughout the county, followed. After two weeks the husband and children returned to their farm, near Republic, Kansas.

As she read, theories popped up. One, the woman had been kidnapped but fingerprints and DNA found in the shower room had no match to the national sexual predator database.

Another theory: the woman set up her disappearance, had taken other clothing and left by bus to parts unknown. No bus driver remembered a woman fitting that description. Many articles in the paper repeated the same information. Later a feature told more about the young farm wife, aged thirty, loving mother of two, a boy aged six and a girl four. Loved by all who knew her, she was a Sunday school teacher and a frequent blue and purple ribbon winner at the County Fair, where she entered her jams, clothing she had sewn and

157

flowers she'd grown. In late September she and her family had rented an RV to go to the funeral of her husband's uncle in Dallas. Afterwards they wanted to do some fall sightseeing, and Marjorie requested a side trip to her hometown, Harmon in Arkansas.

From that feature Maria had to concede the age didn't match with that of the Missing Dr. Rhonda. Of course the two children hadn't sounded likely. The body must belong to the Kansas woman, given the body's proximity to the RV Park. *Once again, I have come up empty-handed; but I have learned more about investigative work, and I met two cool women in my field.*

Later on the way back to Little Rock, Maria stopped at the site of the discovery of the body and surveyed the RV Park. She found there was no way to lock the shower cubicles. She shuddered. *I'd never go in one of them unless armed.*

Back in the car she sighed. How she had hoped DNA collected in Corpus Christi would match that of the dead woman, and the case would be concluded. *Another dead end, pun notwithstanding. But something has bothered me from the time I entered the motel. Why did I feel a strong presence of Dr. Rhonda throughout my time in Harmon?*

* * *

When Sandra reached their home, she found Rhonda absolutely giddy. She kept telling Sandra that she had a surprise for her. Sandra didn't find out what until Wayne dropped by to say, "Good-bye."

"Wow! Moby Dick," as he had nicknamed Sandra's van, "has never looked better." Perplexed, Rhonda, who had the van serviced and washed in preparation for the trip, didn't think getting rid of a little Arkansas mud improved it that much.

Rhonda burst out laughing at the comment, and that's when Sandra knew something was afoot. She left down the stairs with Rhonda and Wayne on her heels and found the van covered in painted designs of daisies, hearts, stars, moons, rainbows, smiling suns and puffy letters saying, "Girls' Road Trip" and "Corpus Christi or Bust!" Rhonda explained that she had talked Andrea into getting frothy paint kids used for cars and helping her decorate it.

There was nothing for Sandra to do except join in the laughter. *How can my Texas plan possibly fail with such a gaily decorated mode of transportation? A million ways, at least.*

Wayne embraced her and whispered in her ear, "I'll be counting the days until you come back, sweetheart. We could have a beautiful future together."

They kissed, and Sandra had an uncomfortable thought. Why do I feel as if I'm kissing him and any future together good-bye? Returning there is a terrible idea but it's too late to back out now.

Chapter Thirty-nine

Handling Danger

Maria reached the outskirts of Little Rock and approached railway tracks. She could hear a train far in the distance, too soon for the red lights and descended safety arm. Without any prior warning the rental car shook and stalled on the tracks. Maria's heart pounded as Xavier's voice taunted her, "I told you that this job is too dangerous for women".

The train came closer with whistle screaming and the crossing lights flashing while the arm hit the car. Maria grabbed her phone and briefcase. She had to abandon the rental. Hearing the explosion of a car reduced to its parts, she let out a feral scream.

A police officer who looked just like Stan drove her to the airport and she barely made her flight. She was exhausted and fell asleep before the plane was in the air.

A flight attendant touched the shoulder of the young uniformed woman passenger having a bad dream. "We'll be landing soon."

Interlude

After asking you to hop on a bus that crashed, you may be reluctant to accept this invitation. Ride with me as the three Jackson sisters travel to Corpus Christi. Be prepared to be confused by more name changes. Sandra, playing dead, takes the name of lost sister **Midge.** To pretend to be the beneficiary in Dr. Collins' will, Rhonda must become **Sandra**. We're in for a roller coaster ride with good breaks and bad breaks as they reach a region overtaken by Spring Break.

PART TWO

Chapter One

Road Trip

Spirits were high, at least the first morning of the road trip to Corpus Christi. As her sisters and niece filled the back with an excess of luggage, a cooler, a picnic basket besides George's litter box and carrier, Sandra laughed, "Now I know why I bought this big old van."

Three sisters who shared the same good looks couldn't have been more different: Sandra, poised, calculating and focused; Rhonda, self-centered, living for the moment; Rainey, serious, aloof and moralistic. Their outfits reflected their personalities. Sandra dressed in a silk shirt and slacks, Rhonda, beach ready in shorts and tank top, and Rainey in a crisp matched gingham blouse and pants. The cast of travelers in addition to the three sisters included a crabby cat and an equally irritating twelve-year-old, dressed in holey jeans and an oversized sweatshirt with a hood that pretty much hid her face.

"Rhonda, you sit in the front. Andrea and I will sit in the back," Rainey insisted.

"Oh, no, I get the back because I want to become better acquainted with my niece," Rhonda countered and pushed her sister aside as she climbed in with George, protesting that he wanted no part of this.

Andrea already had tuned out. With ear buds to hear her music and fingers flying as she kept up constant texting to her friend, Holly, the pre-teen didn't care who sat beside her.

Three miles out of town, Rhonda shrieked. "Stop! I have to get out."

Sandra, back in doctor mode, stopped the van and rushed to her sister, who vomited out the window.

"Are you carsick?"

"Maybe," conceded Rhonda as she exited the car before hit by another spasm.

"Then you need to sit in the front," Sandra advised. Rainey and Rhonda changed places while Andrea sent a text message to Holly: Crazy aunt puked.

A few miles later Rhonda asked Sandra to stop again and this event repeated itself every few miles. Sandra warned, "Rhonda, you're going to get dehydrated. You have to drink some water. Rainey, hand her a bottle from the cooler."

The ailing sister drank too fast, which meant another stop by the side of the road. Andrea texted: Gross. We have to keep stopping for Aunt. We'll never get to the beach.

"Take sips, only, Sweetie," Sandra advised and when her sister couldn't keep that down, she made a decision. "At the first town we come to that has a hospital, I'm taking you to the ER."

"Andrea," her mother beseeched as the child pulled out one ear bud, "could you check for the nearest hospital?"

Andrea rolled her eyes but found the right app and told Sandra to turn left at the next intersection. That took them miles in the wrong direction, and George, ending a short nap in his carrier, woke up and sang endless Italian arias.

"It's not my fault," protested Andrea though no one had chided her. "George just made me nervous and my battery is low." Then she texted Holly: Everyone blames me for everything. Now we have to take Aunt to hospital. We'll never get there.

Poor Rhonda looked wretched. She had perked up with the suggestion of a hospital but now wailed, "I know I'll die before I get medical attention."

Both her sisters had learned how Rhonda, a drama queen, liked being the center of attention, and a trip to ER suited her well. Each sister had a different idea of what could be wrong. Rainey: *She drank too much, probably partied last night.* Sandra: *Could it be a strain of flu we'll all get, making this the official barf-mobile?*

A blue highway sign for a hospital appeared in a hub for small towns. "There's no reason for all of us to traipse into ER," Sandra decided. "I'll take her and you two can take the

164

van and see the sights. I'll call when we need to be picked up."

"Don't leave George alone," pleaded Rhonda, who leaned against Sandra as they headed toward the ER entrance.

Sandra, using professional medical terminology, convinced the triage nurse that her sister's problems could be life threatening. The head nurse put Rhonda in a room, started an IV to replace fluids, and called for a doctor. The patient did enjoy the attention and Sandra saw the nurse and nursing assistant give each other looks. One asked, "Is there a chance that you're pregnant?"

As Sandra looked astonished that she hadn't considered this, the patient settled it, "Definitely not. I was told I couldn't have children."

When the two were alone, Sandra commented, "I think your doctor was mistaken. Is it Ray's?"

"I sure hope not." A bit later the patient mused, "I'd prefer Ben but not possible."

The ER team decided they should admit Rhonda to the hospital for observation and rest. Not news her surly niece wanted to hear.

"Can't we leave her behind?" whined the tween. "We'll barely get to the beach before we have to come back home."

"Andrea, that's unkind," rebuked her mother. "We are not deserting your aunt when she's ill." Then addressing her daughter's disappointment, she added, "We'll find a motel with a pool and then you can have some fun."

They found a motel with a pool that didn't take pets, but when Andrea protested, they smuggled George in and kept him caged. In no time Andrea found the pool and flirted with a teen hunk, also a guest at the motel, who was much too old for her. The sisters took turns being at the hospital with Rhonda.

Later the sisters softly discussed Rhonda as Andrea slept.

"Is she pregnant?" asked Rainey.

"She insists she isn't because she lost a baby to a premature birth when she was married in her late teens and was told she wouldn't be able to have more children."

"There is little I know about my secret half-sister. And what about you, Sandra? I know nothing about you except that you ran away."

"All you don't know is I thought of you and Midge every day."

Rainey looked as if on the verge of tears. Sandra put her arm around her sister. "I don't know how we will convince Mama to remember us, but I'm determined to find our baby sister; and we three, and our bonus sister, can be connected again."

Chapter Two

On the Road Again

The next morning the hospital released Rhonda with a bottle of pre-natal vitamins, an anti-nausea preparation, and a booklet, "Healthy Moms, Healthy Babies". The Corpus Christi-bound bunch hit the road. They had discovered the day before that George stopped singing if someone, Rainey or Rhonda, took him out of the carrier and petted him a little,

An hour later Rhonda muttered, "They're wrong. I can't be. I want to get a pregnancy test at a drugstore."

"But, Sis, they examined you," Sandra explained as if her sister was one of her former pediatric patients. Then seeing the look of stubbornness on her sister's face, she made a concession. "You're pregnant, but if it will give you peace of mind, we'll stop at the next town."

"We need to stop soon. I have to pee."

At the next rest stop, they pulled into a slot. As soon as Rainey opened the backdoor, George bolted. Andrea let Holly know: Stupid cat is on the run. Don't blame him. I'd like to run off too. Wish I'd stayed with hunk at the motel. While Sandra and Rainey chased the cat, Andrea continued her texting: Watch Mom and other aunt run. LOL

"Rhonda will be devastated if we don't capture him," gasped Sandra as the cat led them around and around the rest stop, finally disappearing into a wooded area.

Rainey, also lacking breath, gave up. "This is impossible. We'll have to find Rhonda a new cat after we're home."

The two went to the restroom to break the news. Rhonda sobbed as the three returned to the van. Opening the door all three chorused, "George?"

Andrea honored them by pulling out the ear buds. "A dog got loose from his owner. He chased the dog into some trees where George was hiding. The dog chased George and I just opened the back door. He jumped right in."

All praised her quick thinking, and her mom hugged her and gave her a smooch on the cheek.

"We need to get a leash for him if he doesn't stay in his carrier," Sandra insisted.

"Add that to the list with pregnancy test," Rainey added, wondering why in the world she had come and brought her child, not the only time she was to question this.

Andrea texted: I caught the cat. Another stop. Forget the beach.

Thankful for a vehicle with a sound system, Sandra turned on the radio to calm everyone. At the next town, all got out. Andrea said she didn't need anything and said she'd take George in his carrier for a walk. Around the corner at the end of the block she stopped for a smoke, something the hunk at the motel had taught her, even giving her a pack.

After stopping at Walgreen's, the sisters spotted an enticing vintage boutique and went inside. This is just what we are going to need," exclaimed Sandra, picking up a blue Ginger jar decorated with sprigs of white cherry blossoms tinged in pink.

"Why?" asked Rainey but before Sandra could answer Rhonda appeared and asked the proprietor if she might use the restroom.

The other two sisters, knowing why Rhonda went in there, hovered by the door. Rhonda came out, looking devastated. "I bought two pregnancy tests and tried them both. They agree. I'm pregnant." She burst into tears.

Both sisters hugged her. "We'll be there for you, Sis." Sandra promised while Rainey concurred.

Meeting Andrea and George at the van, Sandra smelled cigarette smoke on Andrea and whispered in her ear, "Did you let George smoke a cigarette while we were shopping?"

Andrea blushed and realized her mother would be able to smell it, too. She did. "Andrea, why do your clothes smell like smoke?"

"I was standing outside, taking care of George, uh, in front of a bar, I think it was, and, uh, it was really smoky and . . ." trying to make this credible . . . "the door was open, and they had some great music playing and that is why I was standing there."

"Let me see you backpack."

Andrea surrendered it. Her mother found the pack of cigarettes and tossed the full pack minus one cigarette into a sidewalk trash receptacle. Firmly her mother dictated, "There will be none of that."

All were in the van now. Rhonda took a deep breath and exclaimed, "I smell smoke and I think I'm going to throw up again."

Sandra reassured her that the pills would take care of that and then said to all, "It's almost time for supper and we haven't reached Texas yet. I think we'd better eat and stay the night here in Oklahoma because it's still a long way to the coast. And there is something I need to explain to all of you" Andrea started to grumble but knew she was in no position to complain.

After a good southern meal of fried chicken with biscuits (for all but Sandra who opted for fish) and a prolonged stay in the Cracker Barrel Gift shop, the four and George headed to a third-rate motel that took pets. As soon as they were settled, Sandra began her explanation. "When I was in Corpus Christi, I accumulated quite a bit of wealth, a townhouse, art, BMW, bank accounts. I had reason to worry about someone threatening me; and I wanted to be able to have easy access to my assets and that's why I made out my will. This is where it's complicated. I borrowed Rhonda's name while I was in Texas and said my beneficiary was Sandra, really me. My plan, and I know this isn't honest, was to pretend I was dead and then I, as Sandra, could collect the money".

Rainey broke in, "But apparently you didn't do that, if the purpose of this trip is to regain your assets."

Sandra sighed. *It would have been easier if Rhonda hadn't insisted we bring Rainey and Andrea.*

"I didn't want to go into it, but when we reach Corpus Christi Rhonda becomes Sandra. This means I will have to stay out of sight while Sandra presents the death certificates I will provide her. Then my assets, which I earned, will be given to Sandra, who will return them to me in exchange for her room and board, etc."

"You mean a dead woman is driving us to Texas?" quipped Andrea, who quickly texted to Holly, who always sent a sympathetic reply: 2 crazy aunts #1 is pregnant #2 thinks she's dead and she's driving! Let me out of here!

Rainey looked shocked at all her sister had explained, and Sandra wanted to reassure her. "I worked hard and earned all of my money; it rightfully belongs to me; but someone from my past, for some reason, wanted me to lose everything. That's when I cut my hair and dyed it brown and fled Texas."

Rainey shook her head. "You're dead until we leave Texas? Somehow you faked death certificates and what if someone finds out?"

"We'll just have to deal with it. As I told you, we'll be staying in my townhouse. I have to stay in my room while our sister does just what I tell her to collect the money. Andrea, stop texting and listen."

Andrea ignored her aunt: and texted: How can I escape these crazies?

Rainey broke in, "Andrea. You are being very rude. Listen to Aunt Sandra. It's important."

"Thank you." Sandra continued, "You and your mom must pretend I'm deceased, and you two came along with Sandra for Spring Break."

"That's exactly why I came," snarled Andrea.

Sandra answered with kindness, "I know, dear, and they'll be sure to take you to the beach. Port Aransas is a cute town across the ferry, where you can watch dolphins."

"Dolphins!" Andrea rolled her eyes and reattached her ear buds. "I'm done listening, Dead Auntie."

Rainey, lost in thought, didn't even reprimand her daughter for her rudeness. *What have I gotten my daughter and me involved in? This dishonesty goes against everything I believe.* "I hope you know what you're doing, Sandra."

"Rainey, I hate this more than you'll know, but I'm running out of money. This is the only way."

170

"Can't you deal legally with the person who wanted you to lose everything?"

Sandra paused before answering. *She probably thinks it's an ex-husband or lover I left and who is out to get me, not a batty old woman in Tulsa who was a client when I had my beauty salon. I don't want to tell them I'm a wanted felon for practicing without a legal medical license, among other things.* "Rainey, unfortunately this is the only way. I wouldn't do it and involve all of you if there was any alternative."

Andrea broke in, "If everyone is changing their names I'm changing mine. From now on I want to be Tiffany."

"Absolutely not," interjected Rainy. "I'm not changing my name, and you are not changing yours, especially to Tiffany."

"Okay, I'm not changing it but from now on I want everyone to pronounce my name An-dray-a."

"Personally, I like 'Tiffany'," commented Sandra, "but the new way to pronounce your name is classy."

Rainey sighed as the dead aunt shushed everyone. "Enough! We all better get some sleep. I want to get an early start."

With one bathroom and four females an "early start" had little chance.

Chapter Three

Salsa and Sadness

The same night the sisters were in a huddle in a motel in Arkansas, Xavier and Maria had gone to a benefit barbecue and dance. This event was designed to aid the family of a Corpus Christi firefighter killed doing his job at a house fire. Maria had known the fire fighter slightly when she began her law enforcement career as a uniform with the Corpus Christi PD. She was exhausted from her travels but rested all she could during the day because she wouldn't have missed this benefit for anything.

Maria and Xavier proved how much they loved to dance. When the attractive, talented couple danced to salsa music, they cleared the floor. Everyone enjoyed watching the happy couple. Obviously in love.

After the last dance the couple drove across the ferry to Port Aransas to sit on the beach. Spring Breakers had begun to gather, and they decided to stay in the car to watch the moonlit gulf waters.

They talked about their summer wedding and agreed the reception after the ceremony at their parish church would include dancing. After talking and such for hours, Xavier became very serious. "Maria, all the time we were at the benefit, I kept thinking that I don't want people giving me and our kids a benefit because you were killed by a criminal."

"That's very sweet, Xav, but don't worry, I won't let a criminal harm me."

"You can't promise that."

"I know, but I'm trained, and I will take care of myself for you and our babies."

"It's not enough, Maria. As soon as we marry, you have to give up police work."

Maria scooted away from her fiancé and looked him in the eye, "You can't ask me to give up my career. I love my job and I'm good at it."

"I'm not saying you aren't good. What I am saying is that I will not allow my wife to work in such a dangerous field."

Maria thought of the words of the divorced detective from Missouri and burned with fury. "Won't allow? Won't allow? Xavier. I love you, Xavier, but marrying you is a mistake."

"Now, Maria, you don't mean that," soothed Xavier. "You're just tired and stressed from that last fruitless trip"

"I do mean it. I think you should marry someone whom you can dominate, and it won't be me."

With tears in her eyes, Maria slipped Great-grandma's exquisite heirloom ring from her finger. "Please, take me home."

Chapter Four

Broken Hearts

The last thing Xavier had said to Maria was, "You better keep the ring. I'm sure you will come to your senses."

Maria refused the ring and she felt no differently Sunday morning. Ignoring calls from Xavier, she told her housemate and best friend, "You know there were red flags. First he said I could not take Big Boy or ever have a cat because his mother is paranoid about cats. Then he let her choose my engagement ring,"

Sydney broke in. "But it's a gorgeous ring."

"True, and he's one gorgeous man, but the ring is not what I'd have chosen. And that's what I realized. Xavier, abetted by his mother, wanted to make all the choices for me. He constantly has been negative about my being in law enforcement, but when he said last night that he would not allow me to keep my job, I wanted it over."

"I don't blame you. I've wondered for a long time how someone as independent as you could put up with this outdated male domination."

"That's how he was raised. His parents still hold on to the old customs of the domineering patriarch and the subservient wife as Zavier's dad made clear at the engagement party. I sure wasn't raised that way, and I don't want to bring up my children that way."

Maria teared up and her friend put her arm around her. "I know it hurts, but you did the right thing."

Composing herself, Maria stated, "Down to business: I need to call my parents and the attendants besides you and make a list of things to cancel tomorrow like the church, hall, and cake."

* * *

Xavier repeatedly called Maria. Now he was at a friend's house watching the Cowboys game with several men friends.

One asked, "What's wrong, Xav? You haven't said word one. Just keep popping the top on one can of Bud after another."

"I broke off my engagement."

No one commented until a play was completed. One unglued his eyes from the television long enough to say. "Not your engagement to Maria? She's one hot babe."

"Why?" asked another.

"Cheatin on you?" came from still another.

Xavier glared at the author of that. "No," he slurred a little, "I realized she isn't the right wife for me."

"You did the right thing, man," another friend said.

All eyes returned to the game, and not one noticed tears formed in Xavier's.

* * *

Tears flooded from Maria's eyes Monday morning when all Stan said was "How are you?" Stan had never seen his partner this way and wanted to hold her like he would his daughter, but he just handed her a wad of Kleenex. Haltingly she told him about the broken engagement.

"He's a fool," Stan said, trying to be consoling. "You're a darned good detective. There more of women detective all the time. They get married, get pregnant. Take a leave when they have the baby and then come back as mothers that also are cops."

"He just doesn't get it."

"Maria, you could really go places in this field. Don't let that Neanderthal stop you."

Stan's phone rang. The chief had a Spring Break assignment for the two detectives. Like everyone else, including the Chief, they would draw major Spring Beak duties during this time SSPD had come to dread because most of the action was in their jurisdiction on Mustang and Padre islands.

Chapter Five

Cop Stops

By the time they'd all had a turn to primp in the bathroom, had breakfast, and pulled George from a hiding place under a desk, it was 11:00 AM, checkout time. Monday's drive would be a long one if they reached their destination.

Heavy traffic heading towards the coast, mused Sandra. *I need to watch my speed. There are bound to be extra patrols with all the Spring Breakers. I fear I might be identified and arrested if I'm stopped. I just can't think that way.*

Rhonda-now-Sandra, to everyone's relief, felt much better with the medicine, which meant they hadn't had to stop every few miles yesterday or today. The mother-to-be slept most of the time, but when awake, the real Sandra lectured her on not drinking while pregnant and reassured her that together they would bring up this child.

The real Sandra suddenly decided something. "This is confusing with two of us being Sandra now. How about I change my name to Midge while we're in Texas?"

No one disagreed; Rhonda was Sandra and Sandra was Midge.

The van jerked and bounced, shaking up the driver and passengers. Sandra pulled to the side. A flat. Changing a tire was something her foster mom taught her when she let Sandra drive the old pick-up. Rainey possessed the same skill. Though they both got dirty, they put on a spare. They must have looked competent because no Good Samaritans in the heavy traffic zooming by them stopped to help. Both wondered where they'd find a filling station that fixed tires.

Andrea let Holly know: Stupid van has a flat. Any more problems and Spring Break will be over.

Back in the car, Midge worried about how long they could travel on the spare. She forgot to watch her speed. Flashing lights pulled her over. Panic-stricken, Midge silently prayed: *Dear* God, *I pray they aren't still looking for Dr.*

Rhonda, especially since I've grown my hair out and am back to my original color.

"In a big hurry to get to the beach, ladies? "asked the sun-tanned Texas Ranger with crooked teeth and darting eyes.

Midge used all her charm. "I'm horribly sorry, sir. We are going to Corpus Christi but just for business."

Andrea grimaced at that but otherwise was too scared to move.

"What kind of business?"

Midge urged out a tear. "We're settling a family estate."

"Mind if I check your vehicle?"

"Of course not*." I know Andrea smokes but surely, she doesn't have drugs.*

"Please put George on his leash. We don't want to risk his escaping," said to the backseat, and to the officer explained, "George is the cat."

The Arkansas travelers and cat vacated the van.

The three sister look-alikes stood together on the side, all wishing they were invisible. Andrea, today in her holey pants and a tie-dyed T-shirt, stood as far from the others as possible while George tried to wiggle out of the collar attached to his leash. Traffic was heavy, and carloads of kids hooted and honked at what looked like drug-bust suspects standing near their boldly painted van. With a little imagination the kids would swear the women had been shackled together.

It seemed to take the trooper forever to check everything in the van, especially the back end. The women and Andrea grew more embarrassed as time passed. They all stifled a giggle when the trooper reached inside into the recently used litter box.

"All seems well," the trooper announced, wiping his hand off on a handkerchief. "Y'all look alike except the young-un and the cat. Are you a singing group?" He laughed at his attempt at humor.

"No, just sisters who look just like our Mama," explained Sandra.

"My daughter looks like her daddy," Rainey volunteered.

"You purty ladies can be on your way. Y'all still have a long drive. Best you be careful, and you can pay that speeding ticket by mail."

Midge protested the ticket. "I just changed a tire and maybe the spare threw off the speedometer. How far is the next town where we could have it fixed?"

"You changed the tire?" The officer couldn't contain his amazement.

Pointing to Rainey, Midge replied, "That sister and I did." She hoped her voice didn't reveal her feelings towards the chauvinist Texas Ranger.

The trooper inspected the spare and said, "You definitely need to fix the tire soon. That spare is in bad shape, and I doubt it did a thing to your speedometer. There's a Texaco station not too far down the road. They can fix it but it's going to be costly. You were going almost 25 over the speed limit and even though you're a blonde, you should know better than to speed   on a spare. Afraid I have to write the ticket to include speeding and careless driving."

Midge took the ticket with a grimace and all piled back into the car; actually, she felt relieved it was only a traffic ticket. Andrea texted: Never been this embarssed (sic). Cop stopped us to look for drugs. We had to stand by the side of the freeway for hours. I thought I was going to die with people in cars gawking at me.

It wouldn't be too many days before the twelve-year old would experience even worse humiliation, but for now she had plenty to complain about to Holly.

Next stop, a station in the middle of nowhere for the tire repair. Andrea asked for change to buy bags of cheese puffs and Reese's Pieces from one vending machine. Midge and Rainey bought diet sodas from another while Rhonda opted for a "gourmet latte" from a dispenser.

Two hours later a state trooper pulled over Midge for speeding but checked nothing but her Arkansas driver's license. After issuing the ticket and returning her license, he

178

looked her and asked her to let him look at her license again. He stared at her and at the license, made out to Sandra Lewis. He asked her to get out of the van and accompany him to his squad car. Midge's legs turned to jelly, and she wondered how she could walk on them. She smiled bravely and waved to her passengers as she followed the trooper's directions.

He radioed to his station. "Did they ever find that 'Missing Doctor' from Corpus Christi?" The officer had taken a special interest in that case and wondered if he had the famed good-looking missing woman in his patrol car right now.

Midge had never known such fear, even when detained at the SA airport as a suspected terrorist. *What will happen to everyone if I'm arrested?*

Rainey and Sandra both froze. Neither could say a word as they wondered just what their sister had done. Andrea texted Holly: OMG. I think Dead Auntie Sandra just got arrested for more than speeding. Wait, I'm supposed to call her Auntie Midge now and Auntie Rhonda is now Auntie Sandra. See why they are driving moi bonkers?

"Case closed" came over the radio, and Sandra started breathing again. The officer turned to Sandra. "You look like a woman who was missing in Corpus Christi. I was really interested in the case. I have a friend in the South Corpus Christi Police Department and the last I heard they were looking for the woman's sister, who happened to have the same name as you do."

Midge shook her head as if completely confused by the officer's tale and smiled when he told her she was free to return to her vehicle. Questioning looks met Midge who merely shrugged and said, "If that doesn't beat all. The police were looking for another 'Sandra Lewis'? Don't you think that would have occurred to that first trooper? Anyone else want to drive? I'm tired of getting speeding tickets."

No one volunteered except Andrea, who was voted down. Midge split her concentration between the traffic and the speedometer. Andrea's complaints of extreme hunger brought them to a Taqueria for lunch. Andrea had become a

179

vegan since breakfast and pouted that the menu had nothing she could or would eat. The server brought her salsa and tortilla chips and didn't mention the latter was made with animal fat.

The rest of the trip the four of them tried hard to remember who was who now though no one gave Andrea's name her preferred pronunciation. The tween continued listening to her tunes and texting Holly while the sisters sang to the radio and discussed how they might find out where the real Midge's adoptive family had taken her and what they could do to convince their mother she had given birth to four beautiful daughters.

"By the way, Sis, you never told us what the ginger jar's for," mentioned Sandra.

"That's for my ashes. I'm sure we can find some in the barbecue pit on my patio."

Chapter Six

Spring Breakers, Law Breakers

The two detectives' assignment was to patrol Corpus Christi's North Beach. This was in CCPD's jurisdiction, but most of their officers had headed to Padre Island to help SSPD with crowd control.

Unusually warm weather had brought hordes of visitors, high school and college kids on break as well as families with younger children. Also school dropouts and kids that hadn't seen a college door. In their jacked-up trucks with enormous tires, they cruised the beach offering beads to any gal willing to pull down her bikini top.

Stan pointed out all the girls had multiple Mardi Gras beads in various colors around their young necks. "Of course, the girls could have bought them at a souvie shop," offered Maria, defending many gals unnecessarily as yells and applause heralded another young woman earning more beads.

Stan responded, "And those losers probably got the giant Confederate Flags hanging from their trucks at the same shops."

They checked I.D.s of kids drinking on the beach, and found no one under-age drinking because seeing badges approaching, they handed their brew to someone of age. CCPD personnel patrolled the beach in cars and on foot and made a few arrests. "It's cop presence that diffuses most trouble," pontificated Belkin.

Maria gave first aid to a woman with a cut on her foot from a broken bottle in spite of glass containers being banned on all beaches. Otherwise, the biggest excitement was in one of the souvenir shops. They busted a four-year old for shoplifting and remanded him to the custody of the parents, who paid the $2.00 for the shark tooth their son was seen pocketing.

"This may be as bad as it gets on our shift. After a day or two on North Beach most decide to head to Padre and Mustang Island, and we may be sent there tomorrow. Of course, new visitors come here all week. There's plenty to do for families near the beach with the museums, the aquarium."

Maria knew all about the attractions. She had lived in Corpus all her life, but she conceded not knowing much about what happened during Spring Break because, like at Christmas, the Gonzalez family always drove to Mexico.

The detectives' shift had ended before Midge et al approached the "Sparkling City by the Sea". Sandra turned off on North Beach, an area crowded with pedestrians and cars. "I know a great restaurant called Blackbeard's. They have the best crab cakes. I bet you'd love those, Andrea."

"Weren't you listening? I'm vegan. I don't eat meat of any kind and even before I became a vegan, I wouldn't eat anything that had been in the foul, filthy ocean."

Rainey interrupted "Watch your mouth, Andrea. You can order a salad,"

Parking seemed impossible, but Sandra found a place for "The Mother Ship", as they had taken to calling the van, a few blocks from the restaurant. Andrea could hear the music and happy rowdiness from the beach and couldn't wait to be part of that energy.

The line at the restaurant stretched around the block but when Midge gave the hostess her name, the woman happened to remember a table for a party of four in the back room, and a waitress seated them rather than another obnoxious male foursome from the beach that was far ahead of Midge's party.

They studied the menu. Midge and Rainey had the crab cakes and Sandra had chowder. Deciding maybe she wasn't a vegan today, Andrea had chicken tenders.

Midge looked around the dining room where she and Linda had eaten many times. She noticed a large party of women who sat at long table along one side of the side of the room. One whispered loudly, "It's her! The Missing Doctor." She pointed at Rainey. "I'd know her anywhere. After all I waited on her at Wal-Mart, and I found the bag with her hair and the bloodstained blouse. I wonder how she got that scar? Maybe her kidnapper had a knife."

182

Midge gulped at hearing the woman and felt relieved the others at her table weren't paying any attention to the woman's stage whisper. She suggested they finish and go to her home. *I never thought through how my actions would impact others. That woman waited on me when I bought clothes and scissors and hair dye? She must have reported the encounter. I didn't think anyone would find the bag with the blouse and hair. I just wanted them away from the motel and out of the car.*

Chapter Seven

Squatters

As Midge pulled into her driveway, she was appalled when she saw a "For Sale" sign on the lawn. Forgetting momentarily that she had named Linda Hernandez executive of the estate, she pondered: *How can it be for sale? I never authorized selling it. I've paid the mortgage, taxes, and all the insurance. This could be more complicated than I thought it would be.*

To her sisters, who stared at the sign, she said, "This is a mistake." Hopping out of the car, she yanked up the sign and threw it on the porch. Calmly she unlocked the door.

The sisters couldn't contain their admiration for the home and its exquisite interior decorating. As the sisters oohed, Andrea tried hard not to be impressed. Not wanting to incur the wrath of the Homeowners Association, Midge put the decorated van in the garage

Joining her relatives, she made room assignments. "For now, Rainey and Andrea can take the guest room," Midge pointed towards the hospitable room with its own bath, "and Sandra-my-Beneficiary will sleep with me. Stash your luggage accordingly."

Midge checked the kitchen for any food. Someone had cleaned out the cupboards and refrigerator. She couldn't help thinking about her one-time lover when she entered her beautifully appointed bedroom. She opened the door to the walk-in closet, about the size of her bedroom in the Arkansas apartment, to hang up her clothes. She spotted two huge packing boxes. Someone had written on one with black marker "Consignment Shop".

It contained all her designer clothes, including the tan jacket that matched the pants in her suitcase. The other box had a word that looked as if angrily scrawled: "Trash". Sandra had no doubt who sorted her clothing when she opened the box and found all the lingerie and costumes she used to wear for the husband of her best friend, Linda. *How could I have had an affair with her husband and how could I have left without telling her I had to leave? I've done some terrible things but it always comes to my betrayal of her being the worst.*

She heard a knock on the door, and pulled the bedroom door shut. Being dead is going to be hard. Why couldn't I have stuck to my intention of being totally honest once I reached Arkansas?

Andrea didn't hear the door as she involved herself in texting Holly: I'm close to loosing (sic) my mind. They better take me to the beach tomorrow.

The **Beneficiary** was in the bathroom. Rainey took a deep breath, opened the front door and made a dive but missed the cat, posed for escape. She screamed, "George!"

The tall fair-skinned man on the porch raced after the feline, grabbed it and calmed the frightened animal. He looked over the animal resting on its back in his strong arms. It resembled one of his cats, a Russian Blue, ironically also named "George".

Handing the cat to Rainey, he paused and then forged ahead. "Ma'am, I'm a cat person, and I think you should change George's name. He's a she and, if I'm not mistaken, will have a family soon."

Rainey shook her head, tightened her grip on the cat and remembered to ask the kind man how she could help him.

"I'm Tim Sylte, the realtor. Why was my sign taken down and who are you?"

"I'm with the beneficiary to the estate of the former owner. We're here for Spring Break".

Sylte raised his eyebrows. "This doesn't make sense. I was hired two months ago by the executor of the estate to sell this townhouse, and I have a couple coming back for a second look in a few minutes. I'm sure they intend to make an offer tonight."

"I'm sorry. There must be a mistake. I know for certain the beneficiary has not put the house up for sale."

When a young couple drove up, their realtor walked over to tell them there was a small irregularity that he intended to take care of with a phone call.

"Good! We're ready to make an offer," the wife cooed.

While Sylte called Dr. Hernandez, Rainey shut and locked the door.

"What was that all about?" asked Sandra.

"George is a girl, and she's pregnant."

Sandra-the-Beneficiary burst into tears.

* * *

Dr. Hernandez couldn't believe what the realtor said—squatters in Rhonda's house? When the court had closed the case of the Missing Doctor, they froze all of Rhonda's assets. The judge had instructed that Linda, as executor, liquidate all assets including the house, its contents with its extensive art collection, and the BMW. She put the townhouse on the market. The car sold through a police auction.

"Mr. Sylte, I will have to get back to you as soon as I talk to my attorney. Could you tell me anything else about the people in the house?"

"The woman I talked to said she and the beneficiary of the former owner are there for Spring Break, and that the beneficiary did not authorize the sale of the property."

"This is weird but I will do what I can."

"I must tell you that time is of the essence. I have an excellent offer on the townhouse, and the buyers want to purchase most of the paintings and pottery separately."

"As I said," Linda said as firmly as she could," I will get back to you as soon as possible."

The thoroughly baffled woman hung up and dialed her brother-in-law, the esteemed Corpus Christi attorney. She remembered that he and her sister had gone on a cruise and wouldn't be back until next week. *What to do? I don't feel right about calling Rhonda's attorney at home.*

Linda tried to puzzle it out. *How can this be? They'd proved Rhonda and Sandra were the same person. DNA can't be wrong, but what if they never had Sandra's DNA? I spoke with Sandra on the phone. She always maintained she was not Rhonda, but Rhonda's sister Sandra. Based on the findings of Maria and her detective partner, Rhonda ran away and is still alive. But did something happen to her since then, and her sister has come to claim everything but doesn't know the court froze all because of Rhonda being a fugitive?*

The court earlier had awarded Linda, as executor, a fixed amount plus a percentage of sales. A nice nest egg for her children's education, but Linda wasn't worried about the money. She remembered the last time she was at the townhouse when she packed up personal items. The townhouse where she had spent relaxed, happy times with her best friend. Where she learned her husband also had spent quality time alone with Rhonda. She had vowed to put that behind her but seeing all of Rhonda's seductive negligees had brought it all back. She had tossed them in a box for the trash haulers, which she had neglected to put out for them, and she hadn't found time to take the other clothing to a consignment shop. *The only thing I can do is call to see if Dave's mom can watch the boys while I go to the townhouse myself.* The phone interrupted her thoughts.

The realtor, having taken his clients to Coffee Waves by HEB, insinuated another buyer had a bigger offer. They really wanted the townhouse and agreed to up the ante. Sylte excused himself to phone Dr. Hernandez again. "The buyers will pay the full asking price and buy all the art. This is the big fish I can't let get away!"

"I'm sorry, Mr. Sylte. I tried. My attorney is out of town and I won't be able to reach another until tomorrow. It upsets me to tell you this, but the house may not be for sale after all."

Sylte, steamed about his sizeable endangered commission, ended the call. He couldn't bring himself to tell the clients the last thing the executer of the estate had said. Instead full of smiles, he said she would have information in the morning and he promised to call as soon as the seller got back to him, He showed the couple two more great townhouses that had just come on the market.

He went to sleep that night wondering what the squatters had renamed their cat.

* * * *

"What was that all about?" Midge asked, coming from her room after she heard Rainey lock the front door.

"A realtor wanting to have a showing," answered Rainey. Usually with little to say, Rainey repeated word-for-word everything that happened.

"Thanks for saying the beneficiary hadn't authorized the sale of the house. George is pregnant, too?"

"Yes. I told Rhonda—I mean Sandra—and she's sobbing."

"Undoubtedly, about her, not George's, pregnancy," Midge said before announcing, "Okay, tell everyone to come to the dead woman's room. We have things to discuss." Midge added, "Turn off the lights. In case the realtor or anyone else comes, we're not home."

With all assembled, Midge began, "Okay, accomplices."

"I don't like that title," protested Rainey.

"You filled the role very well tonight, Rainey. I'd say you're in on this."

"I'm not 'in'," pouted Andrea.

"That's okay, honey, you're too young anyway," Midge conceded.

Andrea changed her mind. "I'm not too young. I want to be an accomplice."

Everyone else sighed while Andrea rolled her eyes.

"Tomorrow I'd like Sandra to go to the bank and credit union to close out both accounts. There probably will be a waiting period before we can get the cash. I want all my CDs to be transferred to my Chicago bank. I will give you all the account numbers tomorrow, Sandra-my-Beneficiary."

"What? I thought we were going to the beach tomorrow," shouted Andrea.

She is as self-centered as any teen I knew in my practice, was what Midge thought while Sandra mused, *She's just like I was at that age.*

188

Midge looked hard at her niece. "Sweetie, you will go to the beach, but tomorrow we must get started on regaining my money."

"Why can't I take her to that beach over in Port Aransas after I go to the banks?" asked Sandra.

"Why not, indeed! The banking won't take long. You three can go to the beach while I find out why my place is for sale."

That met with agreement. The doorbell forestalled conversation for a while.

With no answer, Linda sighed and went back to her car. As Midge heard a car pull away, she exclaimed, "Now for the important business. What shall we re-name George?"

Chapter Eight

Tuesday Tidbits

On a break, Linda called a non-emergency number at SCCPD and asked for Maria. The clerk told her, "Detective Gonzalez is out on the island patrolling the Spring Breakers. She'll be hard to reach this week unless it's an emergency."

Linda thanked her and said her question didn't constitute an emergency. *Spring Break. We used to close the clinic during Spring Break. Rhonda and I had such fun going to Matzalan during one Spring Break.*

* * *

Desk Sergeant Angela pondered: *I know Dr. Hernandez was involved in the case of the Missing Doctor. Wonder if this has anything to do with that?* The case was on her mind because she had found a message on the tip line from the Wal-Mart clerk who insisted she had waited on the run-away doctor and who had found a bag with hair and a blouse. The woman, Marlys Something, said she had spotted the doctor at Blackbeard's when she and her church circle were having supper out last night. "Even if it is Spring Break," she'd added, "we're not letting those kids run us off." The clerk hadn't given the message to the detectives since they'd left before she'd reviewed the phone messages.

* * *

As promised, Linda called the attorney who handled Rhonda's will. His secretary said he had gone skiing in Colorado to escape Spring Break.

Call the courthouse next? That would be logical. I have to get back to Mr. Sylte as to how he should proceed.

A nurse notified Dr. Linda that she had a patient.

* * *

Rainey awakened before the others. She remembered seeing a Stripes convenience store not too far from the townhouse complex and walked there to buy rolls and juice for breakfast. *After we come home from the beach, we will have to do some serious grocery shopping.*

When she returned to the town home she felt as if she was the "Slightly Tardy Good Fairy" because Sandra and Andrea already were up scouring the empty cupboards and refrigerator and muttering. They were overjoyed to see her though Andrea asked why she hadn't gotten donuts instead of rolls. The Good Fairy counted to ten and then prayed her daughter would someday outgrow her current contrary stage.

Everyone had eaten and started to gather their beach necessities when Midge appeared. She handed Sandra directions to the credit union and bank and all the bank numbers she would need plus a map of the city and surrounding towns and copies of the death certificate. She paused as she looked at Sandra who looked a little peaked.

"Are you feeling okay?"

"Sure. I'm fine, just pregnant."

"That's good. I also wanted to tell you when you go to the parking ramp at the bank, look around to see if you see a black BMW with lots of notices tucked under the windshield wipers. *I threw away the keys but I have a spare set here some place.* No, forget that. No doubt it has been towed. *But maybe I can find out where.*

"Anything else?" Sandra asked, sounding perturbed as she put sunscreen, bikini, towel and other supplies into a beach bag.

"No, that's it, and I am incredibly grateful to you, Sis. It all will be worth it, you'll see."

Sandra did not look convinced and was much more interested in going to Port Aransas. She urged the other two to hurry to get the van packed with beach necessities.

They said good-bye to Dead Rhonda. "Make certain the cat doesn't get out," Rainey cautioned.

Andrea capitalized on that saying, "Dead Auntie, take good care of Georgy Girl."

They'd decided on the name, based on a song the sisters all remembered when they heard it on the van radio the day

191

before. Andrea had heard the announcer say on what she called the Prehistoric Station a group called the Seekers recorded it way back in 1966, in the Dark Ages. She was disgusted when her mom and aunties sang to it, and then did the same thing when they named the cat and now as they left for the van, they were doing it again.

How much can I stand? Andrea texted her best friend who answered: This sucks.

Before they left, Midge, trying not to be conspicuous, stuck a jug of vinegar out the door.

"What for?" asked Sandra

"Stingray encounters. And remember not to take your cell phones into the water!"

A neighbor biking by saw the woman with the vinegar and stopped. "Rhonda, you're back! Wonderful to see you and that you're okay. We've all been worried sick about you."

Sandra stepped up to the plate and introduced herself to the woman. "I'm Sandra, Rhonda's sister, and this is my sister Rainey and her daughter, Andrea. The woman you saw is another sister, Midge. We're all here for Spring Break and to settle Rhonda's affairs. Rhonda is . . ." Sandra's voice broke, "Rhonda died."

The neighbor looked horrified. "I'm devastated. She was a wonderful neighbor and everyone who went to her said she was a terrific doctor."

A looked passed between Rainey and Sandra. *Doctor?*

As the woman continued to express her condolences, Andrea did everything but stomp her feet in impatience. Once in the van, she texted: Finally on the way!!! She threw a fit when they stopped at the credit union, and her mother admonished her.

The sisters looked but saw no BMWs. Andrea and her mom stayed in the car and were amazed that Sandra emerged almost instantly.

"Sis won't be happy to hear this. The court has frozen all her accounts No sense in going to the bank. We're off to the beach!"

Chapter Nine

Day at the Beach

Andrea, with visions of cute boys surrounding her the moment she walked onto the sand in a new two-piece swimsuit, shouted, "Hurray!" *Of course, that won't really happen because Mom made me buy this one-piece little kid suit.*

The traffic thickened as they reached S.P.I.D., the main artery that connected Corpus Christi to the causeway and bridge. The route currently resembled a parking lot filled with boisterous Spring Breakers, yelling out their windows, sound systems blaring. Midge had suggested this route because otherwise they would wait all day to get on the ferry.

"How much worse could the ferry be?" asked Sandra as they approached a left turn, which took them seventeen miles on a two-lane road with bumper-to-bumper traffic to Port Aransas. The little town was alive with Spring Breakers going into liquor stores, bars, tattoo parlors, and restaurants. They saw an IGA and Rainey suggested they buy soda and food for a picnic lunch.

Andrea complained about another stupid delay, but Rainey ignored her. They stopped at IGA, the little grocery store that had everything a beach-going tourist could possibly need plus groceries. Rainey looked at the wide variety of wines, but assumed alcohol wasn't allowed on the beach; besides she made a practice of never drinking in front of her children. *Knowing how dull my sisters consider me, a bottle of Barefoot or Sea Glass would be a nice surprise for tonight, but Rhonda, I mean **Sandra**, shouldn't drink, and come to think of it, I've never seen the real Sandra drink alcohol.*

Rainey put the bottle of Barefoot she was holding back on the shelf and finished up the shopping. As a prolific reader whose only desire was to sit on the beach and read, Rainey noticed a rack of books by local authors. She loved to know more about the history of towns and found one by Guthrie Ford about Port Aransas's first family called The

<u>Mercer Diaries</u>. She put that in the cart. Meanwhile Sandra and Andrea selected food for all of them.

Adequately supplied for the day the three decided they'd have the beach to themselves with all the people they saw in the store and in general downtown. Following slow-moving beach buggies and golf carts to the beach, they found more cars and people than imaginable. They had no way of knowing that without the Breakers, Port A would be a ghost town today because all the locals had left town or were hunkered down in their homes with two weeks' worth of groceries, waiting for the Breakers to go home. These heavily taxed homeowners hoped their places wouldn't catch on fire because the fire fighters were directing ferry traffic. They prayed no one had a heart attack because how would the over-extended EMTs –be able to treat them or get through the traffic in time to take them to a Corpus hospital? Fortunately, tourists were spared such dour information as they came to have fun at the coast while contributing heavily to the community's economy.

Sandra and Andrea went right into the water while Rainey, who had never learned to swim, settled under a rented umbrella to read. The other two soon grew bored and decided to go shopping.

They returned hours later. "I got hungry—already started the picnic," Rainey said with a smile.

Her smile faded as Andrea, oblivious to the food she personally had selected for lunch, began, "That's okay. We stopped for Snow Cones and burgers at Pelican Pete's." Rainey smiled again as she daughter continued in a positive vein. "The owner, Richard, is a funny guy, but he and his wife are ready to move on. Wouldn't it be great if we could buy it and live on this island forever?"

"I'm sure your father might have something to say about that…" Before she could finish, Andrea added, "Look what my favorite Aunt Rhonda--I mean Sandra bought me." She pointed to the tattoo of a fleur de lis on one thigh.

"Rhonda—uh, Sandra, what were you thinking? She's only twelve!" *Her father will have seven fits.*

"Don't freak. It's just Henna."

"But it lasts, Mom. And look, what else-—a toe ring!"

"And?" prompted Sandra.

Aunt and niece put their feet side-by-side and chorused, "Yellow Box flip flops."

"$75 but 30% off," bragged Andrea, as if she had paid for them.

"The jewels have to be real," kidded Sandra.

"Your aunt certainly has spoiled you, Andrea. I hope you have thanked her."

"Of course, she has. Honey, show your mom what else."

Andrea pulled up the big t-shirt she wore over her swimsuit. Rainey looked as if she could have killed her sister when she saw her little girl wore a teeny-weeny bikini. As she pulled the shirt off, numerous strings of gold, green and purple Mardi Gras beads appeared

Rainey noticed her sister wore them, too. "You're not going to tell me you got them…."

Andrea and Sandra laughed and laughed at the look on Rainey's face.

"Gotcha, Mom! We bought them!"

Chapter Ten

Being Dead is Boring

Rhonda was ravenous and grateful to find a caramel roll and juice in the kitchen. Sandra handled the neighbor extremely well. *While they are gone I plan to spend my time on the computer and see if I can find anything about why my house was put up for sale, Maybe in public court notices. I also want to make another thorough search to see if I can find Midge with the info I received from the Harmon reporter. Actually, I need to prove that woman from the RV Park wasn't our baby sister.*

It didn't take long to realize her desktop computer had vanished, just as she had. *Did the police confiscate it?*

What was she supposed to do until the other three returned? For a while she'd reveled in the peace and quiet and finished <u>Detour,</u> a book by her favorite author Devorah Fox. She loved the main character, Archie, a big rig driver. Such a nice man who reminded her of Wayne. *He never can never find out what I'm doing to obtain the money to invest in his project. I know a good relationship shouldn't have secrets, but there are things he can't know or he never will accept me I've been unable to keep my pledge of honesty.*

She picked up her cell and called Sandra, Rainey, and even the Queen of Texting, but no one picked up. She hoped they were having fun. She wished they had called after they picked up the money. She picked up Georgy Girl and imagined she was her little dog, Poppy, which led to more magical thinking.

If I can find the BMW, Rainey can cancel the plane reservations and she and Andrea can drive the Mother Ship back to Arkansas. I can call the realtor—Rainey put his card on the kitchen counter—and he can resume selling my house. I think I'll put the art and furnishings I want into storage until I settle for good and then have them shipped to me. We all should be able to leave in a couple days if everything goes smoothly. She sighed and remarked to Georgy Girl, "As if anything has gone remotely well since I first tried to leave Texas."

She spied the ginger jar on the counter and filled it with a cup of ashes from the barbeque pit on the patio. Officially, Dr. Rhonda Collins was dead.

By afternoon, close to climbing the walls, Midge turned on the television and heard an inaccurate, unofficial, and sensationalized "Breaking News" segment. One of Rhonda's favorite anchors, thrilled her channel was the first to report this news, chirped, "The Missing Doctor case may be reopened. The public is putting pressure on the SCCPD to do more with the Dr. Rhonda Collin's case. The belief of many is the South Corpus Christi Police Department didn't try hard enough to find out what happened to the 'Missing Doctor". Now new evidence has surfaced. Listen at 6:00 when we hope to have received some response to our calls to Chief Ortiz. For now, a viewer sent us an i-Phone photo of Dr. Collins and three other women eating at the Blackbeard's on North Beach".

"What on earth?" asked Midge, her voice panicky, "Did that woman I overheard at the restaurant report seeing me? Will the police be here any moment to arrest me?"

The cat listened to her rant on until she got bored and went to the kitchen to find her food dish.

Midge decided not to share this with the others but intended to watch the 6:00 news.

* * *

Andrea yearned to stay until it was dark enough to have a beach fire but her "jailers" as she referred to her mom and aunt in a text had enough sun and wanted to go home.

They drove south on The Island Road/Highway 361, lined with Beer and Bail Bond billboards. The adults commented on the trouble teenagers could get into during Spring Break, never dreaming they would find out about that first-hand.

Belkin halted the stream of cars led by a decorated white van going south. He needed to let cars turn left on the road

197

from the beach access on the Corpus Christi portion of Mustang Island. He did a double take when he saw the van driver and called to Maria, who stared at the driver and said, "I know what you're thinking! Ask her."

Friendly-like, Belkin asked Sandra, "Don't I know you?"

"No. Maybe you're thinking of my sister, Rhonda Collins."

"Right! That's just who I thought you were. May I see your license?

Sandra fumbled in her bag and came up with her sister Sandra's license.

Andrea piped up from the back, "We're here for Spring Break from Arkansas."

"I see that!" commented Belkin who added, jokingly, "Where did you get those beads, young lady?"

Andrea blushed and not waiting for an answer, Belkin boldly asked, "Where's Rhonda?"

A car rear-ending another stole his attention, but he thought he heard someone say, "She passed, officer." Or did they ask, "Can we pass, officer?"

By the time he had finished with the accident, a Corpus Christi Officer had allowed the right lane to proceed.

Belkin swore. He had been unbelievably close.

On the way to the townhouse, while Andrea, per usual, listened to her tunes and texted her friends, Rainey asked Sandra, "Did you hear Midge's neighbor call her 'Doctor'?"

"Yes, I've been thinking about it a lot today. I bet some patient wanted to sue her for something, but it wasn't her fault. That's why she made out the will the way she did."

"Did you know she's a doctor?"

"No, she owned a hair salon in Tulsa when we reunited, but I know she went to college because she used to be a teacher. I don't know why she changed her name to mine, except really it was her name. I changed mine to honor her, but now I wonder if she took my name to guarantee I'd be the one who would get in trouble."

"Oh, Sis, she'd never do that to you."

198

"But since I found her again, I've gotten the idea she doesn't like me very much."

"That's untrue. She wants to take care of you and the baby."

That's what she says, but I wonder if that's because she feels guilty about making me do the dirty work."

"I don't think that's true. I don't know what happened to her after she ran away, but I've never seen anyone as desperate to have family around her."

The conversation ended. Passing a Mexican restaurant with a drive-through, they stopped for carry out.

* * *

Panicked after hearing the news bulletin, Midge decided to call towing companies to see if any remembered towing a black BMW from the Vega Building parking ramp in late September. If she could locate her car, she could leave the van with Sandra and get out of town until things cooled down.

"Hello, I'm Midge Collins and I'm trying to find out what happened to the car of my deceased sister." She described the car and where it had been parked.

Midge received the same negative answer until she reached the last towing company listed in the phone directory. The driver of the tow truck answered the phone. He definitely remembered towing such a car in September because "That lot has got to be the trickiest place in South Texas for towing a car."

"Do you remember where you towed it?"

"Sure do. SCCPD."

"What do you think they did with it?"

"Ma'am, I don't have the foggiest idea except they wouldn't have it towed there if there wasn't some crime connected to it."

"Thank you." Midge's voice revealed the hopelessness she felt.

"Wait, Ma'am, I know sometimes they have police auctions. Maybe they sold it."

That didn't help. Maybe she would have to rent a car, after borrowing Rainey's license, as she wanted to go a couple places before she left town.

She next called Mr. Sylte. "This is one of the sisters of the deceased owner of the townhouse. Do the people still want it?"

The realtor didn't sound happy. The executor hadn't called but he had heard from the prospective buyers. "No thanks to all of you. They thought I was jerking them around and backed out of the deal."

Having a sudden inspiration Midge questioned, "Mr. Sylte, you know the townhouse well and I wonder if you would like to buy it?"

"I certainly do but it's a little too cashy for my boyfriend and me."

"If we lowered the price considerably, would you buy it directly from me as the current owner?"

"If we could agree on a great price, I'm all for it but I definitely don't want the artwork. They're nice pieces, but I'm an artist myself and want to display my own paintings."

"Not just a realtor but an artist, too. I can understand why you'd want your own creations. What price are you thinking?" After Sylte suggested a reasonable figure, Midge hesitated, "Let me talk to my sisters and decide on a price we'd consider, and I'll make certain someone else takes the artwork."

Midge's next call was to a storage rental. Climate controlled, it was worth the price. She had a hundred thousand invested in the collection. She heard the van and forgot about the 6:00 PM news.

The beach-goers arrived with cartons suffusing the air with tantalizing scents of Mexican food. Midge babbled, "Oh, terrific, I haven't eaten since the breakfast you left. I'm starving. I don't know why I didn't walk to Stripes for lunch. They have the most delicious burritos, but good thing I resisted or I would be too full for this wonderful feast."

"Enough chatter! Let's eat," came from Andrea, whom Midge noted was wearing Yellow Box jeweled flip-flops. *Adorable but pricey.*

"Look, Auntie Sandra bought us twin shoes!"

Rainey had set the table and opened up the cartons of a wide variety of Mexican specialties, even some that suited Andrea, now a vegetarian but definitely not a vegan after she learned vegans don't eat dairy products, including ice cream, which she had learned from the owner of Pelican Pete's. All feasted while they told Midge about their fun day.

After they'd eaten and Andrea had left to watch television, Sandra sighed. "We have some bad news."

"What could it be?" Midge, in a good mood because of the house and art coup, asked with a laugh. "You withdrew my money and spent it all in Port A? I know how they raise prices every place for the Spring Breakers on gas, food, everything."

"Not quite, but when we went to the Credit Union, they said your account has been frozen. I showed them the death certificate, but they said they couldn't do anything without a court order."

Midge looked thunderstruck. *What happened? Wouldn't they keep the account open until there's a death certificate or was it frozen because they found out what I did?* All she said to the others was, "I'm not certain what to do."

Sandra shrugged. "I'll go to the courthouse tomorrow." Midge patted her shoulder. "It'll work out."

Andrea wandered out of the living room and expressed her opinion that they should return to the beach the next day. "I want to go to that one where all the cars were coming from yesterday when we had to stop. It's closer."

"Oh, honey," Midge said, "I don't think it will work tomorrow. I need the Mother Ship most of the day, and your mama wants to get groceries."

"Okay, Aunt Midge. We can go to the beach another day. There's still time. What you have to do is way more important." Andrea's tone dripped with honey.

"Andrea, that sounds very mature," praised her mom.

"We'll make certain there's time for another beach day before you leave," Midge promised.

Andrea shrugged and walked away, plotting. Holly had given her a great idea.

The three sisters continued to talk. "Do you think Georgy-Girl is fatter?" asked Rainey.

"When I was holding her today, I noticed her nipples seem swollen. We need to take her to the vet to get a due date," offered Midge, "and you, my dear sister, need to see an OB as soon as we go home."

Sandra sighed. She didn't believe in ending the life of unborn babies, but if only she could just turn back the clock to prevent conception, whenever that was. She looked into a mirror to see if she was fatter.

"By the way." Midge commented, "I could use some help wrapping up the paintings, pottery and statues. Then I think with the back seat down we can transport them to the storage unit I rented. Either tomorrow or Thursday."

"But I thought," said Rainey, conscience of the group, "they go with the house."

"No! I sold it today and the guy didn't want them."

The sisters applauded.

Later Midge called Sylte to tell him he had a deal.

The sisters already were wrapping the paintings and pottery and within a couple hours they moved the sizeable collection to a large storage unit.

Chapter Eleven
Fun and Fear

The next morning Andrea slipped away right after Sandra left for the courthouse. She wanted her mother and other aunt to believe she had gone with her now favorite Aunt Sandra.

The twelve-year-old had paid more attention than her mother and aunts realized when she rode in the Mother Ship. She knew exactly how to find S.P.I. D. and walked to it and then walked forever until she could see the big mall she remembered passing. She imagined kids would be there and she could hitch a ride to a beach with some girls. Instead a carload of boys saw her waiting to cross at the lights and asked if she wanted a ride.

She smiled and got in the back, which was crowded with three hunky guys. She sat on the lap of one, and the driver told her to duck if they saw a cop since she wasn't wearing a seatbelt. The guys asked her lots of questions about where she was from, why she was alone and how did she get that cute! Andrea made the guys laugh with her story of coming to CC in a clunky old van with one aunt who kept barfing and one who thought she was dead but kept driving. They roared when she told them that they believed the cat was a boy, but it turned into a pregnant girl cat.

It never occurred to Andrea that anything bad could happen to her with these cute guys, who seemed really nice. Nice or not, the guys weren't dumb. Only one wasn't of age, but all planned to do some serious beer bong drinking on the beach. They figured out the girl, who gave her name as Tiffany from Oklahoma, was younger then the age they gave them, fifteen. They thought having her hang out with them might attract attention from the CC cops who patrolled the beach, and they didn't want that.

They stopped the car after driving on the beach and said Tiffany would have to get out because they had to meet some other people. "Have a great day, Tiffany," they all yelled. The one whose lap she sat on handed her some more beads as she exited the car.

Perplexed, the young girl stood by a bollard for a while watching groups of kids on the beach. She finally approached a mixed group of teens and worked up some tears. One empathetic girl noticed her immediately and came up to her, "What's wrong, sweetie?"

"My boyfriend and I had a fight and he dumped me. I want to stay on the beach for a while until I call someone to pick me up, but I'd feel better if I could be with other people."

"No problem. What's your name?"

"Tiffany."

"Hey, everyone, this is Tiffany. She's hanging with us.

"One girl trilled, "Are those Yellow Box?"

Tiffany looked at her flip-flops and answered nonchalantly, "Yes, they're my favorites. I have two other pairs at home."

Impressed, the girl said, "We're glad you're with us."

Andrea smiled broadly. *I'm in.*

* * *

"Have you seen Andrea?" Rainey, returning from the walk to Stripes, asked Midge.

"I assumed she went to the courthouse with Sandra," answered her sister.

"That makes sense. They sure had fun together yesterday."

Sandra, after being gone most of the morning, came up the walk alone. She looked at Midge with a hopeless look, "I'm afraid that I'm not being very successful at being you. The clerk told me they couldn't say anything about a specific case but there are two main reasons why an estate is unavailable to beneficiaries: no proof of death or an invalid will. Another reason for the will being declared invalid is that the one who wrote it is wanted as a felon. She suggested we go to the police station and ask to talk to the detectives on the case."

204

"Then that's what you'll have to do, but first, where's Andrea?"

"I have no idea."

"She wasn't with you?'

"No, I thought she was still asleep when I left. Maybe she went to Stripes for ice cream or something."

* * *

The group of kids shared their food and sodas with Andrea, and she had a ball. They also shared their smokes, both e-cigs and old-fashioned, and she had her first beer in a red paper cup. She didn't like the taste of the beer and was thinking of calling her mom when a really dreamy guy, maybe the oldest in the group, sat next to her and asked if she wanted to swim. They went into the water together. As a rogue wave knocked her down, Andrea realized she had forgotten to remove her cell phone, suspended from a chain around her neck.

* * *

Rainey checked out the room she shared with her daughter. Right away she noticed her daughter's brightly colored beach bag did not hang on a hook as it had the night before. There was no sign of her swimsuit, baggy t-shirt, flip-flops or beach towel. She tried to call her wayward daughter, but by then Andrea's phone wasn't in service.

* * *

Andrea's "hero", named Luis, rescued her from being knocked down into the water and gave her another beer to "revive" her. This one tasted way better. He also shared a joint with her; like all beginners, she choked on the burning garbage-smelling weed. He helped her to do it the right way. She achieved a lighter-than-air feeling before she thought she was going to be sick. Tiffany said she'd be right back and headed toward the bank of mobile toilets. She entered one that was beyond gross and smelled worse than anything her delicate nose had encountered. She couldn't bend over the opening. Backing out and breathing sea air, she no longer felt sick.

Seeing her return, Luis asked what took her such a long time. She smiled. Taking her hand, he led her into one of the tents the group had set up; no one seemed to notice. Luis told her she was a hottie. He gave the Arkansas girl her first kiss, followed by many more. They found themselves together on a camp cot.

* * *

Rainey returned to her sisters and expressed her suspicion that Andrea had headed to a beach on her own. Rainey wanted to call her husband Dan but decided not to alarm him for now.

The sisters jumped into the van to look for the girl. It took them two hours to reach the Mustang Island beach because of the traffic. Sandra's phone rang and they all jumped. Only a robo-call about a credit card with less interest.

They turned onto the beach off Island Road, the beach Andrea had mentioned. They walked from one group of kids after another to ask if they had seen a girl fitting Andrea's description. A group of five college men, too wasted to be credible, said they had given a little kid a ride from SPID but hadn't seen her since they arrived.

All the things that could have happened to Andrea tortured mother and aunts. "Sex, Drugs and Rock-n-Roll," muttered Sandra under her breath. The thought of her hitchhiking brought back terrible memories to Midge of her experience when the run-away accepted a ride with a truck driver. Rainey prayed to find her daughter unharmed.

* * *

Luis ran his hands over the young girl's face, neck, tummy, legs, anything not covered by her bikini. He put one of her hands on the front of his trunks, and with alarm she felt something harder than anything anticipated when whispered about at school with other sixth grade girls. When he clumsily attempted to remove her bikini, she panicked and kicked and flailed her arms. *Oh, no. It's going to hurt me!*

If the truth were known, the fifteen-year old boy had no more experience than the girl. With relief he sighed, "It's okay, little gal. I'm afraid I went too fast. Let's go out in the water to cool off a bit."

They left the tent and a few of the kids stared at them though most were too under the influence of the pot and beer to notice or care. "Jelly because you weren't the ones kissing in the tent?" Luis boasted as they ran past to the gulf, which wasn't all that warm in March.

After they left the water, Luis wandered off. Andrea danced with some other girls to the music blasting from one of the big trucks parked near them. One girl asked Andrea if she and Luis had "done the big one". Andrea gave her a secretive smile; then thinking they might reject her, confessed that all they did was kiss.

The afternoon blurred as Bud and Mary Jane exerted their presence. At some point a girl who had arrived a short time earlier came up to Andrea and smacked her across the face, "I hear you have been flirting with my boyfriend all day."

Stunned both by the slap and by the fact Luis already had a girlfriend, Andrea hit the girl back. Pretty soon they rolled around on the sand pulling hair and scratching each other. The angry girlfriend ripped the front of Andrea's t-shirt. A gathering crowd circled and chanted, "Chick fight, chick fight!"

"Go chicky, chicky!" they shouted until someone spotted a patrol car and shouted, "Cops!"

They dispersed and one of Andrea's new friends started a bonfire. The group gathered around it. They discussed what they saw in the colors of the flames: dragons, ballerinas, sunsets, poinsettias. Andrea felt absolutely blissful. This was much better than being stuck with the aunts and her mom. *Except for that mean girl, I'm with really cool kids from Corpus Christi.* Another thought floated past Andrea: *phone home*. Andrea quickly discovered her phone hadn't survived its dunk in the Gulf.

* * *

The three sisters continued to look and were sure they spotted the missing Andrea numerous times. They talked to a police officer, who promised to alert officers on other beaches in Padre as well as North Beach and the Port Aransas beach. "Otherwise, you ladies would have to search for a needle in several haystacks."

Sandra shared her thoughts. "Maybe she'll be home because she didn't come to the beach after all. She just went for a walk and got lost and her phone wouldn't work because the battery was low, but by now she found her way home and wonders where we are."

The last thing Midge wanted was being involved with the police, but there was no question that she would blow her cover to find her niece. "We'll call the police department if she isn't home and have them issue an Amber Alert."

Rainey sobbed in the backseat as they headed to the townhouse. No Andrea awaited them. Midge placed a call to SCCPD to report a missing child.

* * *

It didn't occur to Andrea to borrow a phone. Besides she didn't want to go home. Even a fight hadn't ruined the best day of her life. Besides, someone had told her that later there would be birthday cake for one of the kids. She couldn't wait to text Holly about this spectacular day but, *Oops, my phone is ruined*. That made her laugh. After another hit on a marijuana pipe, she laughed hysterically. Everything was fabulously funny.

Was it her crazy laughter that drew the attention of two cops patrolling the beach? They smelled the pot, saw paraphernalia and beer cans and calculated that no one in the group was of age. Over youthful opposition that not one of them had smoked pot or drunk beer, the officers loaded all ten of them into a "paddy wagon" and transported them to the SCCPD.

The officers knew that a huge percentage of American teens and kids even younger already drank and smoked dope. They just weren't as sly as older kids about hiding evidence. *These kids are damaging their undeveloped brains and need this lesson*, thought one of the officers as he placed all ten in a holding cell. Most, boys and girls, blubbered and expressed the fear: "My parents will kill me."

An officer interviewed each one at a time. Several named the person who had purchased beer and pot for them. A clerk called each parent.

When Andrea's turn came, she was mortified because she didn't know the address of the townhouse where she, her mother, and aunts were staying, and she never memorized any of their phone numbers, among all the lost data kept on her phone. She, knowing better than to lie to cops, told them her real name, age, and Arkansas address. She confessed she had run away and hitchhiked to the beach.

Unaware that Stan and Maria already were looking for the child, one officer said to the clerk, "Better check to see if there is a report of a missing child. I have a feeling someone will come looking for her. She's the youngest one in this round-up."

They put her back in holding where she sat, alone, as the last of the unhappy parents had come to retrieve their kids and pay fines for their misdeeds. Some kids hugged friends as they left holding, but no one, not even Luis, said good-bye to Andrea—the ultimate humiliation.

Chapter Twelve
Amber Alert

Stopping back at headquarters after a long day on the beach, Maria and Stan found the Chief waiting for them. He waved a newspaper in front of them. It held the same information that Midge had heard on television the day before with the headline, MISSING DOCTOR SEEN AT BLACKBEARDS.

The chief, employing a barrage of colorful expletives, wanted to know what "new evidence" the detectives had. He said he had checked the nuisance line, as he called the tip-line, with the message from the broad who found the hair and said she saw the missing doc the night before at the North Beach restaurant.

"New evidence? We don't have any new evidence. The tipster probably went to the media with her news because we sure don't have any," protested Stan.

Not wanting to reveal her trip to Chicago and the further info she'd found about Brian, Maria retorted with false bravado "If we had uncovered more, we most certainly would have told you, not the media, and asked you to re-open the case."

"Why do I doubt that with you two?" stormed the Chief. Peppered with more profanity, his response included the accusation that detectives had been digging around a closed case. Finding more evidence, he'd projected, the detectives had gone to the media in hopes the public viewpoint that the police hadn't done enough would convince him to open the case.

Both continued to deny the accusations as the dispatcher broadcast over the PA: "Possible Amber Alert. Twelve-year old girl is missing."

Maria and Stan wanted to go their respective homes, shower off the sand stuck to their bodies with sweat, eat supper, drink a longneck and go to bed. But neither turned down the order of the Chief that both go find the kid. The dispatcher gave them the phone number and address of the distraught mother.

A horde of reporters made it almost impossible to leave. "Hey, smart detectives, what are you doing about the new evidence in the Missing Doctor case?" "Where have you been hiding her?" "Why didn't you tell us she's been found?" What about the lost kid?"

Belkin grabbed a mic. "We have spent the day on the beach keeping your kids and kids from all over Texas and the nation safe. Now one's missing and we don't have time to talk to you jackals."

The "jackals" parted to let them through. Studying the address as they drove there, Maria erupted, "Stan, this is the address of the Missing Doctor's townhouse."

Almost too beat to be sarcastic, Stan responded, "What? Maybe she's returned, and we can bust her and then go find the kid staying with her."

As they pulled up to the townhouse, once the object of their search in the Missing Doctor case, both recognized the van from Arkansas.

"Dr. R's relatives," realized Maria, "are staying here."

"The missing kid must be the one I talked to in the back seat," added Stan, fear knotting his stomach as the missing child became all too real.

Three distraught women, in mid-to-late thirties who looked remarkably like each other, burst out the front door.

"I'm the mother, and we haven't seen my daughter since early this morning. We've called her phone repeatedly, but she hasn't answered."

"Aren't you the people we saw yesterday in the fancy van on the Island Road?"

Sandra nodded. "We're Rhonda Collins' sisters. "I'm Sandra" and pointing, "She's Rainey and she's Midge. You met all of us, but Midge and you met Andrea who's missing."

"We have a good idea what she looks like, but we need to ask you endless questions to help us locate her."

The questioning barely had begun when Belkin received a call from the jail warden. "I have a twelve-year-old in

211

holding. Picked up on Mustang Beach for underage drinking and using illegal drugs. I believe she is the missing child." The warden gave other details of what they were calling the "Middle School Spring Break Bust".

"I think we've already found her. She's at the police station."

Tears of joy came to Rainey's eyes. "Praise God."

"I must advise you that she was found on the beach with nine other kids drinking beer and using pot."

"But Andrea wasn't, just the other kids, right?"

"No, your daughter was high when we picked her up. There will be a fine that you must pay before law enforcement releases her. Because of her age and no other recorded first-time offenses, she will be given educational materials and not allowed on city beaches for the length of Spring Break. Further discipline is left to the parents. A second offense will not be treated as lightly, regardless of age."

Rainey fought back tears. All that mattered was that Andrea had been found, but her embarrassment and the feeling of being a parental failure were in conflict with her joy

The van followed the patrol car to the police headquarters. Both detectives were thrilled that this case had ended quickly and well. They checked in and left work for the day while the sisters went to the wing which housed the jail.

There they found a sobbing, remorseful Andrea. The women gasped at scratches on her cheeks and one shoulder, exposed by a torn T-shirt. Andrea wailed, "I didn't know the address of the townhouse and everyone else got picked up to go home; and my phone got ruined."

With pursed lips, Rainey paid the fine, and a guard released Andrea. Seeing the scratches didn't look serious, mother held daughter and said, "No matter what you have done, I love you. But there will be consequences for your behavior."

Both aunts embraced their niece. "We've all been worried to death, and this was terribly hard on your mom," lectured Midge while Sandra reassured her niece that what she'd done wasn't that terrible and would turn out fine.

Rainey wanted the help of her husband to decide how they would discipline their young daughter with the big ideas. She called him and changed the plane tickets purchased for Saturday to the earliest possible flight. Late that Wednesday night she and Andrea left Corpus Christi.

Chapter Thirteen

Sleepless in Corpus Christi

Though exhausted by another grueling day in the sun, Maria couldn't sleep. She wished Sydney hadn't left for San Antonio; she needed to talk. Working the beaches had prevented Maria from thinking about Xavier, but the Chief's suspicions had made her remember the trip to Chicago she and Xavier had taken. It had been a wonderful weekend, but life with Xav wouldn't be like that. If they were married and she told him about a day of unusual heat for March, of arrests for drug use, under-age drinking, driving violations, weapon possession and the Amber Alert, he would have shrugged it off and told her it was no work for a woman and that she was lucky none of those kids high on dope had stabbed her. He would have reminded her that he never wanted her to be in law enforcement. The point was they never would marry because he demanded she give up her job, and she refused. Even though the week had been difficult the number of problems was nothing compared to crowds of good kids they saw having a wonderful time.

She heard Big Boy, who had been having a nap on the couch, hit the floor in the living room and knew he'd soon join her. He didn't care what career she'd chosen, and now she wouldn't have to worry about finding a home for him for the sake of Xav's controlling mother. *I've done the right thing, but why, why is it almost unbearably painful?*

After marching on her chest for a while, the cat with the locomotive purr settled in bed in the crook of her arm, and Maria's thoughts turned to another worry. Something didn't seem right at the townhouse. The story the women had given was that they were staying in their deceased sister's townhouse, which one had inherited.

One had said she was Sandra, the sister named in the will, but all the doctor's assets were frozen. *We know Sandra and Rhonda are the same person. We proved that, didn't we? DNA doesn't lie— but lab techs make mistakes. Rhonda was*

214

one of those women in the townhouse. I just know it. This case is far from over.

Her last thought as she drifted off to sleep after midnight was one of gratitude: *At least they found their child.*

* * *

Linda Hernandez was among the sleepless. She had left a message for the realtor to call and was surprised she hadn't heard from him, but without being able to talk with either of the attorneys or Maria, what could she tell him? She had no way of knowing that Mr. Sylte avoided her because he didn't want her to know that he had gone ahead and with an attorney, who hadn't left town during Spring Break, drew up documents to enable him to purchase the townhouse directly from the deceased owner's beneficiary. He had moved to Corpus in late November and knew nothing about the "Missing Doctor".

* * *

Before she and her disgraced child left, efficient Rainey had changed the linens in the guest room to convert it to Sandra's room. Shortly after 3:00AM the next morning Midge, troubled about the looks the female detective had given the sisters, had finally fallen asleep. A loud scream erupted from the guest room.

The possibility that someone had broken into the townhouse and caused the scream didn't occur to Midge. Her doctor instincts had kicked in. *Oh, no, something has happened to Rhonda's baby!*

Midge rushed across the townhouse, flinging open the guest room door. Georgy-Girl had just given birth on the bed.

Once Sandra had gotten over the shock, she and her sister watched the miracle of birth, as the cat delivered four more tiny grey and white kittens. She purred proudly as she washed each baby and let it nurse.

"She knows just what to do," Rhonda said in awe.

"And, you will, too, Sis."

Sandra spoke softly and slowly, "I'm not sure. When I lost my first baby, I was sad for a long time. Then I decided it

215

meant I wasn't supposed to have children, and I developed no interest in babies." Her voice became shrill as she lay her head in her hands, "I am scared to death."

Holding her sister, Sandra soothed her by whispering, "You're bound to find out sometime. I was a doctor for eight years. I will help you to have a fine healthy baby."

Chapter Fourteen

Reckless Endeavors

Sandra couldn't bear to leave the little family, which gave Midge the opportunity to go to the SCCPD herself early Thursday morning. When she told the clerk she wished to talk to the detectives, who had worked on her deceased sister's case, she heard the same thing the clerk had told Linda: Detectives Belkin and Gonzalez would not be in the office this week because they were part of Spring Break Law Enforcement.

"May I leave something for them?" Midge asked, handing Angela an envelope with a death certificate inside.

As she left, Midge had another idea. *Linda is the executor. I, as Midge, am going to ask her*. She started to call the clinic. *No! I'm going there in person!*

A voice in her head warned, Sandra Lewis, you know that is an insane idea.

Soon after, she walked into the clinic. Low murmurs among adults and a shout from a child filled the waiting room:

"Dr. Rhonda."

"It's Dr. Rhonda."

"She's back."

"My Docker Wanda!"

Two receptionists, overcome by emotion, had tears in their eyes as the woman whom they knew as Dr. Rhonda approached the counter.

With a knot in her stomach and a great feeling of loss, the former doctor kept her back to patients she had treated. The person causing all the commotion smiled and spoke for the benefit of all in the room, "Actually, I'm her sister. Is it possible to see Dr. Hernandez?"

Sounds of disappointment pervaded the waiting room, as one of the women at the desk answered, "She is with a patient but you may wait in her office. I will show you."

Midge walked down the halls, dearly familiar to her as Dr. Rhonda Collins. She peeked into the office that had been her own. Three doors down she thanked the receptionist and sat down on the seat where she had sat countless times before, chatting with Linda before the workday began.

How I loved working here, being a doctor, making sick people well.

Dr. Linda Hernandez walked into her office and froze. *Rhonda.*

Midge spoke first, lowering Rhonda's real voice, "Dr. Hernandez, I am one of Rhonda Collins' sisters, and I have a couple questions I hope you can answer."

Dr. Linda waited. *She looks just like Rhonda; she sounds a little different. Her hair is blonde, a little shorter than it was but not the brown she was said to have dyed it.*

Midge went on, "Another sister and I came to Corpus Christi to settle Rhonda's affairs, but we have run into some irregularities."

"Such as?"

"We are staying at Rhonda's home, which we learned is for sale but actually now it isn't because our sister, Sandra, who is the beneficiary, sold it."

"But she can't do that!"

"Why?"

"The court froze all of Rhonda's assets. She had named me executor and I'm fulfilling my job of selling the house and adding the proceeds to her frozen accounts."

"That's not right. My sister Sandra is beneficiary but gets nothing? Why?"

"It's complicated."

Midge swallowed. "Tell me why the estate is frozen."

"Because ——I don't want to be the one to tell you this. Your sister is a felon. All charges were dropped but her assets eventually will go to the state."

"But she's dead. I have her death certificate." Midge withdrew it from her purse and presented it.

"This says she died in Arkansas, a few weeks ago. Of a heart attack." *Rhonda never had heart problems.*

"That's right. After she left Texas, she went to see friends in Chicago and then she came home to Arkansas." Her eyes filled, "Finally we were together, and then she died."

"I'm sorry for your loss. She used to be my . . . my best friend." *Why am I having trouble believing her?*

Midge thanked her for her time and left the office just as Dr. Ron walked by.

"How dare you show your face here."

In spite of her doubts, Linda interrupted, "This is Rhonda's sister. Rhonda passed away."

Dr. Ron, with a look of disbelief, slammed the door to his office.

Holding her breath, Midge left by a side door and took a deep breath. She'd pulled it off though nothing she learned, even the news of having charges dropped, helped her need for money.

The distant siren of a police car caused her to panic. *Did Ron call the police?*

She wished she wasn't driving something as conspicuous but left the lot and turned down an alley. She sat until the police car went past the clinic. She started the van. There was one more place she wanted to go. She felt emboldened by the other two stops.

She wanted to see her little dog again. She didn't know how she was going to manage this, but she was determined to go to the Hernandez' home. It's *Thursday. That's when their housekeeper comes.*

Midge rang the bell. The housekeeper answered. Her eyes grew huge and fear showed in her voice, "I know who you are. You're the Missing Doctor."

"No, I'm the sister of Dr. Collins, but don't be embarrassed, everyone makes that mistake because we look enough alike to be twins. Is Mrs. Hernandez home?"

"No, she's at work." *Hmm, Dr. Collins would know that but I'm still suspicious.*

Midge had stopped at a florist and gave the housekeeper, Betty Chen, a large spring bouquet, with a card saying, "I'm

219

sorry, Rhonda". Please give this to Dr. Hernandez. My sister wanted me to drop it off."

The fake sister spotted Poppy and caroled, "Oh, what a cute dog. I love animals."

Betty knew Poppy had been the Missing Doctor's dog. She knew a lot more than most people about the case because of her association with the Hernandez family. She knew Dr. Collins was not to be trusted, and she was certain this woman was Dr. Collins, when the little Chihuahua, afraid of strangers, ran up to her. His tail wagged with such vigor that his whole body vibrated.

It didn't occur to Betty that the woman might steal the dog as she ran into the kitchen to call the police. They put her on hold on the non-emergency line. She waited a while but had to give up because she had housework to finish.

As soon as she held the little dog again, Midge knew she could never part with him. She took advantage of Betty's absence. As Midge turned to leave with the dog held tight in her arms, the youngest Hernandez burst through the door with all the energy of a four-year-old. "Auntie Rhonda, Auntie Rhonda you came back!" Teddy hugged her around her legs.

Midge was overcome. She loved that little boy and though she lied easily and smoothly, she couldn't lie to him about who she was.

"You can't take Poppy back," declared the boy. "He's mine now."

I can't take his dog either. "I won't take him, sweetheart; I just came to say 'hi'." She put Poppy on the floor as Teddy jabbered on. He had beaten his dad to the door and wondered why he was a slowpoke. He couldn't wait to tell him his "auntie" was back.

Dave Hernandez had picked up his youngest son from pre-kindergarten. While his son ran to the house, Dave stopped to check the mailbox on the street. He contemplated calling the police to tow that ridiculous van he assumed had broken down and was abandoned by Spring Breakers in front of his house. He picked up a basketball belonging to one of his sons and tossed it into a bin in the garage. He opened the door to his home and saw the last person on earth he ever expected to see.

"Rhonda. What a surprise!" he said as evenly as possible not wanting to make a scene in front of his child. The woman looked at her former lover with a mixture of shame and passion.

Teddy darted away. Dave roughly grabbed the woman he had loved by both shoulders and said in a stern but quiet voice, "Part of me wants to strangle you for what you did." Then loosening his grip, he resumed, "And part of me …"

"Wants to take me to bed?"

Dave couldn't respond as Teddy came back with cookies Betty had given him, "Want a cookie, Auntie Rhonda?"

"No thank you, sweetheart, you eat mine."

Steering her out the door, Dave told Teddy, "She can't stay, Sport, and lowering his voice he hissed to his former lover, "I plan to pretend I never saw you."

She smiled brightly and said, "I'll do the same." *I'm marrying someone twice the man you'll ever be.*

After he left, Dave said to his son, "Hey, Buddy, let's have a secret from Mommy. Let's not tell her that Auntie Rhonda came to see us."

"Why?"

"I think it will be fun if just you and I have a secret. Not Mommy or anyone—just you and me.

Teddy glowed. "Okay!"

Dave saw the bouquet the housekeeper had arranged on the dining room table. "Did the woman I saw leaving bring that bouquet?"

"Yes, Mr. Hernandez." Not wanting to come right out and tell him her suspicions, she added, as a hint, "The funniest thing. You know how Poppy is with strangers, but he ran right up to her. I called the police." If she had told him she didn't reach them, he would have called.

Betty returned to the kitchen and didn't see Mr. Hernandez take the card attached to a decorative holder in the bouquet and without looking at it, tear it into little pieces, and dispose of it and the plastic holder.

* * *

Midge drove back to the townhouse. Finding her sister in the guest room with Georgy-Girl and the kittens, she asked, "Have you moved all day, Sis?"

"Not much. It's just fascinating to watch those poor little blind things squirm around and what a good mother Georgy-Girl is even though she's hardly more than a kitten herself. She doesn't leave them except to eat and use the litter box, and she keeps them sparkling clean."

"Did you ever have a pet before?"

"Not growing up. My stepmother wouldn't allow a pet in the house. My last husband had dogs, big black labs. They were good dogs but not exactly lap dogs."

"I had a little Chihuahua I had to leave behind when I left Texas. I loved my little dog, and I did something stupid today. I went to see him at the home of people who have him now. I thought only the housekeeper would be there, but the little boy and dad were there, and they recognized me."

"Didn't you tell them you are Midge?"

"It didn't work."

"Oh, no!" Sandra boiled over. "What are we going to do?

"Now that I've been recognized, I think it would be best for me to leave town for a few days. I'll rent a car because you have the van."

"Well, okay. How long will you be gone?"

"It depends. I probably will go to San Antonio. If you need me I can get back quickly; and I'll keep in touch. It seems as if all my plans to retrieve my hard-earned money are not going to be realized."

"Too bad. I like it here and hoped maybe the sale wouldn't go through. Then you, Georgy-Girl and family, and I could live here forever."

Midge didn't comment. She packed, and Sandra took her to a car rental.

* * *

222

Linda arrived home after her long day of work at the clinic. Teddy met her at the door, "Mommy, Auntie Rhonda came for a visit and said I can keep Poppy forever." Then seeing his dad, he froze into an exaggerated pose with his hand over his mouth. "Oh, Daddy, I'm sorry. It was our secret."

"It's okay, Buddy. Why don't you feed Poppy? I need to talk to your mom."

Alone with her husband, Linda asked, "Why are you trying to keep it secret?"

"The housekeeper let Rhonda in before I got home."

"She has a name, Dave."

"For crying out loud, I'm trying to tell you what happened, and you give me a lesson in political correctness." Then lying expertly, "Okay, Betty let Rhonda in and suspecting who she was, Betty called the police. They probably have found Rhonda by now and they might decide to reopen the case and charge her for all she did."

"Why didn't you want me to know?"

"I didn't want to upset you."

"Don't worry. I saw her, too. At the clinic."

Hanging up her jacket in the closet, she noticed the gorgeous flowers on the table. "Flowers?"

"Why not? For the woman I love." Dave took Linda in his arms, but all she could think of was the guilty flowers she'd figured out he used to bring to her after a tryst with Rhonda.

Chapter Fifteen

Nightmare on the Beach

Early Thursday morning the clerk had called both detectives to say, "The good news is you're not out on the blazing beach today. The bad news is the chief wants you to take the night shift, which starts at 6:00 and lasts until Corpus Christi beaches close at midnight. Check in here by 4:00 if you want to get there on time because I hear the traffic is horrendous.

Thursday evening two detectives made their way slowly through traffic congestion to the island and complained about the night shift.

"The Chief really must want to punish us for all that evidence we've dug up that will solve the Missing Doctor case."

Maria agreed.

"Just be glad we aren't in Port A. Their beaches are open until 2:00, though in time I bet they'll change that because they're sick of our beaches closing and emptying on to theirs," Belkin commented on the way out. He suddenly noticed Maria seemed quiet, and he asked, "Your ex still trying to talk you into coming back to him?"

"No! In fact, he's told everyone it was his idea to break off the engagement."

"Ah, the frail male ego. I'll tell you again you're smart to be rid of him."

Maria didn't respond. It still hurt too much.

The evening started out to be a calm one. Lots of fires to monitor but, in general, well-behaved kids. "Just hope we don't have to be here tomorrow night," voiced Belkin.

"Oh, St. Patrick's Day! Another reason to go wild."

Mostly they patrolled in the car and talked about the possibility of starting their own private investigating firm, that wouldn't include Spring Break patrol.

Maria smiled as Belkin said, "You're great with details while I have the experience. We could do it!"

224

Maria had been thinking all day about the three women at the townhouse and was ready to bring that up when about 11:00 they saw what looked like a fight on the darkened beach. Ponderous clouds covering the moon as well as those famous Texas stars made it especially hard to see. They left the patrol car with its lights flashing and walked over to break it up. With illumination from their high-beam beacons, they saw the glint of a knife. A kid dropped to the sand with blood spurting from an artery while the crowd disappeared into the darkness. Someone had notified 911 and distant sirens sounded. Stan applied pressure to the arm of the bleeding youth with a rolled-up beach towel as he awaited EMTs.

Another fight broke out further down the beach. With Stan busy, Maria called for back-up and gave the mile marker. She waited until she saw two officers jump out of their CCPD car and run towards her. One hand on her revolver, she started towards the second fight with the two officers behind her. *Have to be gang members* was her thought as out of the shadows someone crouched behind a tent jumped up and hit Maria in the head with a one-liter vodka bottle, a glass bottle that all beaches banned, this one filled with sand. The blow knocked her out cold and broke the bottle. Blood trickled from head wounds, embedded with broken glass and sand. One of the officers knelt beside Maria while the other chased the offender, caught him and arrested him. The drug-impaired cop-hating kid's fate depended on whether his victim lived.

Stan had watched it all, shouted to an onlooker to take over pressing the towel on the wound until the ambulance came, and rushed to his partner's aid. At first look he thought she was dead, also suspected by the CC officer, but she groaned and fought to sit up. Stan helped her back to the ground with his jacket under her head and cautioned her to keep her eyes open and talk to him. She again lost consciousness.

The ambulance arrived and EMTs loaded her and the kid with the arm wound into an ambulance and raced to the closest Corpus hospital. Stan rode along though one of the

225

EMTs said he's probably better stay on patrol. "No, she's my partner. Let those animals kill each other for all I care."

Chapter Sixteen

Second Flight

Night fell Thursday. The real Sandra was on the run again. The second flight from Corpus was much more pleasant than the first—no torrential rains, no need to dispose of evidence, no cops, plus Sirius Radio brightened the journey. She sang to the music from a gospel station, music she remembered from going once or twice to church with her mother when she was a little girl. She switched to NPR for news and left it there because she couldn't figure out how to return to Sirius without pulling over.

I have more to think about than the radio. What am I going to do? Obviously, Dave will tell Linda I was at their home, and one or the other will report me to the police. I can't wait to get back to Arkansas but somehow, I have to get my money. I have to be able to support my little family, my sister, the baby, and me. Somehow, we have to convince the courts to reopen the case, accept the death certificate, and give Sandra the money. If not, I'm counting on Mr. Sylte to get his loan and pay me quite a sum of cash. Oh, and I'll have to find a lawyer to make my personal sale to him legal.

Sandra snared the last vacancy at La Quinta in San Antonio, near the airport. She hadn't realized that Corpus Christi wasn't the only place in the state where Spring Breakers came; the hotel bulged with happy noisy vacationing families.

The motel had Wi-Fi, which inspired Sandra to splurge. She'd missed her own computer: it was a blow to find it gone from her townhouse. I really want to use my time away to track down Midge. *I don't want to waste time waiting my turn at the computer in the lobby—done that before, and I did not hog it like some people do. I need my own computer now and I'll need one when I return to Arkansas, especially if I work with Wayne.*

She'd convinced herself and found the Apple Store at the upscale Shops of La Cantera Mall and put a laptop on her credit card. She passed a rack of phone adapters without even seeing them.

After an early supper at a nearby restaurant crowded with the vacationing families, she returned to the hotel and checked out Facebook, which she joined in hopes her sister or someone who knew her might respond to her search. Nothing led her to her baby sister. She prepared to go to bed when she had a thought. *I should call my sister; I promised to check in.*

Before she had a chance, her phone rang. Wayne.

"Hi there, Sweetheart. I vowed I wasn't going to call you on your vacation with your sisters, but I am missing you terribly tonight and had to call."

Sandra, as the day's events flashed in front of her, stumbled around trying to think of what to say. "I— I should have called you at least to tell you that we arrived but it's been . . ." Her voice trailed off and then she explained, "Yesterday we thought Andrea had been kidnapped. She hitchhiked from Corpus Christi to the beach over on the island. Anyway, Rainey flew home with her after we finally found her."

"That had to be traumatic. I hope nothing else bad happens, and you'll be back home, and we can start up where we left off."

Lulled by his sweet words, Sandra wanted to tell him everything, but she couldn't do that on the phone. She wanted to tell him she missed him and couldn't wait to get home to see him but before she had a chance her phone quit. Dead battery. She looked around frantically for her adapter and realized she hadn't packed it. She didn't want Wayne to think she had hung up on him. She just sat there exhausted, too tired to do anything about it. *I'll use the car adapter first thing tomorrow and call to explain.*

* * *

Wayne immediately called back. No answer. He called Sandra's sister, Rhonda to voice his concern. *Sandra sounded upset. What can be wrong?*

* * *

228

Sandra went to bed. *Another sleepless night. What kind of person am I? I vowed I'd tell only the truth when I returned home and instead I've involved my whole family in this charade. I've even stolen the name of my poor innocent baby sister for this fiasco. I've loved having family again, but I've used my sisters and for what? I may not get a cent of my money. I say I want to care for Rhonda and her baby, but how? I learned to be a good person from Lurene, but I've failed miserably.*

I dream of a future with Wayne, but I'm afraid our relationship won't withstand my whole story. I know I'll never be able to live up to his expectation. I'm not the woman he deserves. Brian has shown where his loyalties lie, even after giving me false hope when he said we belong together. No matter what he promised, he could solidify the case against me.

Sandra Lewis continued with "the sorries". *My own mother doesn't know me and Lurene is gone. My whole life since she died has been a lie, a sham. It's not worth it. My sisters would have been better off if I'd never found them. Andrea wouldn't have been arrested. I'm toxic to everyone I love. Maybe the only solution is to return to Corpus Christi and put an end to the mess I've made of my miserable life. Just put something heavy in my pockets like Virginia Woolf, walk out into the Gulf, and keep walking.*

Despairing, Sandra got out of bed. She put her computer in its case and began picking up her other belonging, leaving San Antonio at 2:00 AM Friday. She found she was too tired to drive and stopped at a rest stop. She saw, illuminated by the restrooms' outside lighting, plants and landscaping rocks. She put a couple fist-sized rocks in the car. She plugged her phone into the charger in the rental car.

When Sandra reached the beach on Mustang Island at dawn the scene was unlike what they had seen, smelled, and heard when they searched for Andrea. Quiet tents covered the beach, trash barrels overflowed, joining drifts of litter on the sand, portable toilets reeked, a few embers glowed in fire pits. Soon public servants would some to clear out much of the daily mess as they thought about tonight when the beach would swarm with under-age drinkers celebrating St. Pat's Day while older Spring Breakers crowded the islands and Corpus Christi bars.

The real Sandra Lewis sat on the sand and watched the sun come up. She noticed an older woman near the shore, picking up shells. She looked amazingly like Lurene.

"Isn't it a shame all those kids will sleep until noon and miss this sunrise, beautiful and filled with hope, Sandra?"

"How do you know my name?'

"Don't you recognize me? I'm here because you look forsaken."

"Lurene! It is you."

"Honey, I never wanted you to get mixed up with Brian. But it's too late for regrets. He is the root of all your problems now. I always said you could accomplish anything you wanted, and now it's time for you to prove it. You're smart. You're strong. Do what you have to do, Sandra, to close the door on your past. Take hope from the sunrise; things are going to change. It won't be easy but you're not alone. Your family will do anything for you because of their love for you, and there's a man in Arkansas who wants to marry you. Call him."

"Lurene, you make everything seem simple. "Lurene? Lurene?"

The woman had vanished into sea fog rolling in from the Gulf.

Chapter Seventeen

Mutual Attraction

Sandra had fallen asleep Thursday night worrying about her sister. Midge hadn't called like she promised. Sandra had tried to call her a few times, but her calls didn't go through. Wayne called and told her that her he was talking to her sister when her phone went dead. And that she sounded upset.

Friday morning Sandra opened the door to one of the neighbors, who handed her a condolence card and a plate of cookies. Sandra thanked and invited her to come in. She declined but before she left, Sandra asked when Spring Break ended. The neighbor laughed, "Well, it depends. The biggest week is this week, the week all the Texas colleges have Spring Beak but there is a less frantic week before or after this week when northern colleges have their breaks. That will be next week, but the crowds are nothing like this." She went on, "You picked quite a week to come here!"

Sandra had a reason for asking. She wanted to know when the detectives would be free because she believed she could convince them it wasn't fair that her sister could lose all her money for both of their sakes.

As the neighbor rambled on and on about how much wilder Spring Breaks used to be back in the 80s, Sandra had a better idea. She would take matters into her own hands and go back to the Police Department today. This time she would go straight to the top and talk to the one in charge, the Chief of Police.

She finally told the neighbor she had an appointment, checked on the feline family, grabbed a couple delicious cookies, and headed for SCCPD. She asked the clerk on duty if she could talk to the Chief of Police. After checking to see if he was available, the clerk directed Sandra to his office.

The chief already had endured a terrible morning. One of his two top-notch detectives were hanging on to life at a local hospital after some thug had hit her on the head on beach patrol last night.

"What the...!" the Chief spouted when the famed and gorgeous Missing Doctor walked into his office. "Heard you were dead, but you're looking mighty good for a corpse, Dr. Collins."

Sandra had a reputation for being a ditz, but she could rise to the occasion and present herself well. The gruff, wise-cracking chief didn't bother her a bit. "I'm not who you think I am; I'm Sandra Lewis, Rhonda Collin's sister. She named me beneficiary to her estate, but I am having trouble obtaining any of what she willed me because I have been told her assets have been frozen."

"And?" asked the Chief.

"When I tried to find out why," Sandra began and then fibbed only a little, "someone at the courthouse referred me to you to explain what happened."

The Chief leaned back in his chair with his hands grasped behind his head. "That was quite a case! One of our detectives busted it wide open . . . Wait! DNA proved you and the doctor are the same person."

Sandra bristled, "That's wrong. I'm her sister, actually half-sister; we both look like our Mama. She willed everything to me because I was the only relative she thought she had. When she left Texas, she went to Chicago for a while and then we both came home to Arkansas. There we found . . ." Sandra hesitated, trying to get this right, "... our other two sisters. You see we were all placed in different foster homes when we were young." Sandra managed a catch in her throat. "That was when Daddy Jack went to prison and Mama abandoned us."

"That a very interesting story, Miss . . .?"

"Lewis."

"Did you know your sister is a felon, who practiced as a doctor with false medical credentials?"

"I didn't know that" Sandra responded honestly. "All I know is that I have her death certificate, *the false certificate burning in my purse*, and feel I'm entitled to what she willed me."

"She's really is dead?"

232

"Yes. We all were together for a while and then she died," Sandra lied as she wiped away tears with a tissue from her purse. She reached back in her purse and handed the death certificate to the Chief.

He said under his breath, "This is the evidence that surfaced that my detectives denied knowing about, but the media found out about." He spoke to Miss Lewis, "Usually when a missing person is found dead, assets are released; but as I explained, in your sister's case, she was a fugitive and even though the case was dropped, her will became null and void when the court froze all your sister's assets."

"But she earned the money, bought her home, and . . ." sobbed Sandra.

The Chief interrupted. "The only thing you can do is try to get the court's decision overturned."

"How do I do that?" Sandra looked at the Chief with such a long-lashed beseeching look.

The tough-guy Chief gave her an uncommon smile, "You file a petition and you'll get a hearing and that usually takes weeks, but I happen to know there is a brand-new judge in town and she's dying to sink her teeth into a case here." The Chief, obviously taken with the beautiful blonde, continued," Someone in the court system owes me big time. I'll pull some strings and the judge could hear your case as early as Monday. You won't need an attorney; the court will appoint one."

Sandra looked even more bewitching. "I can't thank you enough."

The Chief looked at her with great sympathy, "The court will decide if you should thank me, little lady. They'll get in touch with you. Leave all your information with the clerk, including the death certificate."

Sandra couldn't wait to tell Midge. As soon as she climbed into the van, she called on her cell. Distracted as she backed out the van, she ran into a parked police car. Resisting the urge to hit and run, a sobbing Sandra went back inside police headquarters, weeping and ready to beg for mercy. *Oh, no, I've ruined everything.*

233

It was the chief's car, but he assured the woman drowning in her own tears that she had done more damage to her van than his and on a whim invited her to go out to dinner.

Chapter Eighteen

After Surgery

Late Friday afternoon after early morning emergency surgery to release pressure on her brain, and the day in ICU, Maria awakened. The first person she saw sat by her bed next to a vase of roses. Her mind was fuzzy as her eyesight, but she remembered her parents, brother and Stan were there after surgery as she drifted in and out of consciousness. Now she saw Xavier, and her life could have changed course depending on what he said.

"Hello there, sweetheart. That is quite a turban you're wearing. And you're a television celebrity on all channels. And the paper. SCCPD Officer Suffers Attack On Beach. "

Xavier took her hand, "When I heard you'd been hurt, I knew I couldn't live without you. I was wrong trying to tell you that you had to give up your career. Please forgive me and marry me as soon as you can get out of the hospital."

That might have been what Maria would have liked to have heard, but what Xavier really said as he took her hand, "Hello there, sweetheart. That's quite a turban you're wearing. And you're a television celebrity on all the channels. Officer attacked on the beach." When I heard your got hurt in the line of duty, all I could think was now my girl will change her mind, give up her career and marry me."

Maria spoke slowly and with effort, "No, Xav…" Her weak voice trailed off.

Xavier wouldn't give up: "I see that crack on the head didn't knock any sense into you, honey. Please reconsider when you feel better."

"I won't." Maria mouthed and turned her head away, even though that created more pain. When he gave her a kiss on the cheek and left, she closed her eyes and a thought that had reoccurred throughout the night slowly surfaced: *One of the women at the townhouse really was Rhonda.*

Belkin, stopping by before he had to show up for Friday night at the beach, saw Xavier coming from Maria's room.

He gave the detective a smile contrived to say everything was going his way.

Maria's eyes were closed but she opened them as Stan spoke. "What some cops won't do to get out of Spring Break Patrol."

Marie managed a small smile, unlike her usual big contagious one, and asked, "Call Linda?"

* * *

Linda had tried to call Maria at home earlier Thursday evening but reached only the answering machine. She needed to tell her about Rhonda visiting the clinic and the Hernandez home. Maria always returned her calls

One positive thing regarding Rhonda's disappearance was becoming friends with the smart young detective. Linda wished their schedules allowed them to spend more time together and felt remiss for not calling her sooner to ask how wedding plans progressed.

Between her last two patients late Friday afternoon Linda took a call from Detective Stan Belkin, Maria's partner.

"Maria asked me to call you. She received a severe head injury while we were on the island patrolling the beach last night."

"Is she all right?" gasped Linda, as a friend not a doctor.

"It was touch and go; her family and I were here all night and until noon when the surgeon told us she will make it. She's still in ICU and I just stopped back on my way to night patrol. She wakened long enough to ask me to call you."

He agreed to give Linda the room and phone number, but he would have refused that if he known that in all her waking moments Maria had been thinking about the Missing Doctor case.

Linda came to visit as soon as she could leave work. "I'm so distressed this happened to you, Maria," she said as she took her young friend's hand. Immediately she noticed the vintage engagement ring was gone but chalked that up to hospital procedure.

"Need to tell you something." Maria's mind was less fuzzy, but her throat was raw from tubes that she had trouble speaking. "Dr. Rhonda —is back."

"Yes, I know. She came to my office yesterday but said she was one of her sisters. She showed me a death certificate for Rhonda. It said she died a few weeks ago of heart failure in Arkansas. I knew she's Rhonda."

"False. Like her creden—" Her voice gave out.

"Don't try to talk. I know it's hard for you. Rhonda's trying to get her accounts unfrozen with the death certificate and I know it's her because she came to our house and admitted who she was to Teddy and Dave."

"Tired." Maria closed her eyes.

"Of course, sweetie. I'll leave and you sleep. I'm going to write down everything I told you and you can review it when you awaken."

Linda left and ordered a bouquet for Maria.

Chapter Nineteen

Voicemail

Throughout the day Midge's voicemail box filled up.

Wayne, the first to find the phone working, was disappointed Sandra didn't pick up but left a message: "Sweetheart, you sounded upset before I lost contact with you last night. I miss you even more today than I did last night. Please give me a call when you can. I know you're busy because I talked to Rhonda and she mentioned you are in San Antonio having some art pieces appraised. I love you. Please call when you can."

Sandra left a message soon after and was careful what she said because she wasn't ready to tell her about the dented van: "Sis, I hope it's okay if I borrow one of your fancy dresses. I have a date with the Police Chief tonight! By the way, you might want to stay put until Monday because I have a hearing with a judge at 10:00 AM to see if I can get the will reinstated. Bye bye—oh wait, be sure to call Wayne. He's worried about you and FYI you're in San Antonio getting your art stuff appraised. Quick thinking, huh? I didn't want to tell him you're hiding out."

Wayne called back: "I have some news, Sandra. The husband of the woman missing from the RV Park identified the body as hers. He said her birthday is tomorrow. I know what a relief it will be if that isn't you sister Midge's birthday. Please, sweetheart, call me as soon as you can."

Another caller added a voice mail: "Sandra, it's Brian. I have great news. Today is the day I decided would be the day I would turn myself in, but now I'm not going to do that. Grace and Sadie came home yesterday. She has forgiven me, and I'm not going to do anything to mess that up. That means there is no chance you'll be investigated. Call us soon!"

Several more calls from Wayne, each sounding more concerned, filled up the entire voice mail. He would call Saturday and Sunday, but always received the same recorded message: "The recipient's voice mail box is filled."

Chapter Twenty

The High Life

Not having brought anything appropriate to wear for her big night out, Sandra borrowed something from Rhonda's closet, an emerald green Jersey dress that draped from one shoulder, leaving the other bare. Perfect for St. Pat's Day! *Thank goodness I'm not showing. It fits perfectly.*

In the gorgeous dress and her hair in an upsweep Sandra looked quite amazing when her date arrived. She showed him the kittens, and not one person at headquarters would have dreamed the man was a cat person, who talked baby talk to tiny little kittens and their devoted mother. He'd laughed at the name change and said as a kid he'd had a tomcat called Herman, who became Hermione. He said his last wife despised cats and cigars. Things didn't work out even though he had quit smoking and re-homed his tomcat Oscar. Since the divorce he'd been thinking about going to the shelter to find a replacement cat. Sandra promised him the "pick of the litter" but he'd have to wait a while.

The Chief turned on his lights and siren, and they maneuvered quickly through the traffic of Spring Breakers and other St. Pat's Day celebrants. Over dinner the two hit it off as they regaled each other with bad marriage choices. Sandra told him more of the history of the crazy family that had produced four sisters who looked like clones of their mother. Sandra laughed appreciatively when the Chief told her the story about a dog that limped into a bar and said, "I'm here to find the man who shot my paw."

A reporter hanging around the Club wondered who the hottie was with Chief and spied on them all evening. It took him a while, but he realized the woman looked like the Missing Doctor. The Chief was quite aware of the reporter and as he and Sandra left, he grabbed the man by the collar and told him if he dared publish anything about the Chief's private life, "I will. . ."

Sandra couldn't hear what the Chief whispered to the reporter, but the man quickly handed over his digital camera. After removing the media card, the Chief returned the camera. On T.V. police just wrecked the camera, and this made Sandra admire her date even more. *Actually, I wouldn't have minded having a photo of the good-looking Chief and me on the front page of the newspaper. It had been refreshing to date a mature man.*

Both hated to have the evening end. The two exchanged a lingering kiss at the doorstep. Sandra unlocked the door and turned to the Chief. She wanted to invite him in to say good night to the cat family but thought better of it because she didn't know if where that might lead was a good idea. On second thought, it could be very good for the case.

A phone call received by the Chief ended that thought. The Assistant Chief reported more officers needed to be called in to handle the St. Patrick's Day celebrants on the beaches. He'd received a call from Belkin, again on night duty, that Port A already had called in back-up from Aransas Pass, Rockport, and other small coastal towns. This explanation, another quick kiss, a wish for all to go well on Monday, and he left.

Sandra mused, *I wonder how he feels about children?*

Chapter Twenty-one

Over-Achiever

Saturday morning Maria had two requests when she saw her dad. "Please call Xavier and ask him not to visit me because it just upsets me and bring me my laptop". Her doting father did both though wouldn't have brought the laptop if he'd known she had wanted to do more than check Facebook. She wanted it because of a call from her boss.

The Chief, in an unusually jovial mood called to check on her. She told him she wasn't sure when she'd be released and back to work He told her to "take it slow" and she might have listened to him except he mentioned to her about his visitor from Arkansas and his call to the courthouse. He added the new judge was willing to have a hearing on Monday; he was certain it would be overturned.

That fanned the fire in Maria, who set about to prove the death certificate Linda had seen was a phony. In her opinion that might have been the last thing Brian created for his friend Sandra. If she could prove the certificate was fraudulent, the judge couldn't overturn the other case and Maria would introduce the Cavendish connection. Next, she'd prove Dr. Collins was alive. One thing at a time. First the fake death certificate.

Using phone and laptop, Maria checked every death she could find in Arkansas in the last two months. She found no newspaper or online obituaries and no records of the death of Rhonda Collins or Sandra Lewis. She called Linda to see if she remembered the town on the death certificate, but she said she had no time to read anything but the date of death and state of Arkansas. She scolded Maria for working. Maria thanked her for the flowers. She woke up Stan who had worked all night at the beach and was catching a few winks. He was intrigued that Dr. Rhonda had visited the Hernandez home on Thursday, but he also lectured Maria about not working on solving the case.

Every time a nurse came to take her vitals, he or she threatened to remove Maria's laptop, while admonishing her that she needed to rest her brain to recover. Ignoring them, Maria called Stan a second time. She begged him to bring her the file she had on Cavendish in her middle desk drawer.

Stan was on Padre Island where a drowning victim had been recovered when Maria called the second time. Reluctantly, still arguing Maria needed to rest, he agreed to bring the file later. He didn't tell where he was and all the media hype, but she heard about it from a nurse, who had no idea of her patient's pursuit of the doctor.

Chapter Twenty-two

Drowning victim

When an angler found a woman's, body floating near Packery Channel early Saturday he hailed a passing Corpus Christi patrol car. In no time emergency vehicles and the media had arrived. Uniforms diverted traffic from the area, which only added to the congestion of Spring Breakers determined to make the most of their last full day on the coast.

Many feared the body was that of one of the Breakers, but no one had reported a missing friend. It was a reporter who took a quick look at the body and said it was that of someone older than the usual college student. That observation formed the basis of the frenzy that the body belonged to the Missing Doctor.

An autopsy would tell how long the woman had been in the water and cause of death. A database of missing persons could help I.D. the body. The SCCPD had its work cut out for them, but with all their people dealing with Spring Break, there would be a delay in seeking results.

Without autopsy findings or other confirmation, the media had convinced the public that the body belonged to the woman they had made famous. Many reporters jumped on the complaint that the SCCPD hadn't done enough to find the doctor and that in recent days she had been seen dining at a Corpus Christi eatery, possibly with her kidnappers. Stan didn't think the woman resembled Dr. Rhonda but hard to tell because of everything to which nature subjects bodies submerged in sea waters.

Stan left the scene and stopped at headquarters. He picked up the file Maria had requested and stopped in his office where he found a note and death certificate left by Sandra Lewis. It was against his better judgment to take these to Maria, but he knew she wouldn't rest until he brought her what he'd promised.

243

* * *

The Chief called Sandra early Saturday morning. "Hi, kitten," he began and Sandra laughed. He indicated he wanted to see her again. Forgetting she didn't cook, she invited him for supper.

Sandra checked the refrigerator for something she could cook. Georgy-Girl jumped up on the counter to see if food for her was forthcoming. In the process she knocked down the ginger jar, which Rhonda had repeated to all, "This contains 'my ashes' if you need further proof of my death." Sandra cheered that the jar hadn't broken. A few ashes remained inside but most lay scattered all over the kitchen. Sandra vacuumed up the rest.

Deciding she needed inspiration, Sandra turned on the television to a cooking show. In the middle of a demonstration on Mexican shish kabobs, there was a Breaking News bulletin: "A body of a woman fitting the description of Rhonda Collins, the Missing Doctor, has been recovered on Padre Island. Our reporters are on the scene. We will bring you the latest. Stay tuned."

Suddenly, like puzzle pieces, things she had learned about her sister fell into place. Recently the real Sandra had revealed to Sandra that she had been a doctor, and when she told her about the plan to return to Texas she had said something prevented her from claiming her assets. The Chief had insisted her sister was a felon, a criminal. She couldn't imagine her sister doing anything bad, but she had figured out her sister was the Missing Doctor.

Oh, sister, we pretended you were dead and now maybe you really are. No, you can't be dead. You're in San Antonio because someone recognized you. Maybe they followed you to San Antonio and killed you and brought your body back and threw in the Gulf. I have to talk to the Chief.

As she grabbed her phone, the Chief called her, "Kitten, I'm afraid I'm going to have to cancel our date tonight and was looking forward to seeing you and eating a home-cooked meal, bur something has happened in my jurisdiction,

244

and I'm afraid it is going to keep me occupied all day and late into the night."

Sandra wanted to ask many questions including if it was the drowning that occupied him, but the Chief hung up before she could say a word.

"What will I do, what will I do if my sister really is dead?" she asked the cats.

* * *

A newspaper reporter had gained permission to talk to Maria. She told him she remembered nothing of being hit on the head. She suggested he call the Corpus Christi Police Department as she had been told that one of their officers pursued and arrested her assailant. A nurse shooed the reporter out of the room just as Stan arrived. The detective refused to talk to him and chided him for bothering the victim.

Maria's grinned at Stan, who held a Whataburger bag. She managed a small bite but was more interested in the file she's asked him to bring.

"I know I shouldn't be abetting you in working, but I brought your file and something I found on my desk that I think will interest you." He handed her the death certificate, commenting, "Check the place where Rhonda Collins' death occurred."

"Harmon!" Maria exclaimed, and they both laughed in amazement.

"And there's the name of the funeral home. I'll call them right away."

"No! You are here to recover not to solve a case." Maria already was on her phone asking for the number for the funeral home. She spoke to the owner, who happened to be present in the evening for a wake. He was emphatic that in a small town he knew everyone who had died, and he knew he had not signed a death certificate for a Rhonda Collins. "Someone has forged my name."

Maria smiled as she relayed all to Stan. The death certificate definitely was a fraud. Maria sighed with relief and realized her head throbbed badly. She needed to sleep, but she had to ask Stan about the body found near the Packery Channel. "Do you think it's the Missing Doctor and that she is quite recently dead?"

"I saw the body, and I'd say highly doubtful."

Belkin noted that Maria struggled to keep her eyes open and placing a tender kiss on her cheek, whispered, "Good night, partner."

* * *

Stan decided that what he needed to do now before going back on the beach for the last night was to see about an arrest warrant. Stopping at the police station, he tried to reach Ortiz, but the Chief was still occupied with the drowning case. The clerk referred him to the Assistant Chief who agreed to have a judge-signed warrant ready for him in the morning.

A reporter who practically lived at police headquarters overheard the news about a hearing on Monday and vowed to use the media, including social media, to pack the courtroom with Missing Doctors' fans, who believed the SSPD hadn't done enough to find their heroine, the popular doctor who had won the honors.

* * *

When the night nurse checked on Ms. Gonzalez, she found a weak pulse. She pressed the alarm button and personnel thundered down the hall to Maria's room. The physician on duty shouted, "We need to get her to surgery. We're losing her."

Chapter Twenty-three

The Arrest

To keep her mind off the possibility that her sister was dead, Sandra distracted herself Saturday evening by trying on her sister's clothes. On Sunday morning she awakened to a pounding on the door. She answered the door in one of her sister's most revealing negligees to two police officers.

In a cheery voice, the woman asked, "Good morning, officers. May I help you?" Then her heart leapt to her throat. *Maybe they have come to tell me my sister is dead. Don't they always come in pairs to tell you that?*

Both men, Stan Belkin and a rookie officer, tried to look at something except the good-looking woman in the revealing attire. Stan asked without any inflection, "Which one of the sisters are you?"

"I'm Sandra Lewis."

Flashing the warrant, Stan snapped, "Miss Lewis, you are under arrest for trying to gain access to an inheritance with a false death certificate."

The rookie began reciting the right of the arrested to keep silent, but Sandra was anything but silent. "I can't go right now. Can't you see I'm not dressed?"

Sandra could tell by the looks on their faces that they had noticed, and she continued, "And you're wrong. That inheritance belongs to me, and I'm alone and who will feed the cat if you take me away? She's a nursing mother. And besides, the Chief is a personal friend and I have a hearing on Monday to have the first case overturned. I am determined to get what my poor sister earned and I inherited."

"Ma'am, get dressed and feed you cat."

"Don't I get to make a phone call?"

"Most people call a lawyer," came from Stan.

Sandra grabbed her phone and tried again to call her sister as she prayed this time, when she needed her most, she would pick up.

"No one answered. I get another call, don't I?'

The two men waited while she made a second call.

"Rainey, it's me 'Sandra'. If you can believe it, I am being arrested because two police officers say our sister's death certificate is a fake."

On the other end, Rainey said, "I will be there as soon as I can."

"What happened to Andrea?"

"Her dad and I decided she has to turn in her babysitting earnings until she has paid off the $200 I paid for her fine plus what I paid to change flights. Except for babysitting she is grounded."

"Oh, poor girl. I think the policemen are getting impatient. I'll say good-bye and I love you."

Stan reached for her phone.

"Oh, please can't I make just one more to Chief Ortiz? I wasn't thinking straight or I would have called him first."

"No," Stan was out of patience. "Get dressed and feed your cats."

Thinking of a movie, Sandra giggled, "If you're worried I'll crawl out a window when I'm supposed to be, dressing, you can watch."

"No thanks, just hurry," Stan barked, and just in case the ditzy woman did what she suggested, he sent the rookie outside by the window.

Almost half an hour later Sandra reappeared wearing a demure top and tailored slacks with her hair styled and wearing impeccable make-up. She fed the cat as she explained she'd have to find someone to feed her before Rainey could get there from Arkansas. The officers ignored that and cuffed her. They put her in the back of the patrol car, where she wept loudly.

Arriving at police headquarters, the first person they encountered was the Police Chief. He wasn't the least bit happy about being here on a Sunday but the media fall-out regarding the drowned woman required it. When he saw Sandra in cuffs, he exploded, "What the devil are you doing here? I never saw a warrant for your arrest."

Belkin held his temper, "No, you weren't here when I presented evidence Maria found that shows that the doctor's alive and the death certificate's a fake. Your Assistant found a judge to sign it."

"Uncuff her this instant. I think you're wrong and what is Gonzalez doing working when she's supposed to be recovering?"

"Chief, you at least have to look at the proof she found," Stan demanded.

"All right, all right. Sandra, I'm sorry. They will have to fingerprint you and all that."

She batted her eyes at the Chief, "I know it's not your fault, you dear, dear man, but I'm just worried about Georgy-Girl and her babies. She will need food and water this evening."

"You will be out long before that and if there's a snag, I will go feed Georgy myself." Ortiz's sweet tone made Stan want to ask *Who is this man impersonating the Chief?*

Ortiz swaggered away but turned back. "After you're through processing this woman, I, as Chief of this department, want her freed without bond. She is not a flight risk, I guarantee. Maybe her sister has done something wrong, but I know this woman is innocent." Then he whispered to Sandra "I will take you home, honey."

Sandra smiled at her "White Knight" while Stan glowered, "Just read the proof Maria dictated to me."

The Chief read: Funeral home denies that death certificate for Rhonda Collins is authentic and Rhonda Collins proved that by visiting the home of Dr. Linda Hernandez.

After reading the evidence, the Chief had to concede that his sweet Sandra was involved up to her beautiful long lashes. *Obviously, the Missing Doctor manipulated her. She probably thought she had to do it for the sake of her family. Poor kid. She is the sweetest, naturally innocent. She had a rough childhood, and the jerks she married! Regardless of what she has done, I'm a man of my word and she should be free until the hearing.*

249

As soon as Stan had finished the fingerprinting and paperwork, the Chief took Sandra home.

Chapter Twenty-four

Plotting Patient

The hospital had summoned Maria's family Saturday night, and they were still there Sunday morning. The surgeon explained to them that a second very minor surgery, as brain surgeries go, had been necessary to repair a blood vessel, but all went extremely well. They had been keeping her sedated to insure she would rest to help her recovery run smoothly now.

Stan stopped to tell Maria about the arrest and learned that his partner had required another surgery during the night. There was plenty of guilt to go around as each family member felt Maria's working had been the cause for the second surgery. Stan didn't hesitate to say, "I'm to blame. She was determined to crack this case. I tried to talk her out of it, but she can be…"

"Stubborn," supplied Maria's brother.

Stan cracked a smile. "I was going to say determined."

"That too," her father offered.

"She is an incredible detective." Stan offered but his voice broke as he continued. "I need to go but could you keep me in the loop."

"Of course," Maria's mother answered, putting a reassuring hand on the detective's arm. "My girl's tough. She'll be back solving crimes with you in no time."

* * *

At noon Maria awakened and told her mother she was starved. The patient looked much better. After Maria finished most of the food on her tray, her mother asked if she knew what had happened. The last thing she remembered was Stan visiting and bringing her a Whataburger. She thought a minute and said, "I also remember the Chief said there will be a hearing tomorrow on one of our cases. I need to be there to testify."

251

"Maria." Her mother spoke sternly. "Don't even consider that. You need to heal completely before you worry about your job. "

Her mother knew Maria wasn't listening to her. She called Stan as she had promised and asked him if he could come up and talk some sense into Maria. The patient's mom went home for a nap after she made her daughter promise she wouldn't do anything foolish; she said she and the rest of the family would be up later. When the surgeon stopped to see his patient, Maria told him how only she needed to be a witness at the Monday hearing. He repeated what her mother had said, in medical terms, and much more emphatically.

Stan had wound up directing traffic as the Spring Breakers left for home. It was late before he came to do as Mrs. Gonzalez had asked. Maria seemed to be sleeping but as soon as she realized Stan was there, she started talking, "Stan you've got to help me. I feel fine and I have to be at that hearing tomorrow. I need to convince the judge the death certificate isn't authentic."

Stan interrupted, "But, Maria . . ." She spoke over him. "I've been thinking about it all day. All you have to do is find a set of scrubs. I know they have them at Wal-Mart. Go to one that is open 24 hours. There are wheelchairs down by the front door of the hospital entrance. Bring one up here and, if the nurse on duty is at the station, tell her you have to take me downstairs for tests."

She had it all figured out. Only because he was dead tired, he agreed to do everything Maria asked, while later wondering if he'd lost his mind. "Now you need to get some sleep and I have to go out to the airport to pick up my wife."

Chapter Twenty-five

Mama's Girls

Rainey called the mother who had acknowledged only one, Sue-Ella/Rhonda, as her child.

"This is Rainey. I have a bit of bad news. Sue-Ella has been arrested in Corpus Christi, and there will be a hearing tomorrow. I'm making a plane reservation to go there. Would you like to go with me?"

"Of course, Rainey, honey."

Mama had awakened one morning remembering her entire past, which she shared with B.J., who confirmed almost everything she told him. Even though her memory was mostly intact, B.J. worried a bit about some of the bizarre things Mae had done recently like getting up and dancing at church and pulling out flowers and leaving the weeds. Now he heard her say, "If any of my girls are in trouble, I want to be there."

Rainey couldn't believe her ears. *Rainey, honey? Girls, plural!* "I'll make the reservations and call you right back."

It was impossible to find a direct flight to Corpus Christi, which meant Rainey and her mother spent Sunday night in Houston. Rainey had tried to reach Midge with no success and tried again Sunday night without results.

At times her mother seemed completely lucid and now that she remembered she had given birth to four daughters, she was eager to know all about each one. Rainey told her all she knew about her sisters. Skipping the recent episode, she talked about her daughter and about her son. Mama was delighted to know she was a grandma.

Rainey, on the plane to Corpus Christi, explained as well as she could why Sue Ellen had been arrested, trying to help her sister Ronnie Lee. The taxi from the airport deposited them at the courthouse minutes before the hearing began. They found a packed courtroom but Rainey located two empty seats close to the front.

Chapter Twenty-six

Success

Diana Belkin hadn't expected to go shopping as soon as her plane landed, but she helped her husband find a pair of dark blue scrubs like the attendants at the hospital wore. She really got into the charade and found an old I.D. lanyard and typed up a new nametag to put in. She also dug out a black Elvis style wig to complete the disguise. Stan protested but she convinced him he looked super in it.

At the hospital Stan grabbed a wheelchair and tried to be as nonchalant as possible as he pushed it into the elevator and off on the fourth floor, where Maria waited.

Stan clutched when a nurse stopped him. "Are you new? I know all the support staff, but I don't know you. On the other hand, you do look familiar."

"Excuse me, I'm in a hurry. I'm supposed to take the patient in 4322 down for some tests."

"Oh, sure, Maria Gonzalez. Her blood work and everything else has been done——take her away." The nurse threw out her arm expressively as she still wondered where she had seen this man before.

Maria giggled when she saw's Stan's hair and would have laughed out loud as Diana had if she had seen him at home with his air guitar singing "Heartbreak Hotel".

"Sir, would you please close the bathroom door." Even though Maria was expected to use the call button if she needed to get up, she hoped hospital personnel who saw the closed door would guess she was in there and respect her privacy. The patient knew there was nothing she could do but take her "tree" with her.

Without incidence he wheeled the woman in a red fuzzy robe, pulling her tree down the hall, in and out of the elevator and through the main door. Stan knew if they'd found another exit they would be caught, but by being brazen, no one expected a thing. A block from the hospital he turned on the siren and revolving lights in the police van and in minutes was at the courthouse, where he added a gauze mask to his costume.

Chapter Twenty-seven

Call to Order

As the crowd of spectators assembled, Judge Helen Barnes sat in her chambers and looked over the copy of the will she had been handed. She guessed it would be a simple contesting of a will, which should take minutes. Somehow, she had not received the folder with the information that this hearing had been supplanted by the arrest of the plaintiff, making that person the defendant. Stan had explained all that to Maria on the way to the courthouse.

Most of those grabbing seats had followed the story of the Missing Doctor from the first day she disappeared and hoped to find out what really happened to their heroine in the nut-brown suit with the frilly silk blouse that became soiled with blood and thrown in a ditch in a bag with the victim's long blonde hair. Others came for a glimpse of a new heroine, Detective Maria Gonzalez, injured in a Spring Break beach brawl. A rumor circulated on Facebook that she would be released from the hospital to testify. Rubbernecking to see if she really would show up, a communal gasp escaped the crowd when they spotted the detective, who arrived via wheelchair with a hospital attendant.

The tall, imposing African American judge appeared. She seemed astonished at the packed courtroom and spent a few minutes sweeping her eyes over the assemblage, none of whom she had met. The famed prosecutor Tom Cantu sat near Rainey and her mother. He had volunteered his services as the prosecuting attorney but the court clerk told him that for this thrown-together hearing ordered by the South Corpus Christi Police Chief they would use court attorneys. Cantu, brother-in-law of Linda and Dave Hernandez, felt certain the hearing would end up in a trial, and he planned to be the attorney who would exorcize the ghost of Dr. Rhonda Collins and secretly avenge her treatment of his relatives.

Judge Barnes hadn't met Chief Ortiz, though he had recommended her to preside over the hearing. He had a seat towards the front and one news photographer smirked when he saw the chief's eyes glued to the pretty blonde on the defense side.

She certainly noticed the young woman with her head swathed in bandages and attached to an IV tree, seated next to someone in hospital garb. If Chief Ortiz hadn't been fixated on the plaintiff, he might have figured out Belkin was in disguise.

Next the judge focused on the plaintiff, the woman who wanted to contest something about the will. What? She sat on the wrong side of the bench. To her all court cases were theatre productions and she expected this to be a dull one-act performance, but maybe she was wrong about this one. The crowd sat in silence as the judge looked over the room. Tension built until Judge Barnes pounded her gavel and said with sarcasm. "Now, am I to believe all y'all are here to meet me, the new judge?"

Nervous tittering from the crowd. "I thought not. Okay, folks, it's show time."

With that Mae Jackson stood up and yodeled. The judge pounded her gavel, and Mae yodeled louder, in spite of the judge's pounding and Rainey's efforts to restrain her. "But, I yodel when I'm happy," argued Mama.

Pretty soon the whole courtroom broke up in laughter

The judge scowled. "I'm calling for a five-minute break, and this sideshow better be over when I return."

Chapter Twenty-eight

First Act

Order had returned by the time the judge returned. She began again, "This court is now in session and it will stay that way." The judge glowered at all in attendance. "I'm in charge and don't any of you forget it."

"This case is about a will and should be simple. Some poor soul dies, and the will he or she has filed with an attorney is put into effect. Sometimes a survivor contests a will, and that's when the judicial system is needed. This case sounds more complicated. I'm going to let the public prosecutor explain what's going on. I might even learn something."

Aware that this was part of a larger unsolved case, the prosecutor explained only the basic facts of the will in question. "Dr. Rhonda Collins named her only relative, Sandra Lewis, as beneficiary to her estate. However, the so-called proof that Ms. Collins has died is in question." He called Detective Maria Gonzalez as his only witness. She was thrilled to get this out of the way quickly. She'd have a chance to be able to return to the hospital before her absence was noted.

Pushed in the wheelchair by a tall male nurse with a dated hair-cut and scrubs, Maria advanced to the front of the courtroom. The judge used the time to speak in her thunderous voice. "Even though this is supposed to be a simple hearing about a will, I'm curious why this courtroom is filled to the point there isn't room to swing a dead cat."

Sandra began to object to anyone doing such a terrible thing to a cat. The court appointed defense attorney shushed her as the judge narrowed her eyes and shot a fierce look in Sandra's direction. "Bailiff, since these folks think they're extras in a court T.V. drama, let's give them what they want. Swear in the witness."

Marie stated her name and position and the bailiff swore her in. With as much confidence as she could, given her fuzzy robe, Maria began, "The defendant left a death certificate …"

The judge interrupted, "Did you say you're a police detective? Regardless of who you are, you don't look well enough to be here."

Maria ignored the judge's comment, which she knew was true, and prayed she could get through this. She showed her badge and in as strong a voice as she could muster, asked if she could continue. Given permission she began again and said she wanted to introduce evidence to prove "the will in question is invalid". Then she started again, "I have a death certificate for Rhonda Collins, who made out the will. The defendant reported Ms. Collins died in her sleep in Arkansas a few weeks ago due to a heart attack."

"Now, wait a minute, Detective! You are testifying against the defendant, who gave you a death certificate? We need that as evidence, but you folks sure do things different in South Texas. The way it works is that people give others death certificates as proof of death usually to get benefits assigned by the deceased. I'm guessing this woman here …" Her eyes darted towards the defendant and referring to a ginger jar Sandra cradled in her arms, she paused and shouted, "What on earth is that?"

"It's my sister. I mean it's the urn we put her ashes in it, only Georgy, she's my cat, knocked it off the counter, and the lid came off. The ashes scattered all over and I wound up vacuuming her up." Tears welled in Sandra's eyes. "There's just a little bit of Rhonda left."

"Lord love a goose!" Judge Barnes rolled her eyes heavenward. "Clerk, grab that as evidence, too." Sandra openly blubbered as she relinquished the ginger jar they'd bought at that darling little boutique discovered on their road trip.

"Now you hush! I'll give you my full attention in a minute. The detective looks as if she's fading fast." Then, staring at Maria, "You were saying?"

259

"Miss Lewis provided a death certificate to prove the validity of the will, but I called the funeral home that made out the certificate and they confirmed they had no record of Rhonda Collins' death in Arkansas. And they did not make out the certificate, which I showed them via my cell phone. I believe Miss Lewis forged the death certificate and hereby went from plaintiff to defendant."

"I did not forge it," shouted Sandra as the crowded courtroom exploded, Greek chorus style.

The judge pounded her gavel. "Order in the court! And did I give you permission to speak, missy? I already told you that you all get your turn. Honestly, you'd think I was dealing with Kindergartners."

Chuckles erupted, quickly squelched by the judge.

"Detective, I need to see the death certificate." The clerk brought it to her.

"Well, looks real enough but you say her death wasn't verified by Francks Funeral Home indicated on this certificate?"

"That's correct. Miss Lewis may not have produced the form but someone could have created it for her."

"Semantics, Detective. Do you want to change robes with me as long as you are making judgments?"

Maria colored but gaining strength, she added, "I don't wish to make unnecessary judgments, but I do think you might want to have the jar tested to make certain there are traces of human remains."

The judge glared at Maria. "RE-AL-LY? As if I wouldn't figure that out myself! You're done unless you can provide an affidavit from the funeral home saying they didn't sign that certificate. Otherwise, its hearsay and doesn't mean squat."

"There wasn't time to secure that information, but I am sure I can." Maria looked completely beaten. The crowd took exception to the judge's lack of sympathy shown towards the detective, their hometown heroine who had barely survived Spring Break.

Judge Barnes asked the attorney if he had anything to add. "Detective Gonzalez said it all, and I suggest we dismiss and get these ashes tested."

As he spoke the attendant wheeled Maria from the courtroom and back to the hospital. Judge Barnes chastised the attorney. "Now you're trying to be the judge. I want to hear what the defendant and her attorney have to say. Defense?"

"Miss Lewis simply wishes to have what is rightfully hers as the only beneficiary of her dead sister, Rhonda Collins. I will let Miss Lewis explain. Turning to Sandra he said," It's your turn. Come to the stand."

"What's your name?" demanded the judge.

Sandra had been well coached. "My given name was Sue-Ella Jackson, but I now go by my professional name, Sandra Lewis."

"And what is your profession?"

"Uh . . . I'm unemployed." More snickers.

The judge muttered under her breath but audible enough for some in the courtroom to catch it and laugh, "No wonder you want to get your hands on your inheritance." Then loudly, "Swear her in."

After the swearing in, Helen Barnes asked, "Okay, is your sister really dead? And remember you are under oath to tell me the truth."

Before Sandra could answer, the eye-rolling judge had to respond to a huge commotion in the back of the courtroom. Voices buzzed, *"It's her!"* — *"She's alive!"* — *"Praise the Lord, nothing happened to her!"* — *"That's the outfit!"* — *"She and her sister look just alike."*

Dressed in the pecan pants already in her possession, the jacket she had recovered in her townhouse and a Chicago purchase, a blouse similar to the famed ruffled ivory blouse, Dr. Rhonda Collins had succeeded in making the hoped-for grand entrance.

261

Chapter Twenty-nine

Mission Accomplished

Detective Belkin loaded Maria and the wheelchair into the police van and turned on the siren. He drove her as quickly as possible back to the hospital and took the elevator to the fourth floor. There was no one at the desk this time. He wheeled her and the tree to her room and helped her from the chair and into bed.

Maria glanced over at the bathroom door. It remained closed. Lady Luck had been with them. "I can't believe we pulled it off!"

The hospital staff had taken care of everything necessary pertaining to Maria before the attendant had taken her downstairs for tests. Only one nurse poked her head into Maria's room and saw she had managed to get to the bathroom on her own. Another patient was sitting on her buzzer; the nurse went to her aid. When she stopped in again, an exhausted Maria slept in her bed.

Stan changed clothes and ditched his scrubs and mask in a public restroom. He left the hospital as quickly he could. and stashed the rest of his costume in his patrol car. Maria's mission had been accomplished in under an hour. Turning on the siren, Stan rushed back to the courtroom just behind the Missing Doctor.

Chapter Thirty

Act Two

The judge pounded for order. Ignoring her, Dr. Collins projected her voice as she made her way to the front, "Sister, please don't perjure yourself. I'm alive and well."

The judge scowled, "Who do you think you are crashing my courtroom?"

"I'm the one who wrote the will and wanted my sister to have all the benefits in case of my death. Isn't that what you'd call a 'moot point' with my appearance?"

"Court recessed until Thursday," yelled the judge, over the crowd that had gone wild. "All of you, including the crasher, into my chambers."

The real Rhonda was beside herself. The drowned woman couldn't have been her sister because here she was, looking smashing.

Rainey knew she had to do something. She told her mother to sit tight, gave a note to the court clerk and gained admittance into the chamber.

Instead of theatre, the crasher and the crowd had turned the courtroom into a circus, and the judge was furious. She saw Rainey and stopped. "Am I seeing things? Now there are three of them! Who are you?"

"I am Lorraine Butler. My sister didn't know what became of me when we were put in separate foster homes as children. That's why she willed all her assets to Sandra, but Sandra is willing to split them with me and our other sister, Midge."

"And where is she?"

Lorraine pointed to Dr. Collins and both Rhonda and Sandra looked at their sister with disbelief. She continued, "Both my sisters have lied to protect each other out of sisterly love. Rhonda Collins is indeed dead. I don't know why your detective couldn't find anyone to verify this, but it's true. I was there."

The judge raised her voice, "This is a soap opera! I'm about ready to dismiss this case."

The three sisters couldn't believe it. Case dismissed? What did that mean?

"However, if there's more to this story, I'm determined to find out what it is, but for now I am releasing you three." Then the judge grinned wickedly. "How about a jewelry party for sisters? I could arrange for an ankle bracelet for each of you, but somehow I don't think any one of you is a flight risk. However, don't count your chickens before they're hatched and be back her in court Thursday morning at 10:00." Then looking at Sandra, "By the way, didn't you think about dumping the vacuum bag into the jar?"

Sandra reacted with, "Ew! There could have been other nasty things in the bag, those enormous disgusting roaches and——"

The judge snidely inserted, "You threw it in the trash and the haulers already collected it?"

Sandra looked surprised that the judge knew that.

"Now," boomed the Judge, "clear my chambers."

With much to discuss and their mother doing who knows what, the sisters wasted no time in leaving,

Judge Barnes looked at the attorneys, both baffled at what they had just witnessed.

"Okay, you two, give. What more do you know about this? To me it's a waste of time. Obviously these three sisters have acted together to have the will reinstated, and this has been quite a show. To quit wasting the taxpayers' money I'll overturn the first case and throw out the second convoluted one with the plaintiff becoming the defendant. The battered detective has to get the affidavit from the funeral director to convince me the death certificate isn't the real deal. Without evidence I can't accept that when it looks real enough to me, and besides, if the one who wrote the will is alive, who needs a death certificate or a will to get her own assets? That is assuming she told the truth, which another sister disputed; but she wasn't under oath which means she could have lied all she wanted. As far as I'm concerned, the gal and her sisters can take their assets and go back to Arkansas, and we'll never have to deal with them again. I just want them to stew a bit before I give them my judgment."

"Your honor, please; I think you need to speak more to the detective," beseeched the prosecuting attorney and the other attorney concurred.

"And why is that?"

"She and her partner were in charge of a major police investigation into the disappearance of the woman who wrote the will. I think she could give you some valuable insights into this case."

The judge raised her eyebrows. "And that will make me change my mind?"

Chapter Thirty-one

The Whole Story

Maria looked up from her bed. Tuesday afternoon. The formidable judge appeared, smiling broadly. In a colorful dashiki dress and a turban covering her hair looking unlike the judge she's met the day before. "I hear you've had prior experience with what became the 'Amazing Sister Act' yesterday."

Stan had filled her in, "Yes," began Maria, "This past September Dr. Rhonda Collins, a very popular, well respected physician vanished from the clinic where she worked and this caused quite a stir in the community." Then believing the less she tried to explain the better, Maria handed the judge the police report summarizing everything from the doctor's initial disappearance to the discovery that her credentials as a physician had been falsified. An attached DNA form indicated proof of Dr. Collins and Sandra Lewis being the same person. As she read, The Judge's eyebrows shot higher and higher.

"I get it," the judge pronounced. "The doctor made out the will to herself."

"Right. Without a body, she would have had to wait for several years to claim her assets, which are sizeable."

"I see," mused the Judge. "But after her sisters started coming out of the woodwork, she decided she needed to gain access to her money sooner. All she had to do was give her real name, 'Sandra' to one of them, fake her own death, and produce a death certificate."

"Yes!" Maria acted as if the judge had figured it out on her own. "I think you're right."

"It's easy to understand why you thought the death certificate's not authentic with a history of false documents."

Maria nodded.

The judge paused to stir cream into her coffee she had picked up on her way through the waiting room and added, "Detective, you have been extremely helpful. Now all I have to figure out is which of the sisters is telling the truth. They all look alike and they all lie like rugs. Who do you think is the 'doctor'?"

"I'm certain it's the one I heard about who burst into the courtroom, wearing the same suit she wore the day she disappeared."

"Okay. That one confessed, but is she truthful?"

Maria smiled, "I think I know exactly how we can identify the real Rhonda. I need the help of a friend, but I think it will work." She shared her plans, and the judge asked her general questions about living in Corpus Christi and asking her if she knew of any townhouse for sale. She also asked specific ones about Maria's injury.

Maria thought the judge might apologize for being rough on her the previous day. The judge didn't, but as if reading her mind, admitted, "I was rough on you yesterday and I probably didn't score any points with the crowd for that but as a female judge I have to be like iron to be credible."

Marie smiled, "I know just what you mean."

The judge laughed, "Of course you do." Marie began to change her opinion of the judge, who was human after all.

Her Honor became serious again. "You are well aware this meeting is highly irregular," the judge advised, "but I felt like I walked into the middle of a bad movie yesterday and then was hurled into a den of wildcats. The attorneys convinced me I deserved to have more information before I can make any kind of judgment."

* * *

Maria called Linda as soon as her session with the judge ended. "Maria! How are you? I'm sorry I haven't been up to see you, but we are short staffed at work and Dave is out of town which means I'm trying to hold things together on the home front."

"No worries. I have something important to discuss." She gave Linda a brief run-down of what happened in court and explained exactly what she wanted Linda to do.

267

Chapter Thirty-Two

Betrayed by a Gal's Best Friend

The time since the sisters and their mother left the courthouse Monday had been a blur with Mama completely lucid at times and at others wondering where she was and whom the others were. The "woman who yodeled during a court hearing" had become a You-Tube sensation, which had brought national reporters. They camped outside the townhouse, and the trick was keeping Mama from telling them anything.

Mostly the four women watched endless DVDs to avoid discussing what lay ahead for all of them. Rainey prepared simple meals that no one, but Mama, felt like eating. Sandra had several whispered phone conversations with Chief Ortiz, who told her that whatever happened he wanted to keep in touch with the woman he had known as Sandra but now knew as "my sweet, beautiful Rhonda". "

Thursday morning all were up, dressed modestly with subtle make-up and long blonde hair in simple ponytails. They were ready to go to court. To their relief Mama was having a good day.

Sandra's phone rang as they drove to the courthouse. The bailiff directed her and her family to enter the courthouse from a back entrance where he would wait. They could see why. Police officers had set up a roadblock in front of the courthouse, where a huge crowd had assembled. Police officers prevented anyone from entering the courthouse doors.

With the Jacksons in front of her, the Judge drawled, "Good morning y'all. This is a closed hearing, not a reality show. All I want to do is get to the bottom of the shenanigans the Jackson girls and their mother have been trying to pull. I know a lot more about this case than I did Thursday. Don't you think you can put anything past me now."

"First of all," she continued, "I want your names, and I mean real names, not pet names, stage names, or aliases."

The judge paused as she looked over the women before her. "Let me see, we have three women here, and their mother, let's not forget the mother. Ma'am, what is your name?"

Mama jumped up and curtsied to the judge. "Your highness, I'm Martha Mae Jackson, and these are my daughters and-----."

"Just your name, Mrs. Jackson. Maybe we can have a chat later."

Mama sat down with a hurt look as Rainey identified herself.

"Thank you. Now I am going to prove one of you is Dr. Rhonda Collins, who really is Sandra Lewis, who stole the name of her sister Rhonda Collins when she began to impersonate a doctor. You'll never guess where I learned that," she added looking straight at the Police Chief, whom she now had met. He had shared things his sweetie had told him in hopes the judge would treat her kindly.

All three sisters stared straight ahead.

"We could have played that old television show that most of you don't remember called 'To Tell the Truth' from now until kingdom come, but it is a beautiful day and I want to get this settled as quickly as possible. I am taking a shortcut. Bailiff, would you please bring in our star witness."

Baffled, the three sisters, followed the bailiff with their eyes as he went to the side door that led to the judge's chambers. In raced an energetic Chihuahua. He ran right to Sandra Lewis AKA Dr. Rhonda Collins.

With tears running down her face, Sandra picked him up, "Poppy, oh, Poppy."

"As if there is any doubt, is that your dog, Miss Lewis?"

"Yes," admitted the real Sandra, holding back tears and holding tightly to the dog. From her demeanor everyone knew that the only thing that mattered at the moment was the reunion between dog and owner.

"Actually, he isn't your dog. You abandoned him when you fled Corpus Christi," stated the judge.

"It wasn't like that, your honor. I wanted to take him, but it was complicated. I tried to pick him up but . . ." Sandra couldn't compose herself enough to finish.

"Well, Miss Lewis, I want you to take the dog back to my chambers and return him to the rightful owner. The rest of you, take a break. Court will resume in ten minutes."

Both sisters embraced Sandra and the dog she held but with another judicial reminder, Sandra went out the side door with Poppy. Her sisters and mother begged to accompany her but the judge denied their requests.

Linda, expressionless, stood right outside the door. Sandra couldn't stop her tears as she handed Poppy to her. She gulped and said evenly, "I'm very sorry with what I've put you through. Thank you for giving Poppy a home."

Then stoic Linda broke down. Seeing Rhonda, the friend she had held close, she couldn't help herself. In a trembling voice, she said, "I don't understand why you did what you did, and I have been furious with you for not confiding in me that you had problems, not to mention your affair with Dave, but, Rhonda, I'll always remember the great times we had."

The two women, with poor yipping Poppy compressed between them, embraced. Sandra reluctantly let go of Poppy. "Thank you, Linda. I've done terrible things but the worst was betraying you, the best friend I've ever had. I'm sorry."

Linda put Poppy in a carrier. Sandra walked back into the courtroom, knowing she deserved whatever punishment she received.

Justice was swift. The judge said calmly," Since Tuesday I have learned a lot about the Missing Doctor. Today I'm better able to make a judgment against her."

Sandra shuddered.

"First, I have a whole list of charges I can make against Mama, and sisters Rainey and Rhonda. These include obstructing justice, impersonation, perjury and more, but I know a bit about family dynamics and loyalties. Sandra manipulated all of you. I am dismissing all of you but Sandra, the Mastermind."

Mama and two daughters, relieved and obedient, took seats in the courtroom, empty except for a Detective Stan Belkin and Chief Ortiz.

The judge gave Sandra her hardest look "Ms. Lewis, I'd like to throw the book at you but since an unnamed clinic will not press charges, I can't. However, be advised the Great State of Texas could override that and decide to press charges against you for public endangerment, and false credentials. My job, however, is to determine the validity of your will and the disbursement of your assets."

The judge gave her wicked grin. "First of all, for a will to be valid, the maker of that document must be dead. We have plenty of evidence that you aren't. You're here, your dog recognized you, and the detective we met Monday, working from her hospital bed, proved your death certificate is fraudulent. I talked to the owner of Francks Funeral Home and have his sworn affidavit that he did not sign it."

Sandra had sat with no expression but gasped as the judge went on, "As far as I'm concerned you have no assets. You left them behind and those assets were frozen after that same smart young detective determined that your physician credentials are bogus and everything you had you earned fraudulently. Sandra Lewis, you borrowed the name of your sister, Rhonda Collins, and pretended to be a doctor. Thanks to all that's good and holy, you didn't kill a patient."

Sandra's head was bowed as the judge summed up her crimes. "You appointed your friend, Dr. Linda Hernandez, as the executor of your will, and you named your sister, Sandra Lewis as your beneficiary. Only you don't have a sister named Sandra Lewis as proved by DNA. Sandra Lewis and Dr. Collins are the same person. Right?"

Sandra nodded.

The judge glared at her. "It's too bad that as obviously bright as you are, you didn't use those brains to go to med school to become a real physician. With your criminal mind, you intended to collect your own assets. You faked Dr. Collin's death, right?

"Yes."

271

Then you coerced your sister Rhonda to take your name, Sandra Lewis, and come back to Corpus Christi to claim the estate. Is that correct?'

"It is correct. I'm sorry I involved my sisters. They didn't know anything about what I'd done."

Sandra's sisters sobbed while her mother looked more confused than ever.

"Well, Miss Lewis, I don't intend to overturn the ruling that froze your assets; but I will give you two options. The first is a trial, and with all the evidence compiled against you, the jury is bound to find you guilty of multiple counts of fraud. That will enable you to be a guest of the Texas penal system for eight to ten years. This will call you to the attention of Federal Court, which might be quite interested in where you have gotten your false documents."

"The second option."

Sandra had to have the judge repeat the second option as her mind stuck on visiting her dad in prison and the possibility of being sent to prison. Implicating Brian now that he had his family back was in her thoughts, too. Visions of the happy life she and Wayne could have had appeared and vanished.

The judge cleared her throat before repeating the second. Judge Barnes would not have considered this option if not influenced the previous day by Chief Ortiz, who insisted a trial wasn't worth the taxpayers' money. "I repeat: the other option is that you and your family pack your bags and leave immediately. You get nothing."

"Nothing? I can't take belongings from my home?" Sandra wasn't giving up easily though she had made up her mind to take the second option over prison. *It gets down to how can I go to prison when I have Rhonda and the baby in my care? Okay, I've lost all my hard-earned money, but I have my family. I'm starting over to lead a good life,*

"You take only what you and your family brought and leave as soon as possible or face trial and a probable prison sentence, which I'd love for you to have."

Sandra stood as tall as she could. "Your honor, my family and I will leave Texas as soon as we go to my townhouse to pack."

"To pack only what we brought," the judge intoned, putting those words in Sandra's mouth.

Thinking about the fortune that was now in the storage facility Sandra repeated, "We will take nothing from my house except what we brought from Arkansas."

Judge Barnes shook her hear. "This case, the craziest, most bizarre in my entire career, is over." Looking upward she stated, "I pray all cases I have in Texas aren't like this one." Then she pounded her gavel. "Hearing dismissed."

As Sandra and family left, the media swarmed them; reporters from major networks relayed the latest back to national news centers.

Sandra cautioned the sisters and mother to say nothing, but mama grabbed a microphone and began, "I'm Mae Jackson from Harmon, Arkansas. These are my daughters. That one Sue-Ella (she pointed to Rhonda) is the oldest, next to her is Rainey. Midge, the youngest was here but had to leave, I guess, and the last one, Ronnie Lee, did something really bad because the judge yelled at her a lot. But now we're all going back home."

Rainey returned the microphone and hurried her mother along.

Chapter Thirty-three

No Thanks

Midge Brown-Hamilton in Spokane, Washington, turned her kitchen television on to listen to the 5:00 news as she prepared supper for Jeff and their two little ones.

The meat fork she held fell from her hand and clattered to the floor as she stared at the television. She saw a woman who looked just like a faded photo she had of her mother call herself by her mother's name. And her two sisters plus a third one. Did her mother have a love child before the three of them? Her own name was mentioned. She listened with eyes and mouth wide-open as she heard how the sisters—her sisters— had committed fraud in Texas and were just now leaving a courthouse in Corpus Christi.

What terrible thing did they do to make national news? This thought was brushed aside as Midge realized: *My mother, my sisters still live in Harmon. I've wondered about them, but I have had such a good life since my adoption and then marriage, I never have felt the need to search for any of them. Now it will be easy! No matter what they did they are my sisters, my birth mother. We can be reunited after all these years. I'll tell Jeff as soon as he gets home, and I'll call my parents to see if they can come over to babysit, and I need to make travel arrangements right away to go back to my hometown.*

Midge picked up the fork, washed and rinsed it off and returned to browning hamburger. Her two sweet children wandered into the kitchen. Seeing them she thought clearly about what she had just witnessed on television. With determination Midge Jackson Brown-Hamilton said out loud "I've changed my mind. Why would I want any part of that bunch?"

* * *

Stan called Maria to report on the hearing. He could imagine the huge smile on her face when he told her, "Thanks to your determination the Missing Doctor case finally is over, and the judge really bragged about you."

"I'm elated. Now I can concentrate on recovering."

"And by the way," Stan said seriously, "the Houston PD identified the body of the drowned woman. "With the same inflection he added, "It wasn't The Missing Doctor."

Maria laughed.

* * *

The next day Stan stopped to check on Maria. 'Well, partner, you better recover in a hurry. We have another case. I'm on the way to Las Palmas RV Park. There's been a murder, a woman strangled in the shower room."

Epilogue

The four Jacksons and cat family returned without incident to Harmon. Maria and Stan already are working to solve <u>The R.V. Murder,</u> the title of my work in progress.

Sandra sold a couple paintings to invest in Wayne's very successful project. She decided not to tell him anything about her wrongdoing unless he asked. He didn't. Rhonda had her baby, and running out of single men in Harmon, returned to Corpus Christi where she married Chief Ortiz, leaving her baby girl with Sandra. Andrea repaid her parents and no longer is grounded. Rainey is busy caring for Mama, who moved in with her family. Daddy will be released from prison soon; maybe he'll move in, too. The Jackson sisters still search for Midge.

Maria's assailant is serving time. So far Brian hasn't been linked to fraudulent documentation, and Sandra doesn't think too much about her winding up in Federal Court. She is too busy with the baby and working for Wayne and wondering when he'll put a ring on her finger.

The book titles mentioned in this novel are real as are the authors, Guthrie Ford and Devorah Fox. Real-life characters include Dr. Jon Nash, who lives and works in Duluth; and realtor-for-real, Tim Sylte, lives and works in Minneapolis. Connie Harris, authentic church administrator at Island in the Son United Methodist Church, has retired as has Richard Mueller, former owner of Pelican Pete's.

Even I don't know where Sandra was those days before she made her grand appearance at the hearing.

The Author

Author Alice Marks has moved around as much as Sandra Lewis, heroine of her suspense novels <u>Missing</u> and <u>Breaks</u>. Born in Wyoming, she grew up there and received her undergraduate degree at the University of Wyoming. In 1967 She and her husband, Sam, and two babies moved to Minnesota where both had careers in education and reared four children. In 2005 Sam and Alice moved to Port Aransas, Texas, an island town on the Gulf of Mexico. Corpus Christi is accessible by ferry and highway or by highway, JFK bridge and Causeway. After soaking up the sun for eight years and enjoying life in a much different culture, including the energy of Spring Break, the couple returned to Minnesota in 2013 to spend their retirement years. They live in Duluth, where both are involved in music (Sam directs the Duluth Civic Orchestra, and Alice plays flute) and where Alice is involved in many aspects of writing including activities of Lake Superior Writers, leading a writers group, Ink Slingers, and teaching writing workshops and classes. Alice has been published in several anthologies for short stories and poetry. One of her poems will be featured in a dance-poetry collaboration.

Table of Contents

Made in the USA
Columbia, SC
15 February 2020